PRAISE FOR STEPHEN KING

'Not since Dickens has a writer had so many readers by the throat . . . King's imagination is vast. He knows how to engage the deepest sympathies of his readers . . . one of the great storytellers of our time' – *Guardian*

'A writer of exellence . . . King is one of the most fertile storytellers of the modern novel . . . brilliantly done' – *The Sunday Times*

'Splendid entertainment . . . Stephen King is one of those natural storytellers . . . getting hooked is easy' – Frances Fyfield, *Express*

'The true narrative artist is a rare creature. Storytelling – the ability to make the listener or the reader need to know, demand to know, what happens next – is a gift . . . Stephen King, like Charles Dickens before him, has this gift in spades' – *The Times*

PRAISE FOR STEPHEN KING

'The greatest popular novelist of our day, comparable to Dickens' – *Guardian*

'It's being on this familiar territory that makes his fiction so addictive. It's so good you just want more' – *Evening Standard*

'[An] incomparable ability to find the epic in the ordinary' – Michael Chabon

'King has that rare skill of making you believe it could happen' – *Sydney Morning Herald*

'A writer of excellence . . . King is one of the most fertile storytellers of the modern novel' – *The Sunday Times*

ABOUT THE AUTHOR

Stephen King was born in Portland, Maine, in 1947. He won a scholarship award to the University of Maine and later taught English, while his wife, Tabitha, got her degree.

It was the publication of his first novel *Carrie* and its subsequent adaptation that set him on his way to his present position as perhaps the bestselling author in the world.

Carrie was followed by a string of bestsellers including *Hearts in Atlantis*, *Misery*, *Bag of Bones*, *The Dark Half*, the *Dark Tower* series, *On Writing (A Memoir of the Craft)* and *Cell*. Some of his other books have also been adapted into first rate films including *The Shawshank Redemption* and *The Green Mile*.

Stephen King is the 2003 recipient of *The National Book Foundation Medal for Distinguished Contribution to American Letters*.

He lives in Bangor, Maine, with his wife, novelist Tabitha King.

By Stephen King and published by
Hodder & Stoughton

FICTION:

Carrie
'Salem's Lot
The Shining
Night Shift
The Stand
The Dead Zone
Firestarter
Cujo
Different Seasons
Cycle of the Werewolf
Christine
The Talisman (with Peter Straub)
Pet Sematary
It
Skeleton Crew
The Eyes of the Dragon
Misery
The Tommyknockers
The Dark Half
Four Past Midnight
Needful Things
Gerald's Game
Dolores Claiborne
Nightmares and Dreamscapes
Insomnia
Rose Madder
Desperation
Bag of Bones
The Girl Who Loved Tom Gordon
Hearts in Atlantis
Dreamcatcher
Everything's Eventual
From a Buick 8
Cell
Lisey's Story
The Dark Tower I: The Gunslinger
The Dark Tower II: The Drawing of the Three
The Dark Tower III: The Waste Lands
The Dark Tower IV: Wizard and Glass
The Dark Tower V: Wolves of the Calla
The Dark Tower VI: Song of Susannah
The Dark Tower VII: The Dark Tower

By Stephen King as Richard Bachman

Thinner
The Running Man
The Bachman Books
The Regulators
Blaze

NON-FICTION:

Danse Macabre
On Writing (A Memoir of the Craft)

STEPHEN KING

KING

DIFFERENT SEASONS

HODDER

£8.99

Copyright © 1982 by Stephen King

First published in Great Britain in 1992
by Macdonald & Co

This paperback edition published in 2007

The right of Stephen King to be identified as the Author of
the Work has been asserted by him in accordance with the
Copyright, Design and Patents Act 1988.

A Hodder Paperback

4

A CIP catalogue record for this title
is available from the British Libary

ISBN 978 0 340 95260 3

Typeset in Bembo by Palimpsest Book Production Ltd, Grangemouth, Stirlingshire
Printed and bound in Great Britain by
Clays Ltd, St Ives plc

Hodder & Stoughton
A division of Hodder Headline
338 Euston Road
London NW1 3BH

CONTENTS

'Dirty deeds done dirt cheap.'
— AC/DC

'I heard it through the grapevine.'
— Norman Whitfield

It is the tale, not he who tells it.

Hope Springs Eternal

RITA HAYWORTH
AND
SHAWSHANK REDEMPTION

For Russ and Florence Dorr

There's a guy like me in every state and federal prison in America, I guess – I'm the guy who can get it for you. Tailormade cigarettes, a bag of reefer, if you're partial to that, a bottle of brandy to celebrate your son or daughter's high school graduation, or almost anything else . . . within reason, that is. It wasn't always that way.

I came to Shawshank when I was just twenty, and I am one of the few people in our happy little family who is willing to own up to what he did. I committed murder. I put a large insurance policy on my wife, who was three years older than I was, and then I fixed the brakes of the Chevrolet coupé her father had given us as a wedding present. It worked out exactly as I had planned, except I hadn't planned on her stopping to pick up the neighbour woman and the neighbour woman's infant son on the way down Castle Hill and into town. The brakes let go and the car crashed through the bushes at the edge of the town common, gathering speed. Bystanders said it must have been doing fifty or better when it hit the base of the Civil War statue and burst into flames.

I also hadn't planned on getting caught, but caught I was. I got a season's pass into this place. Maine has no death penalty, but the district attorney saw to it that I was tried for all three deaths and given three life sentences, to run one after the other. That fixed up any chance of parole I might have, for a long, long time. The judge called what

I had done 'a hideous, heinous crime', and it was, but it is also in the past now. You can look it up in the yellowing files of the Castle Rock *Call*, where the big headlines announcing my conviction look sort of funny and antique next to the news of Hitler and Mussolini and FDR's alphabet soup agencies.

Have I rehabilitated myself, you ask? I don't know what that word means, at least as far as prisons and corrections go. I think it's a politician's word. It may have some other meaning, and it may be that I will have a chance to find out, but that is the future . . . something cons teach themselves not to think about. I was young, good-looking, and from the poor side of town. I knocked up a pretty, sulky, headstrong girl who lived in one of the fine old houses on Carbine Street. Her father was agreeable to the marriage if I would take a job in the optical company he owned and 'work my way up'. I found out that what he really had in mind was keeping me in his house and under his thumb, like a disagreeable pet that has not quite been housebroken and which may bite. Enough hate eventually piled up to cause me to do what I did. Given a second chance I would not do it again, but I'm not sure that means I am rehabilitated.

Anyway, it's not me I want to tell you about; I want to tell you about a guy named Andy Dufresne. But before I can tell you about Andy, I have to explain a few other things about myself. It won't take long.

As I said, I've been the guy who can get it for you here at Shawshank for damn near forty years. And that doesn't just mean contraband items like extra cigarettes or booze, although those items always top the list. But I've gotten thousands of other items for men doing time here, some of them perfectly legal yet hard to come by in a place where you've supposedly been brought to be punished. There was one fellow who was in for raping a little girl and exposing himself to dozens of others; I got him three pieces of pink Vermont marble and he did three lovely sculptures out of them – a baby, a boy of about twelve, and a bearded young man. He called them The Three Ages of Jesus, and those pieces of sculpture are now in the parlour of a man who used to be governor of this state.

Or here's a name you may remember if you grew up north of Massachusetts – Robert Alan Cote. In 1951 he tried to rob the First Mercantile Bank of Mechanic Falls, and the hold-up turned into a bloodbath – six dead in the end, two of them members of the gang, three of them hostages, one of them a young state cop who put his head up at the wrong time and got a bullet in the eye. Cote had a penny collection. Naturally they weren't going to let him have it in here, but with a little help from his mother and a middleman who used to drive a laundry truck, I was able to get it to him. I told him, Bobby, you must be crazy, wanting to have a coin collection in a stone hotel full of thieves. He looked at me and smiled and said, I know where to keep them. They'll be safe enough. Don't you worry. And he was right. Bobby Cote died of a brain tumour in 1967, but that coin collection has never turned up.

I've gotten men chocolates on Valentine's Day; I got three of those green milkshakes they serve at McDonald's around St Paddy's Day for a crazy Irishman named O'Malley; I even arranged for a midnight showing of *Deep Throat* and *The Devil in Miss Jones* for a party of twenty men who had pooled their resources to rent the films . . . although I ended up doing a week in solitary for that little escapade. It's the risk you run when you're the guy who can get it.

I've gotten reference books and fuck-books, joke novelties like handbuzzers and itching powder, and on more than one occasion I've seen that a long-timer has gotten a pair of panties from his wife or his girlfriend . . . and I guess you'll know what guys in here do with such items during the long nights when time draws out like a blade. I don't get all those things gratis, and for some items the price comes high. But I don't do it *just* for the money; what good is money to me? I'm never going to own a Cadillac car or fly off to Jamaica for two weeks in February. I do it for the same reason that a good butcher will only sell you fresh meat: I got a reputation and I want to keep it. The only two things I refuse to handle are guns and heavy drugs. I won't help anyone kill himself or anyone else. I have enough killing on my mind to last me a lifetime.

Yeah, I'm a regular Neiman-Marcus. And so when Andy Dufresne came to me in 1949 and asked if I could smuggle Rita Hayworth into the prison for him, I said it would be no problem at all. And it wasn't.

When Andy came to Shawshank in 1948, he was thirty years old. He was a short neat little man with sandy hair and small, clever hands. He wore gold-rimmed spectacles. His fingernails were always clipped, and they were always clean. That's a funny thing to remember about a man, I suppose, but it seems to sum Andy up for me. He always looked as if he should have been wearing a tie. On the outside he had been a vice-president in the trust department of a large Portland bank. Good work for a man as young as he was, especially when you consider how conservative most banks are . . . and you have to multiply that conservatism by ten when you get up into New England, where folks don't like to trust a man with their money unless he's bald, limping, and constantly plucking at his pants to get his truss around straight. Andy was in for murdering his wife and her lover.

As I believe I have said, everyone in prison is an innocent man. Oh, they read that scripture the way those holy rollers on TV read the Book of Revelations. They were the victims of judges with hearts of stone and balls to match, or incompetent lawyers, or police frame-ups, or bad luck. They read the scripture, but you can see a different scripture in their faces. Most cons are a low sort, no good to themselves or anyone else, and their worst luck was that their mothers carried them to term.

In all my years at Shawshank, there have been less than ten men whom I believed when they told me they were innocent. Andy Dufresne was one of them, although I only became convinced of his innocence over a period of years. If I had been on the jury that heard his case in Portland Superior Court over six stormy weeks in 1947–48, I would have voted to convict, too.

It was one hell of a case, all right; one of those juicy ones with all the right elements. There was a beautiful girl with society connections (dead), a local sports figure (also dead), and a prominent young businessman in the dock. There was this, plus all the scandal the newspapers could hint at. The prosecution had an open-and-shut case. The trial only lasted as long as it did because the DA was planning to run for the US House of Representatives and he wanted John Q Public to get a good long look at his phiz.

It was a crackerjack legal circus, with spectators getting in line at four in the morning, despite the subzero temperatures, to assure themselves of a seat.

The facts of the prosecution's case that Andy never contested were these: That he had a wife, Linda Collins Dufresne; that in June of 1947 she had expressed an interest in learning the game of golf at the Falmouth Hills Country Club; that she did indeed take lessons for four months; that her instructor was the Falmouth Hills golf pro, Glenn Quentin; that in late August of 1947 Andy learned that Quentin and his wife had become lovers; that Andy and Linda Dufresne argued bitterly on the afternoon of 10 September 1947; that the subject of their argument was her infidelity.

He testified that Linda professed to be glad he knew; the sneaking around, she said, was distressing. She told Andy that she planned to obtain a Reno divorce. Andy told her he would see her in hell before he would see her in Reno. She went off to spend the night with Quentin in Quentin's rented bungalow not far from the golf course. The next morning his cleaning woman found both of them dead in bed. Each had been shot four times.

It was that last fact that militated more against Andy than any of the others. The DA with the political aspirations made a great deal of it in his opening statement and his closing summation. Andrew Dufresne, he said, was not a wronged husband seeking a hot-blooded revenge against his cheating wife; that, the DA said, could be understood, if not condoned. But this revenge had been of a much colder type. Consider! the DA thundered at the jury. Four and four! Not six shots, but eight! *He had fired the gun empty . . . and then stopped to reload so he could shoot each of them again!* FOUR FOR HIM AND FOUR FOR HER, the Portland *Sun* blared. The Boston *Register* dubbed him The Even-Steven Killer.

A clerk from the Wise Pawnshop in Lewiston testified that he had sold a six-shot .38 Police Special to Andrew Dufresne just two days before the double murder. A bartender from the country club bar testified that Andy had come in around seven o'clock on the evening of 10 September, had tossed off three straight whiskeys in a twenty-minute period – when he got up from the bar-stool he told the bartender that he was going up to Glenn Quentin's house and he, the bartender, could 'read about the rest of it in the papers'. Another clerk, this one from the Handy-Pik store a mile or so from Quentin's house, told the court that Dufresne had come in around quarter to nine on the same night. He purchased cigarettes, three quarts of beer, and some dish-towels. The county medical examiner testified that Quentin and the Dufresne woman had been killed between eleven p.m. and two a.m. on the night of 10–11 September. The detective from the Attorney General's office who had been in charge of the case testified that there was a turnout less than seventy yards from the bungalow, and that on the afternoon of 11 September, three pieces of evidence had been removed from that turnout: first item, two empty quart bottles of Narragansett Beer (with the defendant's fingerprints on them); the second item, twelve cigarette ends (all Kools, the defendant's brand); third item, a plaster moulage of a set of tyre tracks (exactly matching the tread-and-wear pattern of the tyres on the defendant's 1947 Plymouth).

In the living room of Quentin's bungalow, four dishtowels had been found lying on the sofa. There were bullet-holes through them and powder-burns on them. The detective theorized (over the agonized objections of Andy's lawyer) that the murderer had wrapped the towels around the muzzle of the murder-weapon to muffle the sound of the gunshots.

Andy Dufresne took the stand in his own defence and told his story calmly, coolly, and dispassionately. He said he had begun to hear distressing rumours about his wife and Glenn Quentin as early as the last week in July. In August he had become distressed enough to investigate a bit. On an evening when Linda was supposed to have gone shopping in Portland after her tennis lesson, Andy had followed her and Quentin to Quentin's one-storey rented house (inevitably dubbed 'the love-nest' by the papers). He had parked in the turnout until Quentin drove her back to the country club where her car was parked, about three hours later.

'Do you mean to tell this court that your wife did not recognize your brand-new Plymouth sedan behind Quentin's car?' the DA asked him on cross-examination.

'I swapped cars for the evening with a friend,' Andy said, and this cool admission of how well-planned his investigation had been did him no good at all in the eyes of the jury.

After returning the friend's car and picking up his own, he had gone home. Linda had been in bed, reading a book. He asked her how her trip to Portland had been. She replied that it had been fun, but she hadn't seen anything she liked well enough to buy. 'That's when I knew for sure,' Andy told the breathless spectators. He spoke in the same calm, remote voice in which he delivered almost all of his testimony.

'What was your frame of mind in the seventeen days between then and the night your wife was murdered?' Andy's lawyer asked him.

'I was in great distress,' Andy said calmly, coldly. Like a man reciting a shopping list he said that he had considered suicide, and had even gone so far as to purchase a gun in Lewiston on 8 September.

His lawyer then invited him to tell the jury what had happened after his wife left to meet Glenn Quentin on the night of the murders. Andy told them . . . and the impression he made was the worst possible.

I knew him for close to thirty years, and I can tell you he was the most self-possessed man I've ever known. What was right with him he'd only give you a little at a time. What was wrong with him he kept bottled up inside. If he ever had a dark night of the soul, as some writer or other has called it, you would never know. He was the type of man who, if he had decided to commit suicide, would do it without leaving a note but not until his affairs had been put neatly in order. If he had cried on the witness stand, or if his voice had thickened and grown hesitant, even if he had gotten yelling at that Washington-bound District Attorney, I don't believe he would have gotten the life sentence he wound up with. Even if he had've he would have been out on parole by 1954. But he told his story like a recording machine, seeming to say to the jury: this is it. Take it or leave it. They left it.

He said he was drunk that night, that he'd been more or less drunk since 24 August, and that he was a man who didn't handle his liquor very well. Of course that by itself would have been hard for any jury to swallow. They just couldn't see this coldly self-possessed young man in the neat double-breasted three-piece woollen suit ever getting falling-down drunk over his wife's sleazy little affair with some small-town golf pro. I believed it because I had a chance to watch Andy that those six men and six women didn't have.

Andy Dufresne took just four drinks a year all the time I knew him. He would meet me in the exercise yard every year about a week before his birthday and then again about two weeks before Christmas. On each occasion he would arrange for a bottle of Jack Daniels. He bought it the way most cons arrange to buy their stuff – the slave's wages they pay in here, plus a little of his own. Up until 1965 what you got for your time was a dime an hour. In '65 they raised it all the way up to a quarter. My commission on liquor was and is ten per cent, and when you add on that surcharge to the price of a fine sippin' whiskey like the Black Jack, you get an idea of how many hours of Andy Dufresne's sweat in the prison laundry was going to buy his four drinks a year.

On the morning of his birthday, 20 September, he would have himself a big knock, and then he'd have another that night after light out. The following day he'd give the rest of the bottle back to me, and I would share it around. As for the other bottle, he dealt himself one drink Christmas night and another on New Year's Eve. Then that one would also come to me with instructions to pass it on. Four drinks a year – and that is the behaviour of a man who has been bitten hard by the bottle. Hard enough to draw blood.

He told the jury that on the night of the 10th he had been so drunk he could only remember what had happened in little isolated snatches. He had gotten drunk that afternoon – 'I took

on a double helping of Dutch courage' is how he put it —
before taking on Linda.

After she left to meet Quentin, he remembered deciding
to confront them. On the way to Quentin's bungalow, he
swung into the country club for a couple of quick ones.
He could not, he said, remember telling the bartender he
could 'read about the rest of it in the papers', or saying
anything to him at all. He remembered buying beer in the
Handy-Pik, but not the dishtowels. 'Why would I want dishtowels?' he asked, and one of the papers reported that three
of the lady jurors shuddered.

Later, much later, he speculated to me about the clerk
who had testified on the subject of those dishtowels, and I
think it's worth jotting down what he said. 'Suppose that,
during their canvass for witnesses,' Andy said one day in the
exercise yard, 'they stumble on this fellow who sold me the
beer that night. By then three days have gone by. The facts
of the case have been broadsided in all the papers. Maybe
they ganged up on the guy, five or six cops, plus the dick
from the attorney general's office, plus the DA's assistant.
Memory is a pretty subjective thing, Red. They could have
started out with "Isn't it possible that he purchased four or
five dishtowels?" and worked their way up from there. If
enough people *want* you to remember something, that can
be a pretty powerful persuader.'

I agreed that it could.

'But there's one even more powerful,' Andy went on in
that musing way of his. 'I think it's at least possible that
he convinced himself. It was the limelight. Reporters asking
him questions, his picture in the papers . . . all topped, of
course, by his star turn in court. I'm not saying that he

deliberately falsified his story, or perjured himself. I think it's possible that he could have passed a lie detector test with flying colours, or sworn on his mother's sacred name that I bought those dishtowels. But still . . . memory is such a *goddam* subjective thing.

'I know this much: even though my own lawyer thought I had to be lying about half my story, he never bought that business about the dishtowels. It's crazy on the face of it. I was pig-drunk, too drunk to have been thinking about muffling the gunshots. If I'd done it, I just would have let them rip.'

He went up to the turnout and parked there. He drank beer and smoked cigarettes. He watched the lights downstairs in Quentin's place go out. He watched a single light go on upstairs . . . and fifteen minutes later he watched that one go out. He said he could guess the rest.

'Mr Dufresne, did you then go up to Glenn Quentin's house and kill the two of them?' his lawyer thundered.

'No, I did not,' Andy answered. By midnight, he said, he was sobering up. He was also feeling the first signs of a bad hangover. He decided to go home and sleep it off and think about the whole thing in a more adult fashion the next day. 'At that time, as I drove home, I was beginning to think that the wisest course would be to simply let her go to Reno and get her divorce.'

'Thank you, Mr Dufresne.'

The DA popped up.

'You divorced her in the quickest way you could think of, didn't you? You divorced her with a .38 revolver wrapped in dishtowels, didn't you?'

'No sir, I did not,' Andy said calmly.

'And then you shot her lover.'

'No, sir.'

'You mean you shot Quentin first?'

'I mean I didn't shoot either one of them. I drank two quarts of beer and smoked however many cigarettes that the police found at the turnout. Then I drove home and went to bed.'

'You told the jury that between 24 August and 10 September, you were feeling suicidal.'

'Yes, sir.'

'Suicidal enough to buy a revolver.'

'Yes.'

'Would it bother you overmuch, Mr Dufresne, if I told you that you do not seem to me to be the suicidal type?'

'No,' Andy said, 'but you don't impress me as being terribly sensitive, and I doubt very much that, if I *were* feeling suicidal, I would take my problem to you.'

There was a slight tense titter in the courtroom at this, but it won him no points with the jury.

'Did you take your .38 with you on the night of 10 September?'

'No; as I've already testified –'

'Oh, yes!' The DA smiled sarcastically. 'You threw it into the river, didn't you? The Royal River. On the afternoon of 9 September.'

'Yes, sir.'

'One day before the murders.'

'Yes, sir.'

'That's convenient, isn't it?'

'It's neither convenient nor inconvenient. Only the truth.'

'I believe you heard Lieutenant Mincher's testimony?'

Mincher had been in charge of the party which had dragged the stretch of the Royal near Pond Bridge, from which Andy had testified he had thrown the gun. The police had not found it.

'Yes, sir. You know I heard it.'

'Then you heard him testify that they found no gun, although they dragged for three days. That was rather convenient, too, wasn't it?'

'Convenience aside, it's a fact that they didn't find the gun,' Andy responded calmly. 'But I should like to point out to both you and the jury that the Pond Road Bridge is very close to where the Royal River empties into the Bay of Yarmouth. The current is strong. The gun may have been carried out into the bay itself.'

'And so no comparison can be made between the riflings on the bullets taken from the bloodstained corpses of your wife and Mr Glenn Quentin and the riflings on the barrel of your gun. That's correct, isn't it, Mr Dufresne?'

'Yes.'

'That's also rather convenient, isn't it?'

At that, according to the papers, Andy displayed one of the few slight emotional reactions he allowed himself during the entire six-week period of the trial. A slight, bitter smile crossed his face.

'Since I am innocent of this crime, sir, and since I am telling the truth about throwing my gun into the river the day before the crime took place, then it seems to me decidedly inconvenient that the gun was never found.'

The DA hammered at him for two days. He re-read the Handy-Pik clerk's testimony about the dishtowels to Andy. Andy repeated that he could not recall buying them, but admitted that he also couldn't remember *not* buying them.

Was it true that Andy and Linda Dufresne had taken out a joint insurance policy in early 1947? Yes, that was true. And if acquitted, wasn't it true that Andy stood to gain $50,000 in benefits? True. And wasn't it true that he had gone up to Glenn Quentin's house with murder in his heart, and wasn't it *also* true that he had indeed committed murder twice over? No, it was not true. Then what did he think had happened, since there had been no signs of robbery?

'I have no way of knowing that, sir,' Andy said quietly.

The case went to the jury at one p.m. on a snowy Wednesday afternoon. The twelve jurymen and women came back at three-thirty. The bailiff said they would have been back earlier, but they had held off in order to enjoy a nice chicken dinner from Bentley's Restaurant at the county's expense. They found him guilty, and brother, if Maine had the death penalty, he would have done the airdance before that spring's crocuses poked their heads out of the dirt.

The DA had asked him what he thought had happened, and Andy slipped the question – but he did have an idea, and I got it out of him late one evening in 1955. It had taken those seven years for us to progress from nodding acquaintances to fairly close friends – but I never felt really close to Andy until 1960 or so, and I believe I was the only one who ever did get really close to him. Both being long-timers, we were in the same cellblock from beginning to end, although I was halfway down the corridor from him.

'What do I think?' He laughed – but there was no humour in the sound. 'I think there was a lot of bad luck floating

around that night. More than could ever get together in the
same short span of time again. I think it must have been
some stranger, just passing through. Maybe someone who
had a flat tyre on that road after I went home. Maybe a
burglar. Maybe a psychopath. He killed them, that's all. And
I'm here.'

As simple as that. And he was condemned to spend the
rest of his life in Shawshank – or the part of it that mattered.
Five years later he began to have parole hearings, and he
was turned down just as regular as clockwork in spite of
being a model prisoner. Getting a pass out of Shawshank
when you've got *murder* stamped on your admittance-slip is
slow work, as slow as a river eroding a rock. Seven men sit
on the board, two more than at most state prisons, and every
one of those seven has an ass as hard as the water drawn up
from a mineral-spring well. You can't buy those guys, you
can't sweet-talk them, you can't cry for them. As far as the
board in here is concerned, money don't talk, and *nobody*
walks. There were other reasons in Andy's case as well . . . but
that belongs a little further along in my story.

There was a trusty, name of Kendricks, who was into me
for some pretty heavy money back in the fifties, and it was
four years before he got it all paid off. Most of the interest
he paid me was information – in my line of work, you're
dead if you can't find ways of keeping your ear to the ground.
This Kendricks, for instance, had access to records I was
never going to see running a stamper down in the goddam
plate-shop.

Kendricks told me that the parole board vote was 7–0
against Andy Dufresne through 1957, 6–1 in '58, 7–0 again
in '59, and 5–2 in '60. After that I don't know, but I do

know that sixteen years later he was still in Cell 14 of Cellblock 5. By then, 1976, he was fifty-eight. They probably would have gotten big-hearted and let him out around 1983. They give you life, and that's what they take – all of it that counts, anyway. Maybe they set you loose someday, but . . . well, listen: I knew this guy, Sherwood Bolton, his name was, and he had this pigeon in his cell. From 1945 until 1953, when they let him out, he had that pigeon. He wasn't any Birdman of Alcatraz; he just had this pigeon. Jake, he called him. He set Jake free a day before he, Sherwood, that is, was to walk, and Jake flew away just as pretty as you could want. But about a week after Sherwood Bolton left our happy little family, a friend of mine called me over to the west corner of the exercise yard, where Sherwood used to hang out, and my friend said: 'Isn't that Jake, Red?' It was. That pigeon was just as dead as a turd.

I remember the first time Andy Dufresne got in touch with me for something; I remember like it was yesterday. That wasn't the time he wanted Rita Hayworth, though. That came later. In that summer of 1948 he came around for something else.

Most of my deals are done right there in the exercise yard, and that's where this one went down. Our yard is big, much bigger than most. It's a perfect square, ninety yards on a side. The north side is the outer wall, with a guardtower at either end. The guards up there are armed with binoculars and riot guns. The main gate is in that north side. The truck loading-bays are on the south side of the yard. There are five of them. Shawshank is a busy place during the work-week – deliveries in, deliveries out.

We have the licence-plate factory, and a big industrial laundry that does all the prison wetwash, plus that of Kittery Receiving Hospital and the Eliot Sanatorium. There's also a big automotive garage where mechanic inmates fix prison, state, and municipal vehicles − not to mention the private cars of the screws, the administration officers . . . and, on more than one occasion, those of the parole board.

The east side is a thick stone wall full of tiny slit windows. Cellblock 5 is on the other side of that wall. The west side is Administration and the infirmary. Shawshank has never been as overcrowded as most prisons, and back in '48 it was only filled to something like two-thirds capacity, but at any given time there might be eighty to a hundred and twenty cons on the yard − playing toss with a football or a base-ball, shooting craps, jawing at each other, making deals. On Sunday the place was even more crowded; on Sunday the place would have looked like a country holiday . . . if there had been any women.

It was on a Sunday that Andy first came to me. I had just finished talking to Elmore Armitage, a fellow who often came in handy to me, about a radio when Andy walked up. I knew who he was, of course; he had a reputation for being a snob and a cold fish. People were saying he was marked for trouble already. One of the people saying so was Bogs Diamond, a bad man to have on your case. Andy had no cellmate, and I'd heard that was just the way he wanted it, although the one-man cells in Cellblock 5 were only a little bigger than coffins. But I don't have to listen to rumours about a man when I can judge him for myself.

'Hello,' he said. 'I'm Andy Dufresne.' He offered his hand and I shook it. He wasn't a man to waste time being social;

he got right to the point. 'I understand that you're a man who knows how to get things.'

I agreed that I was able to locate certain items from time to time.

'How do you do that?' Andy asked.

'Sometimes,' I said, 'things just seem to come into my hand. I can't explain it. Unless it's because I'm Irish.'

He smiled a little at that. 'I wonder if you could get me a rock hammer.'

'What would that be, and why would you want it?'

Andy looked surprised. 'Do you make motivations a part of your business?' With words like those I could understand how he had gotten a reputation for being the snobby sort, the kind of guy who likes to put on airs – but I sensed a tiny thread of humour in his question.

'I'll tell you,' I said. 'If you wanted a toothbrush, I wouldn't ask questions. I'd just quote you a price. Because a tooth-brush, you see, is a non-lethal sort of a weapon.'

'You have strong feelings about lethal weapons?'

'I do.'

An old friction-taped baseball flew towards us and he turned, cat-quick, and picked it out of the air. It was a move Frank Malzone would have been proud of. Andy flicked the ball back to where it had come from – just a quick and easy-looking flick of the wrist, but that throw had some mustard on it, just the same. I could see a lot of people were watching us with one eye as they went about their business. Probably the guards in the tower were watching, too. I won't gild the lily; there are cons that swing weight in any prison, maybe four or five in a small one, maybe two or three dozen in a big one. At Shawshank I was one of those with some weight, and what I thought of Andy Dufresne would have a lot to do with how his time went. He probably knew it too, but he wasn't kowtowing or sucking up to me, and I respected him for that.

'Fair enough. I'll tell you what it is and why I want it. A rock-hammer looks like a miniature pickaxe – about so long.' He held his hands about a foot apart, and that was when I first noticed how neatly kept his nails were. 'It's got a small sharp pick on one end and a flat, blunt hammer-head on the other. I want it because I like rocks.'

'Rocks,' I said.

'Squat down here a minute,' he said.

I humoured him. We hunkered down on our haunches like Indians.

Andy took a handful of exercise yard dirt and began to sift it between his neat hands, so it emerged in a fine cloud. Small pebbles were left over, one or two sparkly, the rest dull and plain. One of the dull ones was quartz, but it was only dull until you'd rubbed it clean. Then it had a nice milky glow. Andy did the cleaning and then tossed it to me. I caught it and named it.

'Quartz, sure,' he said. 'And look. Mica. Shale, silted granite. Here's a piece of graded limestone, from when they cut this place out of the side of the hill.' He tossed them away and dusted his hands. 'I'm a rockhound. At least . . . I *was* a rock-hound. In my old life. I'd like to be one again, on a limited scale.'

'Sunday expeditions in the exercise yard?' I asked, standing up. It was a silly idea, and yet . . . seeing that little piece of quartz had given my heart a funny tweak. I don't know exactly why; just an association with the outside world, I suppose. You didn't think of such things in terms of the yard. Quartz was something you picked out of a small, quick-running stream.

'Better to have Sunday expeditions here than no Sunday expeditions at all,' he said.

'You could plant an item like that rock-hammer in some-body's skull,' I remarked.

'I have no enemies here,' he said quietly.

'No?' I smiled. 'Wait awhile.'

'If there's trouble, I can handle it without using a rock-hammer.'

'Maybe you want to try an escape? Going under the wall? Because if you do –'

He laughed politely. When I saw the rock-hammer three weeks later, I understood why.

'You know,' I said, 'if anyone sees you with it, they'll take it away. If they saw you with a spoon, they'd take it away. What are you going to do, just sit down here in the yard and start bangin' away?'

'Oh, I believe I can do a lot better than that.'

I nodded. That part of it really wasn't my business, anyway. A man engages my services to get him something. Whether he can keep it or not after I get it is his business.

'How much would an item like that go for?' I asked. I was beginning to enjoy his quiet, low-key style. When you've spent ten years in stir, as I had then, you can get awfully tired of the bellowers and the braggarts and the loud-mouths. Yes, I think it would be fair to say I liked Andy from the first.

'Eight dollars in any rock-and-gem shop,' he said, 'but I realize that in a business like yours you work on a cost-plus basis –'

'Cost plus ten per cent is my going rate, but I have to go up some on a dangerous item. For something like the gadget you're talking about, it takes a little more goose-grease to get the wheels turning. Let's say ten dollars.'

'Ten it is.'

I looked at him, smiling a little. 'Have you *got* ten dollars?'

'I do,' he said quietly.

A long time after, I discovered that he had better than five hundred. He had brought it in with him. When they check you in at this hotel, one of the bellhops is obliged to bend you over and take a look up your works – but there are a lot of works, and, not to put too fine a point on it, a man who is really determined can get a fairly large item quite a ways up them – far enough to be out of sight, unless the bellhop you happen to draw is in the mood to pull on a rubber glove and go prospecting.

'That's fine,' I said. 'You ought to know what I expect if you get caught with what I get you.'

'I suppose I should,' he said, and I could tell by the slight change in his grey eyes that he knew exactly what I was going to say. It was a slight lightening, a gleam of his special ironic humour.

'If you get caught, you'll say you found it. That's about the long and short of it. They'll put you in solitary for three or four weeks . . . plus, of course, you'll lose your toy and you'll get a black mark on your record. If you give them my name, you and I will never do business again. Not for so much as a pair of shoelaces or a bag of Bugler. And I'll send some fellows around to lump you up. I don't like violence, but you'll understand my position. I can't allow it to get around that I can't handle myself. That would surely finish me.'

'Yes. I suppose it would, I understand, and you don't need to worry.'

'I never worry,' I said. 'In a place like this there's no percentage in it.'

He nodded and walked away. Three days later he walked up beside me in the exercise yard during the laundry's morning break. He didn't speak or even look my way, but pressed a picture of the Hon. Alexander Hamilton into my hand as neatly as a good magician does a card-trick. He was a man who adapted fast. I got him his rock-hammer. I had it in my cell for one night, and it was just as he described it. It was no tool for escape (it would have taken a man just about six hundred years to tunnel under the wall using that rock-hammer, I figured), but I still felt some misgivings. If you planted that pickaxe end in a man's head, he would surely never listen to *Fibber McGee and Molly* on the radio again. And Andy had already begun having trouble with the sisters. I hoped it wasn't them he was wanting the rock-hammer for.

In the end, I trusted my judgment. Early the next morning, twenty minutes before the wake-up horn went off, I slipped the rock-hammer and a package of Camels to Ernie, the old trusty who swept the Cellblock 5 corridors until he was let free in 1956. He slipped it into his tunic without a word, and I didn't see the rock-hammer again for seven years.

The following Sunday Andy walked over to me in the exercise yard again. He was nothing to look at that day, I can tell you. His lower lip was swelled up so big it looked like a summer sausage, his right eye was swollen half-shut, and there was an ugly washboard scrape across one cheek. He was having his troubles with the sisters, all right, but he never mentioned them. 'Thanks for the tool,' he said, and walked away.

I watched him curiously. He walked a few steps, saw something in the dirt, bent over, and picked it up. It was a small rock. Prison fatigues, except for those worn by mechanics when they're on the job, have no pockets. But there are ways to get around that. The little pebble disappeared up Andy's sleeve and didn't come down. I admired that . . . and I admired him. In spite of the problems he was having, he was going on with his life. There are thousands who don't or won't or can't, and plenty of them aren't in prison, either. And I noticed that, although his face still looked as if a twister had happened to it, his hands were still neat and clean, the nails well-kept.

I didn't see much of him over the next six months; Andy spent a lot of that time in solitary.

A few words about the sisters.

In a lot of pens they are known as bull queers or jailhouse susies — just lately the term in fashion is 'killer queens'. But in Shawshank they were always the sisters. I don't know why, but other than the name I guess there was no difference.

It comes as no surprise to most these days that there's a lot of buggery going on inside the walls — except to some of the new fish, maybe, who have the misfortune to be young, slim, good-looking, and unwary — but homosexuality, like straight sex, comes in a hundred different shapes and forms. There are men who can't stand to be without sex of some kind and turn to another man to keep from going crazy. Usually what follows is an arrangement between two fundamentally heterosexual men, although I've sometimes wondered if they are quite as heterosexual as they thought they were going to be when they get back to their wives or their girlfriends.

There are also men who get 'turned' in prison. In the current parlance they 'go gay', or 'come out of the closet'. Mostly (but not always) they play the female, and their favours are competed for fiercely.

And then there are the sisters.

They are to prison society what the rapist is to the society outside the walls. They're usually long-timers, doing hard bullets for brutal crimes. Their prey is the young, the weak, and the inexperienced . . . or, as in the case of Andy Dufresne, the weak-looking. Their hunting grounds are the showers, the cramped, tunnel-like area way behind the industrial washers in the laundry, sometimes the infirmary. On more than one occasion rape has occurred in the closet-sized projection booth behind the auditorium. Most often what the sisters take by force they could have had for free, if they wanted it; those who have been turned always seem to have 'crushes' on one sister or another, like teenage girls with their Sinatras, Presleys, or Redfords. But for the sisters, the joy has always been in taking it by force . . . and I guess it always will be.

Because of his small size and fair good looks (and maybe also because of that very quality of self-possession I had admired), the sisters were after Andy from the day he walked in. If this was some kind of fairy story, I'd tell you that Andy fought the good fight until they left him alone. I wish I could say that, but I can't. Prison is no fairy-tale world.

The first time for him was in the shower less than three days after he joined our happy Shawshank family. Just a lot of slap and tickle that time, I understand. They like to size you up before they make their real move, like jackals finding out if the prey is as weak and hamstrung as it looks.

Andy punched back and bloodied the lip of a big, hulking sister named Bogs Diamond – gone these many years since to who knows where. A guard broke it up before it could go any further, but Bogs promised to get him – and Bogs did.

The second time was behind the washers in the laundry. A lot has gone on in that long, dusty, and narrow space over the years; the guards know about it and just let it be. It's dim and littered with bags of washing and bleaching compound, drums of Hexlite catalyst, as harmless as salt if your hands are dry, murderous as battery acid if they're wet. The guards don't like to go back there. There's no room to manoeuvre, and one of the first things they teach them when they come to work in a place like this is to never let the cons get you in a place where you can't back up.

Bogs wasn't there that day, but Henry Backus, who had been washroom foreman down there since 1922, told me that four of his friends were. Andy held them at bay for a while with a scoop of Hexlite, threatening to throw it in their eyes if they came any closer, but he tripped trying to back around one of the big Washex four-pockets. That was all it took. They were on him.

I guess the phrase gang-rape is one that doesn't change much from one generation to the next. That's what they did to him, those four sisters. They bent him over a gearbox and one of them held a Phillips screwdriver to his temple while they gave him the business. It rips you up some, but not bad – am I speaking from personal experience, you ask? — I only wish I weren't. You bleed for a while. If you don't want some clown asking you if you just started your period, you wad up a bunch of toilet paper and keep it down the back of your underwear until it stops. The bleeding really is like a menstrual flow; it keeps up for two, maybe three days, a slow trickle. Then it stops. No harm done, unless they've done something even more unnatural to you. No *physical* harm done — but rape is rape, and eventually you have to look at your face in the mirror again and decide what to make of yourself.

Andy went through that alone, the way he went through everything alone in those days. He must have come to the conclusion that others before him had come to, namely, that there are only two ways to deal with the sisters: fight them and get taken, or just get taken.

He decided to fight. When Bogs and two of his buddies came after him a week or so after the laundry incident ('I heard ya got broke in,' Bogs said, according to Ernie, who was around at the time), Andy slugged it out with them. He broke the nose of a fellow named Rooster MacBride, a heavy-gutted farmer who was in for beating his step-daughter to death. Rooster died in here, I'm happy to add.

They took him, all three of them. When it was done, Rooster and the other egg — it might have been Pete Verness, but I'm not completely sure — forced Andy down to his knees. Bogs Diamond stepped in front of him. He had a pearl-handled razor in those days with the words *Diamond Pearl* engraved on both sides of the grip. He opened it and said, 'I'm gonna open my fly now, mister man, and you're going to swallow what I give you to swallow. And when you done swallowed mine, you're gonna swallow Rooster's.

29

I guess you done broke his nose and I think he ought to have something to pay for it.'

Andy said, 'Anything of yours that you stick in my mouth, you're going to lose it.'

Bogs looked at Andy like he was crazy, Ernie said.

'No,' he told Andy, talking to him slowly, like Andy was a stupid kid. 'You didn't understand what I said. You do anything like that and I'll put all eight inches of this steel into your ear. Get it?'

'I understand what you said. I don't think you under-stand *me*. I'm going to bite whatever you stick into my mouth. You can put that razor in my brain, I guess, but you should know that a sudden serious brain injury causes the victim to simultaneously urinate, defecate . . . and bite down.'

He looked up at Bogs, smiling that little smile of his, old Ernie said, as if the three of them had been discussing stocks and bonds with him instead of throwing it to him just as hard as they could. Just as if he was wearing one of his three-piece bankers' suits instead of kneeling on a dirty broom-closet floor with his pants around his ankles and blood trickling down the insides of his thighs.

'In fact,' he went on, 'I understand that the bite-reflex is sometimes so strong that the victim's jaws have to be pried open with a crowbar or a jackhandle.'

Bogs didn't put anything in Andy's mouth that night in late February of 1948, and neither did Rooster MacBride, and so far as I know, no one else ever did, either. What the three of them did was to beat Andy within an inch of his life, and all four of them ended up doing a jolt in solitary. Andy and Rooster MacBride went by way of the infirmary.

How many times did that particular crew have at him?

I don't know. I think Rooster lost his taste fairly early on – being in nose-splints for a month can do that to a fellow – and Bogs Diamond left off that summer, all at once.

That was a strange thing. Bogs was found in his cell, badly beaten, one morning in early June, when he didn't show up in the breakfast nose-count. He wouldn't say who had done it, or how they had gotten to him, but being in my business, I know that a screw can be bribed to do almost anything except get a gun for an inmate. They didn't make big salaries then, and they don't now. And in those days there was no electronic locking system, no closed-circuit TV, no master-switches which controlled whole areas of the prison. Back in 1948, each cellblock had its own turnkey. A guard could have been bribed real easy to let someone – maybe two or three someones – into the block, and, yes, even into Diamond's cell.

Of course a job like that would have cost a lot of money. Not by outside standards, no. Prison economics are on a smaller scale. When you've been in here a while, a dollar bill in your hand looks like a twenty did outside. My guess is, that if Bogs was done, it cost someone a serious piece of change – fifteen bucks, we'll say, for the turnkey, and two or three apiece for each of the lump-up guys.

I'm not saying it was Andy Dufresne, but I do know that he brought in five hundred dollars when he came, and he was a banker in the straight world – a man who understands better than the rest of us the ways in which money can become power.

And I know this: After the beating – the three broken ribs, the haemorrhaged eye, the sprained back and the dislocated hip – Bogs Diamond left Andy alone. In fact, after that he left everyone pretty much alone. He got to be like a high wind in the summertime, all bluster and no bite. You could say, in fact, that he turned into a 'weak sister'.

That was the end of Bogs Diamond, a man who might eventually have killed Andy if Andy hadn't taken steps to prevent it (if it *was* him who took the steps). But it wasn't the end of Andy's trouble with the sisters. There was a little hiatus, and then it began again, although not so hard nor so often. Jackals like easy prey, and there were easier pickings around than Andy Dufresne.

He always fought them, that's what I remember. He knew, I guess, that if you let them have at you even once, without fighting it, it got that much easier to let them have their way without fighting next time. So Andy would turn up with bruises on his face every once in a while, and there was the matter of the two broken fingers six or eight months after Diamond's beating. Oh yes – and sometime in late 1949, the man landed in the infirmary with a broken cheekbone that was probably the result of someone swinging a nice chunk of pipe with the business-end wrapped in flannel. He always fought back, and as a result, he did his time in solitary. But I don't think solitary was the hardship for Andy that it was for some men. He got along with himself.

The sisters was something he adjusted himself to – and then, in 1950, it stopped almost completely. That is a part of my story that I'll get to in due time.

In the fall of 1948, Andy met me one morning in the exercise yard and asked me if I could get him half a dozen rock-blankets.

'What the hell are those?' I asked.

He told me that was just what rockhounds called them; they were polishing cloths about the size of dishtowels. They were heavily padded, with a smooth side and a rough side – the smooth side like fine-grained sandpaper, the rough side almost as abrasive as industrial steel wool (Andy also kept a box of that in his cell, although he didn't get it from me – I imagine he kited it from the prison laundry).

I told him I thought we could do business on those, and I ended up getting them from the very same rock-and-gem shop where I'd arranged to get the rock-hammer. This time I charged Andy my usual ten per cent and not a penny more. I didn't see anything lethal or even dangerous in a dozen 7″ x 7″ squares of padded cloth. Rock-blankets, indeed.

It was about five months later that Andy asked if I could get him Rita Hayworth. That conversation took place in the auditorium, during a movie-show. Nowadays we get the movie-shows once or twice a week, but back then the shows were a monthly event. Usually the movies we got had a morally uplifting message to them, and this one, *The Lost Weekend*, was no different. The moral was that it's dangerous to drink. It was a moral we could take some comfort in.

Andy manoeuvred to get next to me, and about halfway through the show he leaned a little closer and asked if I could get him Rita Hayworth. I'll tell you the truth, it kind of tickled me. He was usually cool, calm, and collected, but that night he was jumpy as hell, almost embarrassed, as if he was asking me to get him a load of Trojans or one of those sheepskin-lined gadgets that are supposed to 'enhance your solitary pleasure,' as the magazines put it. He seemed over-charged, a man on the verge of blowing his radiator.

'I can get her,' I said. 'No sweat, calm down. You want the big one or the little one?' At that time Rita was my best girl (a few years before it had been Betty Grable) and she came in two sizes. For a buck you could get the little Rita. For two-fifty you could have the big Rita, four feet high and all woman.

'The big one,' he said, not looking at me. I tell you, he was a hot sketch that night. He was blushing just like a kid trying to get into a kootch show with his big brother's draft-card. 'Can you do it?'

'Take it easy, sure I can. Does a bear shit in the woods?' The audience was applauding and catcalling as the bugs came out of the walls to get Ray Milland, who was having a bad case of the DT's.

'How soon?'

'A week. Maybe less.'

'Okay.' But he sounded disappointed, as if he had been hoping I had one stuffed down my pants right then. 'How much?'

I quoted him the wholesale price. I could afford to give him this one at cost; he'd been a good customer, what with his rock-hammer and his rock-blankets. Furthermore, he'd been a good boy – on more than one night when he was having his problems with Bogs, Rooster, and the rest, I wondered how long it would be before he used the rock-hammer to crack someone's head open.

Posters are a big part of my business, just behind the booze and cigarettes, usually half a step ahead of the reefer. In the 60s the business exploded in every direction, with a lot of people wanting funky hang-ups like Jimi Hendrix, Bob Dylan, that Easy Rider poster. But mostly it's girls; one pinup queen after another.

A few days after I spoke to Ernie, a laundry driver I did business with back then brought in better than sixty posters, most of them Rita Hayworths. You may even remember the picture; I sure do. Rita is dressed – sort of – in a bathing suit, one hand behind her head, her eyes half closed, those full, sulky red lips parted. They called it Rita Hayworth, but they might as well have called it Woman in Heat.

The prison administration knows about the black market, in case you were wondering. Sure they do. They probably know as much about my business as I do myself. They live with it because they know that a prison is like a big pressure cooker, and there have to be vents somewhere to let off steam. They make the occasional bust, and I've done time in solitary a time or three over the years, but when it's something like posters, they wink. Live and let live. And when a big Rita Hayworth went up in some fishie's cell, the assumption was that it came in the mail from a friend or a relative. Of course all the care-packages from friends and relatives are opened and the contents inventoried, but who goes back and re-checks the inventory sheets for something as harmless as a Rita Hayworth or an Ava Gardner pin-up? When you're in a pressure-cooker you learn to live and let live or somebody will carve you a brand-new mouth just above the Adam's apple. You learn to make allowances.

It was Ernie again who took the poster up to Andy's cell, 14, from my own, 6. And it was Ernie who brought back the note, written in Andy's careful hand, just one word: 'Thanks.'

A little while later, as they filed us out for morning chow,

I glanced into his cell and saw Rita over his bunk in all her swimsuited glory, one hand behind her head, her eyes half-closed, those soft, satiny lips parted. It was over his bunk where he could look at her nights, after lights out, in the glow of the arc sodiums in the exercise yard.

But in the bright morning sunlight, there were dark slashes across her face – the shadow of the bars on his single slit-window.

Now I'm going to tell you what happened in mid-May of 1950 that finally ended Andy's three-year series of skirmishes with the sisters. It was also the incident which eventually got him out of the laundry and into the library, where he filled out his work-time until he left our happy little family earlier this year.

You may have noticed how much of what I've told you already is hearsay – someone saw something and told me and I told you. Well, in some cases I've simplified it even more than it really was, and have actually repeated (or will repeat) fourth- or fifth-hand information. That's the way it is here. The grapevine is very real, and you have to use it if you're going to stay ahead. Also, of course, you have to know how to pick out the grains of truth from the chaff of lies, rumours, and wish-it-had-beens.

You may also have gotten the idea that I'm describing someone who's more legend than man, and I would have to agree that there's some truth to that. To us long-timers who knew Andy over a space of years, there was an element of fantasy to him, a sense, almost, of myth-magic, if you get what I mean. That story I passed on about Andy refusing to give Bogs Diamond a head-job is part of that myth, and how he kept on fighting the sisters is part of it, and how he got the library job is part of it, too . . . but with one important difference: I was there and I saw what happened, and I swear on my mother's name that it's all true. The oath of a convicted murderer may not be worth much, but believe this: I don't lie.

Andy and I were on fair speaking terms by then. The guy fascinated me. Looking back to the poster episode, I see there's one thing I neglected to tell you, and maybe I should. Five weeks after he hung Rita up (I'd forgotten all about it by then, and had gone on to other deals), Ernie passed a small white box through the bars of my cell.

'From Dufresne,' he said, low, and never missed a stroke with his push-broom.

'Thanks, Ernie,' I said, and slipped him half a pack of Camels.

Now what the hell was this, I was wondering as I slipped the cover from the box. There was a lot of white cotton inside, and below that . . .

I looked for a long time. For a few minutes it was like I didn't even dare touch them, they were so pretty. There's a crying shortage of pretty things in the slam, and the real pity of it is that a lot of men don't even seem to miss them.

There were two pieces of quartz in that box, both of them carefully polished. They had been chipped into drift-wood shapes. There were little sparkles of iron pyrities in them like flecks of gold. If they hadn't been so heavy, they would have served as a fine pair of men's cufflinks – they were that close to being a matched set.

How much work went into creating those two pieces? Hours and hours after lights out, I knew that. First the chipping and shaping, and then the almost endless polishing and finishing with those rock-blankets. Looking at them, I felt the warmth that any man or woman feels when he or she is looking at something pretty, something that has been *worked* and *made* – that's the thing that really separates us from the animals, I think – and I felt something else, too. A sense of awe for the man's brute persistence. But I never knew just how persistent Andy Dufresne could be until much later.

In May of 1950, the powers that be decided that the roof of the licence-plate factory ought to be resurfaced with roofing tar. They wanted it done before it got too hot up there, and they asked for volunteers for the work, which was planned to take about a week. More than seventy men spoke up, because it was outside work and May is one damn fine month for outside work. Nine or ten names were drawn out of a hat, and two of them happened to be Andy's and my own.

For the next week we'd be marched out to the exercise yard after breakfast, with two guards up front and two more behind . . . plus all the guards in the towers keeping a weather eye on the proceedings through their field-glasses for good measure.

Four of us would be carrying a big extension ladder on those morning marches – I always got a kick out of the way Dickie Betts, who was on that job, called that sort of ladder an extensible – and we'd put it up against the side of that low, flat building. Then we'd start bucket-brigading hot buckets of tar up to the roof. Spill that shit on you and you'd jitterbug all the way to the infirmary.

There were six guards on the project, all of them picked on the basis of seniority. It was almost as good as a week's vacation, because instead of sweating it out in the laundry or the plate-shop or standing over a bunch of cons cutting pulp or brush somewhere out in the willywags, they were having a regular May holiday in the sun, just sitting there with their backs up against the low parapet, shooting the bull back and forth.

They didn't even have to keep more than half an eye on us, because the south wall sentry post was close enough so that the fellows up there could have spit their chews on us, if they'd wanted to. If anyone on the roof-sealing party had made one funny move, it would take four seconds to cut him smack in two with .45 caliber machine-gun bullets. So those screws just sat there and took their ease. All they needed was a couple of six-packs buried in crushed ice, and they would have been the lords of all creation.

One of them was a fellow named Byron Hadley, and in that year of 1950, he'd been at Shawshank longer than I had. Longer than the last two wardens put together, as a matter of fact. The fellow running the show in 1950 was a prissy-looking downeast Yankee named George Dunahy. He had a degree in penal administration. No one liked him, as far as I could tell, except the people who had gotten him his appointment. I heard that he wasn't interested in anything but compiling statistics for a book (which was later published by a small New England outfit called Light Side Press, where he probably had to pay to have it done), who won the intra-mural baseball championship each September, and getting a death-penalty law passed in Maine. A regular bear for the death-penalty was George Dunahy. He was fired off the job in 1953, when it came out he was running a discount auto repair service down in the prison garage and splitting the profits with Byron Hadley and Greg Stammas. Hadley and Stammas came out of that one okay – they were old hands at keeping their asses covered – but Dunahy took a walk. No one was sorry to see him go, but nobody was exactly pleased to see Greg Stammas step into his shoes, either. He was a short man with a tight, hard gut and the coldest brown eyes you ever saw. He always had a painful, pursed little grin on his face, as if he had to go to the bathroom and couldn't quite manage it. During Stammas's tenure as warden there was a lot of brutality at Shawshank, and although I have no proof, I believe there were maybe half a dozen moonlight burials in the stand of scrub forest that lies east of the prison. Dunahy was bad, but Greg Stammas was a cruel, wretched, cold-hearted man.

He and Byron Hadley were good friends. As warden, George Dunahy was nothing but a posturing figurehead; it was Stammas, and through him, Hadley, who actually administered the prison.

Hadley was a tall, shambling man with thinning red hair. He sunburned easily and he talked loud and if you didn't move fast enough to suit him, he'd clout you with his stick. On that day, our third on the roof, he was talking to another guard named Mert Entwhistle.

Hadley had gotten some amazingly good news, so he was griping about it. That was his style – he was a thankless man with not a good word for anyone, a man who was convinced that the whole world was against him. The world had cheated him out of the best years of his life, and the world would be more than happy to cheat him out of the rest. I have seen some screws that I thought were almost saintly, and I think I know why that happens – they are able to see the difference between their own lives, poor and struggling as they might be, and the lives of the men they are paid by the state to watch over. These guards are able to formulate a comparison concerning pain. Others can't, or won't.

For Byron Hadley there was no basis of comparison. He could sit there, cool and at his ease under the warm May sun and find the gall to mourn his own good luck while less than ten feet away a bunch of men were working and sweating and burning their hands on great big buckets filled with bubbling tar, men who had to work so hard in their ordinary round of days that this looked like a *respite*. You may remember the old question, the one that's supposed to define your outlook on life when you answer it. For Byron Hadley the answer would always be *half empty, the glass is half empty*. Forever and ever, amen. If you gave him a cool drink of apple cider, he'd think about vinegar. If you told him his wife had always been faithful to him, he'd tell you it was because she was so damn ugly.

So there he sat, talking to Mert Entwhistle loud enough for all of us to hear, his broad white forehead already starting to redden with the sun. He had one hand thrown back over the low parapet surrounding the roof. The other was on the butt of his .38.

We all got the story along with Mert. It seemed that Hadley's older brother had gone off to Texas some fourteen years ago and the rest of the family hadn't heard from the son of a bitch since. They had all assumed he was dead, and good riddance. Then, a week and a half ago, a lawyer had called them long-distance from Austin. It seemed that Hadley's brother had died four months ago, and a rich man at that ('It's frigging incredible how lucky some assholes can get,' this paragon of gratitude on the plate-shop roof said). The money had come as a result of oil and oil-leases, and there was close to a million dollars.

No, Hadley wasn't a millionaire – that might have made even him happy, at least for a while – but the brother had left a pretty damned decent bequest of thirty-five thousand dollars to each surviving member of his family back in Maine, if they could be found. Not bad. Like getting lucky and winning a sweepstakes.

But to Byron Hadley the glass was always half-empty. He spent most of the morning bitching to Mert about the bite that the goddam government was going to take out of his windfall. 'They'll leave me about enough to buy a new car with,' he allowed, 'and then what happens? You have to pay the damn taxes on the car, and the repairs and maintenance, you get your goddam kids pestering you to take 'em for a ride with the top down –'

'And to *drive* it, if they're old enough,' Mert said. Old Mert Entwhistle knew which side his bread was buttered on, and he didn't say what must have been as obvious to him as to the rest of us: If that money's worrying you so bad, Byron old kid old sock, I'll just take it off your hands. After all, what are friends for?

'That's right, wanting to drive it, wanting to *learn* to drive on it, for Chrissake,' Byron said with a shudder. 'Then what happens at the end of the year? If you figured the tax wrong and you don't have enough left over to pay the overdraft, you got to pay out of your own pocket, or maybe even borrow it from one of those kikey loan agencies. And they audit you anyway, you know. It don't matter. And when the government audits you, they always take more. Who can fight Uncle Sam? He puts his hand inside your shirt and squeezes your tit until it's purple, and you end up getting the short end. Christ.'

He lapsed into a morose silence, thinking of what terrible bad luck he'd had to inherit that $35,000. Andy Dufresne had been spreading tar with a big Padd brush less than fifteen feet away and now he tossed it into his pail and walked over to where Mert and Hadley were sitting.

We all tightened up, and I saw one of the other screws, Tim Youngblood, drag his hand down to where his pistol was holstered. One of the fellows in the sentry tower struck his partner on the arm and they both turned, too. For one moment I thought Andy was going to get shot, or clubbed, or both.

Then he said, very softly, to Hadley: 'Do you trust your wife?'

Hadley just stared at him. He was starting to get red in the face, and I knew that was a bad sign. In about three seconds he was going to pull his billy and give Andy the butt end of it right in the solar plexus, where that big bundle of nerves is. A hard enough hit there can kill you, but they always go for it. If it doesn't kill you it will paralyze you long enough to forget whatever cute move it was that you had planned.

'Boy,' Hadley said, 'I'll give you just one chance to pick up that Padd. And then you're goin' off this roof on your head.'

Andy just looked at him, very calm and still. His eyes were like ice. It was as if he hadn't heard. And I found myself wanting to tell him how it was, to give him the crash course.

The crash course is you *never* let on that you hear the guards talking, you *never* try to horn in on their conversation unless you're asked (and then you always tell them just what they want to hear and shut up again). Black man, white man, red man, yellow man, in prison it doesn't matter because we've got our own brand of equality. In prison every con's a nigger and you have to get used to the idea if you intend to survive men like Hadley and Greg Stammas, who really would kill you just as soon as look at you. When you're in stir you belong to the state and if you forget it, woe is you. I've known men who've lost eyes, men who've lost toes and fingers; I knew one man who lost the tip of his penis and counted himself lucky that was all he lost. I wanted to tell Andy that it was already too late. He could go back and pick up his brush and there would still be some big lug waiting for him in the showers that night, ready to charlie-horse both of his legs and leave him writhing on the cement. You could buy a lug like that for a pack of cigarettes or three Baby Ruths. Most of all, I wanted to tell him not to make it any worse than it already was.

What I did was to keep on running tar onto the roof as if nothing at all was happening. Like everyone else, I look after my own ass first. I have to. It's cracked already, and in Shawshank there have always been Hadleys willing to finish the job of breaking it.

Andy said, 'Maybe I put it wrong. Whether you trust her or not is immaterial. The problem is whether or not you believe she would ever go behind your back, try to hamstring you.'

Hadley got up. Mert got up. Tim Youngblood got up. Hadley's face was as red as the side of a firebarn. 'Your only

44

problem,' he said, 'is going to be how many bones you still get unbroken. You can count them in the infirmary. Come on, Mert. We're throwing this sucker over the side.'

Tim Youngblood drew his gun. The rest of us kept tarring like mad. The sun beat down. They were going to do it; Hadley and Mert were simply going to pitch him over the side. Terrible accident. Dufresne, prisoner 81433-SHNK, was taking a couple of empties down and slipped on the ladder. Too bad.

They laid hold of him, Mert on the right arm, Hadley on the left. Andy didn't resist. His eyes never left Hadley's red, horsey face.

'If you've got your thumb on her, Mr Hadley,' he said in that same calm, composed voice, 'there's not a reason why you shouldn't have every cent of that money. Final score, Mr Byron Hadley thirty-five thousand, Uncle Sam zip.'

Mert started to drag him towards the edge. Hadley just stood still. For a moment Andy was like a rope between them in a tug-of-war game. Then Hadley said, 'Hold on one second, Mert. What do you mean, boy?'

'I mean, if you've got your thumb on your wife, you can give it to her,' Andy said.

'You better start making sense, boy, or you're going over.'

'The government allows you a one-time-only gift to your spouse,' Andy said. 'It's good up to sixty thousand dollars.'

Hadley was now looking at Andy as if he had been poleaxed. 'Naw, that ain't right,' he said. 'Tax *free*?'

'Tax free,' Andy said. 'IRS can't touch cent one.'

'How would you know a thing like that?'

Tim Youngblood said: 'He used to be a banker, Byron. I s'pose he might –'

'Shut ya head, Trout,' Hadley said without looking at him. Tim Youngblood flushed and shut up. Some of the guards called him Trout because of his thick lips and buggy eyes. Hadley kept looking at Andy. 'You're the smart banker who shot his wife. Why should I believe a smart banker like you? So I can wind up in here breaking rocks right alongside you? You'd like that, wouldn't you?'

Andy said quietly, 'If you went to jail for tax evasion, you'd go to a federal penitentiary, not Shawshank. But you won't. The tax-free gift to the spouse is a perfectly legal loophole. I've done dozens . . . no, hundreds of them. It's meant primarily for people with small businesses to pass on, or for people who come into one-time-only windfalls. Like yourself.'

'I think you're lying,' Hadley said, but he didn't – you could see he didn't. There was an emotion dawning on his face, something that was grotesque overlying that long, ugly countenance and that receding, sunburned brow. An almost obscene emotion when seen on the features of Byron Hadley. It was hope.

'No, I'm not lying. There's no reason why you should take my word for it, either. Engage a lawyer –'

'Ambulance-chasing highway-robbing cocksuckers!' Hadley cried.

Andy shrugged. 'Then go to the IRS. They'll tell you the same thing for free. Actually, you don't need me to tell you at all. You would have investigated the matter for yourself.'

'You fucking-A. I don't need any smart wife-killing banker to show me where the bear shit in the buckwheat.'

'You'll need a tax lawyer or a banker to set up the gift for you and that will cost you something,' Andy said. 'Or . . . if you were interested, I'd be glad to set it up for you nearly free of charge. The price would be three beers apiece for my co-workers –'

'Co-workers,' Mert said, and let out a rusty guffaw. He slapped his knee. A real knee-slapper was old Mert, and I hope he died of intestinal cancer in a part of the world where morphine is as of yet undiscovered. 'Co-workers, ain't that cute? Co-workers! You ain't got any –'

'Shut your friggin' trap,' Hadley growled, and Mert shut. Hadley looked at Andy again. 'What was you saying?'

'I was saying that I'd only ask three beers apiece for my co-workers, if that seems fair,' Andy said. 'I think a man feels more like a man when he's working out of doors in the springtime if he can have a bottle of suds. That's only my opinion. It would go down smooth, and I'm sure you'd have their gratitude.'

I have talked to some of the other men who were up there that day – Rennie Martin, Logan St Pierre, and Paul Bonsaint were three of them – and we all saw the same thing then . . . *felt* the same thing. Suddenly it was Andy who had the upper hand. It was Hadley who had the gun on his hip and the billy in his hand, Hadley who had his friend Greg Stammas behind him and the whole prison administration behind Stammas, the whole power of the state behind *that*, but all at once in that golden sunshine it didn't matter, and I felt my heart leap up in my chest as it never had since the truck drove me and four others through the gate back in 1938 and I stepped out into the exercise yard.

Andy was looking at Hadley with those cold, clear, calm eyes, and it wasn't just the thirty-five thousand then, we all agreed on that. I've played it over and over in my mind and

I *know*. It was man against man, and Andy simply *forced* him, the way a strong man can force a weaker man's wrist to the table in a game of Indian wrestling. There was no reason, you see, why Hadley couldn't've given Mert the nod at that very minute, pitched Andy overside onto his head, and still taken Andy's advice.

No reason. *But he didn't.*

'I could get you all a couple of beers if I wanted to,' Hadley said. 'A beer does taste good while you're workin'.' The colossal prick even managed to sound magnanimous.

'I'd just give you one piece of advice the IRS wouldn't bother with,' Andy said. His eyes were fixed unwinkingly on Hadley's. 'Make the gift to your wife if you're *sure*. If you think there's even a chance she might double-cross you or backshoot you, we could work out something else —'

'Double-cross me?' Hadley asked harshly. 'Double-cross *me*? Mr Hotshot Banker, if she ate her way through a boxcar of Ex-Lax, she wouldn't dare fart unless I gave her the nod.'

Mert, Youngblood, and the other screws yucked it up dutifully. Andy never cracked a smile.

'I'll write down the forms you need,' he said. 'You can get them at the post office, and I'll fill them out for your signature.'

That sounded suitably important, and Hadley's chest swelled. Then he glared around at the rest of us and hollered, 'What are you jimmies starin' at? Move your asses, goddammit!' He looked back at Andy. 'You come over here with me, hotshot. And listen to me well: if you're Jewing me somehow, you're gonna find yourself chasing your head around Shower C before the week's out.'

'Yes, I understand that,' Andy said softly.

48

And he did understand it. The way it turned out, he understood a lot more than I did – more than any of us did.

That's how, on the second-to-last day of the job, the convict crew that tarred the plate-factory roof in 1950 ending up sitting in a row at ten o'clock on a spring morning, drinking Black Label beer supplied by the hardest screw that ever walked a turn at Shawshank Prison. That beer was pisswarm, but it was still the best I ever had in my life. We sat and drank it and felt the sun on our shoulders, and not even the expression of half-amusement, half-contempt on Hadley's face – as if he was watching apes drink beer instead of men – could spoil it. It lasted twenty minutes, that beer-break, and for those twenty minutes we felt like free men. We could have been drinking beer and tarring the roof of one of our own houses.

Only Andy didn't drink. I already told you about his drinking habits. He sat hunkered down in the shade, hands dangling between his knees, watching us and smiling a little. It's amazing how many men remember him that way, and amazing how many men were on that work-crew when Andy Dufresne faced down Byron Hadley. I thought there were nine or ten of us, but by 1955 there must have been two hundred of us, maybe more . . . if you believed what you heard.

So, yeah – if you asked me to give you a flat-out answer to the question of whether I'm trying to tell you about a man or a legend that got made up around the man, like a pearl around a little piece of grit – I'd have to say that the answer lies somewhere in between. All I know for sure is that Andy Dufresne wasn't much like me or anyone else I ever knew since I came inside. He brought in five hundred dollars jammed up his back porch, but somehow that graymeat son of a bitch managed to bring in something else as well. A sense of his own worth, maybe, or a feeling that he would be the winner in the end . . . or maybe it was only a sense of freedom, even inside these goddamned grey walls. It was a kind of inner light he carried around with him. I only knew him to lose that light once, and that is also a part of this story.

By World Series time of 1950 – this was the year Bobby Thompson hit his famous home run at the end of the season, you will remember – Andy was having no more trouble from the sisters. Stammas and Hadley had passed the word. If Andy Dufresne came to either of them or any of the other screws that formed a part of their coterie, and showed so much as a single drop of blood in his underpants, every sister in Shawshank would go to bed that night with a headache. They didn't fight it. As I have pointed out, there was always an eighteen-year-old car thief or a firebug or some guy who'd gotten his kicks handling little children. After the day on the plate-shop roof, Andy went his way and the sisters went theirs.

He was working in the library then, under a tough old con named Brooks Hatlen. Hatlen had gotten the job back in the late 20s because he had a college education. Brooksie's degree was in animal husbandry, true enough, but college educations in institutes of lower learning like The Shank are so rare that it's a case of beggars not being able to be choosers.

In 1952 Brooksie, who had killed his wife and daughter

after a losing streak at poker back when Coolidge was President, was paroled. As usual, the state in all its wisdom had let him go long after any chance he might have had to become a useful part of society was gone. He was sixty-eight and arthritic when he tottered out of the main gate in his Polish suit and his French shoes, his parole papers in one hand and a Greyhound bus ticket in the other. He was crying when he left. Shawshank was his world. What lay beyond its walls was as terrible to Brooks as the Western Seas had been to superstitious 13th-century sailors. In prison, Brooksie had been a person of some importance. He was the head librarian, an educated man. If he went to the Kittery library and asked for a job, they wouldn't give him a library card. I heard he died in a home for indigent old folks up Freeport way in 1952, and at that he lasted about six months longer than I thought he would. Yeah, I guess the state got its own back on Brooksie, all right. They trained him to like it inside the shithouse and then they threw him out.

Andy succeeded to Brooksie's job, and he was head librarian for twenty-three years. He used the same force of will I'd seen him use on Byron Hadley to get what he wanted for the library, and I saw him gradually turn one small room (which still smelled of turpentine because it had been a paint closet until 1922 and had never been properly aired) lined with *Reader's Digest Condensed Books* and *National Geographics* into the best prison library in New England.

He did it a step at a time. He put a suggestion box by the door and patiently weeded out such attempts at humour as *More Fuk-Boox Pleeze* and *Escape in 10 EZ Lesions*. He got hold of the things the prisoners seemed serious about. He wrote to three major book clubs in New York and got two of them, The Literary Guild and The Book of the Month Club, to send editions of all their major selections to us at a special cheap rate. He discovered a hunger for information on such small hobbies as soap-carving, woodworking, sleight of hand, and card solitaire. He got all the books he could on such subjects. And those two jailhouse staples, Erle Stanley Gardener and Louis L'Amour. Cons never seem to get enough of the courtroom or the open range. And yes, he did keep a box of fairly spicy paperbacks under the checkout desk, loaning them out carefully and making sure they always got back. Even so, each new acquisition of that type was quickly read to tatters.

He began to write to the state senate in Augusta in 1954. Stammas was warden by then, and he used to pretend Andy was some sort of mascot. He was always in the library, shooting the bull with Andy, and sometimes he'd even throw a paternal arm around Andy's shoulders or give him a goose. He didn't fool anybody. Andy Dufresne was no one's mascot.

He told Andy that maybe he'd been a banker on the outside, but that part of his life was receding rapidly into his past and he had better get a hold on the facts of prison life. As far as that bunch of jumped-up Republican Rotarians in Augusta was concerned, there were only three viable expenditures of the taxpayers' money in the field of prisons and corrections. Number one was more walls, number two was more bars, and number three was more guards. As far as the state senate was concerned, Stammas explained, the folks in Thomastan and Shawshank and Pittsfield and South Portland were the scum of the earth. They were there to do hard time, and by God and Sonny

Jesus, it was hard time they were going to do. And if there were a few weevils in the bread, wasn't that just too fucking bad?

Andy smiled his small, composed smile and asked Stammas what would happen to a block of concrete if a drop of water fell on it once every year for a million years. Stammas laughed and clapped Andy on the back. 'You got no million years, old horse, but if you did, I believe you'd do it with that same little grin on your face. You go on and write your letters. I'll even mail them for you if you pay for the stamps.'

Which Andy did. And he had the last laugh, although Stammas and Hadley weren't around to see it. Andy's requests for library funds were routinely turned down until 1960, when he received a check for two hundred dollars – the senate probably appropriated it in hopes that he would shut up and go away. Vain hope. Andy felt that he had finally gotten one foot in the door and he simply redoubled his efforts; two letters a week instead of one. In 1962 he got four hundred dollars, and for the rest of the decade the library received seven hundred dollars a year like clockwork. By 1971 that had risen to an even thousand. Not much stacked up against what your average small-town library receives, I guess, but a thousand bucks can buy a lot of re-cycled Perry Mason stories and Jake Logan Westerns. By the time Andy left, you could go into the library (expanded from its original paint-locker to three rooms), and find just about anything you'd want. And if you couldn't find it, chances were good that Andy could get it for you.

Now you're asking yourself if all this came about just because Andy told Byron Hadley how to save the taxes on his windfall inheritance. The answer is yes . . . and no. You can probably figure out what happened for yourself.

Word got around that Shawshank was housing its very own pet financial wizard. In the late spring and the summer of 1950, Andy set up two trust funds for guards who wanted to assure a college education for their kids, he advised a couple of others who wanted to take small fliers in common stock (and they did pretty damn well, as things turned out; one of them did so well he was able to take an early retirement two years later), and I'll be damned if he didn't advise the warden himself, old Lemon Lips George Dunahy, on how to go about setting up a tax-shelter for himself. That was just before Dunahy got the bum's rush, and I believe he must have been dreaming about all the millions his book was going to make him. By April of 1951, Andy was doing the tax returns for half the screws at Shawshank, and by 1952, he was doing almost all of them. He was paid in what may be a prison's most valuable coin: simple goodwill.

Later on, after Greg Stammas took over the warden's office, Andy became even more important – but if I tried to tell you the specifics of just how, I'd be guessing. There are some things I know about and others I can only guess at. I know that there were some prisoners who received all sorts of special considerations – radios in their cells, extraordinary visiting privileges, things like that – and there were people on the outside who were paying for them to have those privileges. Such people are known as 'angels' by the prisoners. All at once some fellow would be excused from working in the plate-shop on Saturday forenoons, and you'd know that fellow had an angel out there who'd coughed up a chuck of dough to make sure it happened. The way it usually works is that the angel will pay the bribe to some middle-level screw, and the screw will spread the grease both up and down the administrative ladder.

Then there was the discount auto repair service that laid Warden Dunahy low. It went underground for a while and then emerged stronger than ever in the late fifties. And some of the contractors that worked at the prison from time to time were paying kickbacks to the top administration officials, I'm pretty sure, and the same was almost certainly true of the companies whose equipment was bought and installed in the laundry and the licence-plate shop and the stamping-mill that was built in 1963.

By the late sixties there was also a booming trade in pills, and the same administrative crowd was involved in turning a buck on that. All of it added up to a pretty good-sized river of illicit income. Not like the pile of clandestine bucks that must fly around a really big prison like Attica or San Quentin, but not peanuts, either. And money itself becomes a problem after a while. You can't just stuff it into your wallet and then shell out a bunch of crumpled twenties and dog-eared tens when you want a pool built in your back yard or an addition put on your house. Once you get past a certain point, you have to explain where that money came from . . . and if your explanations aren't convincing enough, you're apt to wind up wearing a number yourself.

So there was a need for Andy's services. They took him out of the laundry and installed him in the library, but if you wanted to look at it another way, they never took him out of the laundry at all. They just set him to work washing dirty money instead of dirty sheets. He funnelled it into stocks, bonds, tax-free municipals, you name it.

He told me once about ten years after that day on the plate-shop roof that his feelings about what he was doing were pretty clear, and that his conscience was relatively untroubled. The rackets would have gone on with him or without him. He had not asked to be sent to Shawshank, he went on; he was an innocent man who had been victimized by colossal bad luck, not a missionary or a do-gooder.

'Besides, Red,' he told me with that same half-grin, 'what I'm doing in here isn't all *that* different from what I was doing outside. I'll hand you a pretty cynical axiom: the amount of expert financial help an individual or company needs rises in direct proportion to how many people that person or business is screwing.

'The people who run this place are stupid, brutal monsters for the most part. The people who run the straight world are brutal and monstrous, but they happen not to be quite as stupid, because the standard of competence out there is a little higher. Not much, but a little.'

'But the pills,' I said. 'I don't want to tell you your business, but they make me nervous. Reds, uppers, downers, nembutals — now they've got these things they call Phase Fours. I won't get anything like that. Never have.'

'No,' Andy said. 'I don't like the pills either. Never have. But I'm not much of a one for cigarettes or booze, either. But I don't push the pills. I don't bring them in, and I don't sell them once they are in. Mostly it's the screws who do that.'

'But —'

'Yeah, I know. There's a fine line there. What it comes down to, Red, is some people refuse to get their hands dirty at all. That's called sainthood, and the pigeons land on your shoulders and crap all over your shirt. The other extreme is to take a bath in the dirt and deal any goddamned thing that will turn a dollar – guns, switchblades, big H, what the hell. You ever have a con come up to you and offer you a contract?'

I nodded. It's happened a lot of times over the years. You are, after all, the man who can get it. And they figure if you can get them a nine-bolt battery for their transistor radio or a carton of Luckies or a lid of reefer, you can put them in touch with a guy who'll use a knife.

'Sure you have,' Andy agreed. 'But you don't do it. Because guys like us, Red, we know there's a third choice. An alternative to staying simon-pure or bathing in the filth and the slime. It's the alternative that grown-ups all over the world pick. You balance off your walk through the hog-wallow against what it gains you. You choose the lesser of two evils and try to keep your good intentions in front of you. And I guess you judge how well you're doing by how well you sleep at night . . . and what your dreams are like.'

'Good intentions,' I said, and laughed. 'I know all about that, Andy. A fellow can toddle right off to hell on that road.'

'Don't you believe it,' he said, growing sombre. 'This is hell right here. Right here in The Shank. They sell pills and I tell them what to do with the money. But I've also got the library, and I know of over two dozen guys who have used the books in here to help them pass their high school equivalency tests. Maybe when they get out of here they'll be able to crawl off the shitheap. When we needed that second room back in 1957, I got it. Because they want to keep me happy. I work cheap. That's the trade-off.'

'And you've got your own private quarters.'

'Sure. That's the way I like it.'

The prison population had risen slowly all through the fifties, and it damn near exploded in the sixties, what with every college-age kid in America wanting to try dope and the perfectly ridiculous penalties for the use of a little reefer. But in all that time Andy never had a cellmate, except for a big, silent Indian named Normaden (like all Indians in The Shank, he was called Chief), and Normaden didn't last long. A lot of the other long-timers thought Andy was crazy, but Andy just smiled. He lived alone and he liked it that way . . . and as he'd said, they liked to keep him happy. He worked cheap.

Prison time is slow time, sometimes you'd swear it's stop-time, but it passes. It passes. George Dunahy departed the scene in a welter of newspaper headlines shouting SCANDAL and NEST-FEATHERING. Stammas succeeded him, and for the next six years Shawshank was a kind of living hell. During the reign of Greg Stammas, the beds in the infirmary and the cells in the solitary wing were always full.

One day in 1958 I looked at myself in a small shaving mirror I kept in my cell and saw a forty-year-old man looking back at me. A kid had come in back in 1938, a kid with a big mop of carrotty red hair, half-crazy with remorse, thinking about suicide. That kid was gone. The red hair was half grey and starting to recede. There were crow's tracks around the eyes. On that day I could see an old man inside, waiting his time to come out. It scared me. Nobody wants to grow old in stir.

Stammas went early in 1959. There had been several investigative reporters sniffing around, and one of them even did four months under an assumed name, for a crime made up out of whole cloth. They were getting ready to drag out SCANDAL and NEST-FEATHERING again, but before they could bring the hammer down on him, Stammas ran. I can understand that; boy, can I ever. If he had been tried and convicted, he could have ended up right in here. If so, he might have lasted all of five hours. Byron Hadley had gone two years earlier. The sucker had a heart attack and took an early retirement.

Andy never got touched by the Stammas affair. In early 1959 a new warden was appointed, and a new assistant warden, and a new chief of guards. For the next eight months or so, Andy was just another con again. It was during that period that Normaden, the big half-breed Passamaquoddy, shared Andy's cell with him. Then everything just started up again. Normaden was moved out, and Andy was living in solitary splendour again. The names at the top change, but the rackets never do.

I talked to Normaden once about Andy. 'Nice fella,' Normaden said. It was hard to make out anything he said because he had a harelip and a cleft palate; his words all came out in a slush. 'I liked it there. He never made fun. But he didn't want me there. I could tell.' Big shrug. 'I was glad to go, me. Bad draught in that cell. All the time cold. He don't let nobody touch his things. That's okay. Nice man, never made fun. But big draught.'

Rita Hayworth hung in Andy's cell until 1955, if I remember right. Then it was Marilyn Monroe, that picture from *The Seven Year Itch* where she's standing over a subway grating and the warm air is flipping her skirt up. Marilyn lasted until

1960, and she was considerably tattered about the edges when Andy replaced her with Jayne Mansfield. Jayne was, you should pardon the expression, a bust. After only a year or so she was replaced with an English actress – might have been Hazel Court, but I'm not sure. In 1966 that one came down and Raquel Welch went up for a record-breaking six-year engagement in Andy's cell. The last poster to hang there was a pretty country-rock singer whose name was Linda Ronstadt.

I asked him once what the posters meant to him, and he gave me a peculiar, surprised sort of look. 'Why, they mean the same thing to me as they do to most cons, I guess,' he said. 'Freedom. You look at those pretty women and you feel like you could almost . . . not quite but *almost* step right through and be beside them. Be free. I guess that's why I always liked Raquel Welch the best. It wasn't just her; it was that beach she was standing on. Looked like she was down in Mexico somewhere. Someplace quiet, where a man would be able to hear himself think. Didn't you ever feel that way about a picture, Red? That you could almost step right through it?'

I said I'd never really thought of it that way.

'Maybe someday you'll see what I mean,' he said, and he was right. Years later I saw exactly what he meant . . . and when I did, the first thing I thought of was Normaden, and about how he'd said it was always cold in Andy's cell.

A terrible thing happened to Andy in late March or early April of 1963. I have told you that he had something that most of the other prisoners, myself included, seemed to lack. Call it a sense of equanimity, or a feeling of inner peace, maybe even a constant and unwavering faith that someday the long nightmare would end. Whatever you want to call it, Andy Dufresne always seemed to have his act together. There was none of that sullen desperation about him that seems to afflict most lifers after a while; you could never smell hopelessness on him. Until that late winter of '63.

We had another warden by then, a man named Samuel Norton. The Mather brothers, Cotton and Increase, would have felt right at home with Sam Norton. So far as I know, no one had ever seen him so much as crack a smile. He had a thirty-year pin from the Baptist Advent Church of Eliot. His major innovation as the head of our happy family was to make sure that each incoming prisoner had a New Testament. He had a small plaque on his desk, gold letters inlaid in teakwood, which said CHRIST IS MY SAVIOUR. A sampler on the wall, made by his wife, read: HIS JUDG-MENT COMETH AND THAT RIGHT EARLY. This latter sentiment cut zero ice with most of us. We felt that the judgment had already occurred, and we would be willing to testify with the best of them that the rock would not hide us nor the dead tree give us shelter. He had a Bible quote for every occasion, did Mr Sam Norton, and whenever you meet a man like that, my best advice to you would be to grin big and cover up your balls with both hands.

There were less infirmary cases than in the days of Greg Stammas, and so far as I know the moonlight burials ceased altogether, but this is not to say that Norton was not a believer in punishment. Solitary was always well populated. Men lost their teeth not from beatings but from bread and water diets. It began to be called grain and drain, as in 'I'm on the Sam Norton grain and drain train, boys.'

The man was the foulest hypocrite that I ever saw in a high position. The rackets I told you about earlier continued to flourish, but Sam Norton added his own new wrinkles. Andy knew about them all, and because we had gotten to be pretty good friends by that time, he let me in on some of them. When Andy talked about them, an expression of amused, disgusted wonder would come over his face, as if he was telling me about some ugly, predatory species of bug that was, by its very ugliness and greed, somehow more comic than terrible.

It was Warden Norton who instituted the 'Inside-Out' programme you may have read about some sixteen or seventeen years back; it was even written up in *Newsweek*. In the press it sounded like a real advance in practical corrections and rehabilitation. There were prisoners out cutting pulpwood, prisoners repairing bridges and causeways, prisoners constructing potato cellars. Norton called it 'Inside-Out' and was invited to explain it to damn near every Rotary and Kiwanis club in New England, especially after he got his picture in *Newsweek*. The prisoners called it 'road-ganging', but so far as I know, none of them were ever invited to express their views to the Kiwanians or the Loyal Order of the Moose.

Norton was right in there on every operation, thirty-year church-pin and all, from cutting pulp to digging storm-drains to laying new culverts on state highways, there was Norton, skimming off the top. There were a hundred ways to do it – men, materials, you name it. But he had it coming another way, as well. The construction businesses in the area were deathly afraid of Norton's Inside-Out programme, because prison labour is slave labour, and you can't compete with that. So Sam Norton, he of the Testaments and the thirty-year church-pin, was passed a good many thick envelopes under the table during his fifteen-year tenure as Shawshank's warden. And when an envelope was passed, he would either overbid the project, not bid at all, or claim that all his Inside-Outers were committed elsewhere. It has always been something of a wonder to me that Norton was never found in the trunk of a Thunderbird parked off a highway somewhere down in Massachusetts with his hands tied behind his back and half a dozen bullets in his head.

Anyway, as the old barrelhouse song says, My God, how the money rolled in. Norton must have subscribed to the old Puritan notion that the best way to figure out which folks God favours is by checking their bank accounts.

Andy Dufresne was his right hand in all of this, his silent partner. The prison library was Andy's hostage to fortune. Norton knew it, and Norton used it. Andy told me that one of Norton's favourite aphorisms was *One hand washes the other*. So Andy gave good advice and made useful suggestions. I can't say for sure that he hand-tooled Norton's Inside-Out programme, but I'm damned sure he processed the money for the Jesus-shouting son of a whore. He gave good advice, made useful suggestions, the money got spread around, and . . . son of a bitch! The library would get a new set of automotive repair manuals, a fresh set of *Grolier Encyclopedias*, books on how to prepare for the Scholastic Achievement Tests. And, of course, more Erle Stanley Gardeners and more Louis L'Amours.

And I'm convinced that what happened happened because Norton just didn't want to lose his good right hand. I'll go further: it happened because he was scared of what might happen – what Andy might say against him – if Andy ever got clear of Shawshank State Prison.

I got the story a chunk here and a chunk there over a space of seven years, some of it from Andy – but not all. He never wanted to talk about that part of his life, and I don't blame him. I got parts of it from maybe half a dozen different sources. I've said once that prisoners are nothing but slaves, but they have that slave habit of looking dumb and keeping their ears open. I got it backwards and forwards and in the middle, but I'll give it to you from point A to point Z, and maybe you'll understand why the man spent about ten months in a bleak, depressed daze. See, I don't think he knew the truth until 1963, fifteen years after he came into this sweet little hell-hole. Until he met Tommy Williams, I don't think he knew how bad it could get.

Tommy Williams joined our happy little Shawshank family in November of 1962. Tommy thought of himself as a native of Massachusetts, but he wasn't proud; in his twenty-seven years he'd done time all over New England. He was a professional thief, and as you may have guessed, my own feeling was that he should have picked another profession.

He was a married man, and his wife came to visit each and every week. She had an idea that things might go better with Tommy – and consequently better with their three-year-old son and herself – if he got his high school degree. She talked him into it, and so Tommy Williams started visiting the library on a regular basis.

For Andy, this was an old routine by then. He saw that Tommy got a series of high school equivalency tests. Tommy would brush up on the subjects he had passed in high-school – there weren't many – and then take the test. Andy also saw that he was enrolled in a number of correspondence courses covering the subjects he had failed in school or just missed by dropping out.

He probably wasn't the best student Andy ever took over the jumps, and I don't know if he ever did get his high school diploma, but that forms no part of my story. The important thing was that he came to like Andy Dufresne very much, as most people did after a while.

On a couple of occasions he asked Andy 'what a smart guy like you is doing in the joint' – a question which is the rough equivalent of that one that goes 'What's a nice girl like you doing in a place like this?' But Andy wasn't the type to tell him; he would only smile and turn the conversation into some other channel. Quite normally, Tommy asked someone else, and when he finally got the story, I guess he also got the shock of his young life.

The person he asked was his partner on the laundry's steam ironer and folder. The inmates call this device the mangler, because that's exactly what it will do to you if you aren't paying attention and get your bad self caught in it. His partner was Charlie Lathrop, who had been in for about twelve years on a murder charge. He was more than glad to reheat the details of the Dufresne murder trial for Tommy; it broke the monotony of pulling freshly pressed bedsheets out of the machine and tucking them into the basket. He was just getting to the jury waiting until after lunch to bring in their guilty verdict when the trouble whistle went off and the mangle grated to a stop. They had been feeding in freshly washed sheets from the Eliot Nursing Home at the far end; these were spat out dry and neatly pressed at Tommy's and Charlie's end at the rate of one every five seconds. Their job was to grab them, fold them, and slap them into the cart, which had already been lined with brown paper.

But Tommy Williams was just standing there, staring at Charlie Lathrop, his mouth unhinged all the way to his chest. He was standing in a drift of sheets that had come through clean and which were now sopping up all the wet muck on the floor – and in a laundry wetwash, there's plenty of muck.

So the head bull that day, Homer Jessup, comes rushing over, bellowing his head off and on the prod for trouble. Tommy took no notice of him. He spoke to Charlie as if old Homer, who had busted more heads than he could probably count, hadn't been there.

'What did you say that golf pro's name was?'

'Quentin,' Charlie answered back, all confused and upset by now. He later said that the kid was as white as a truce flag. 'Glenn Quentin, I think. Something like that, anyway –'

'Here now, here now,' Homer Jessup roared, his neck as red as a rooster's comb. 'Get them sheets in cold water! Get quick! Get quick, by Jesus, you –'

'Glenn Quentin, oh my God,' Tommy Williams said, and that was all he got to say because Homer Jessup, that least peaceable of men, brought his billy down behind his ear. Tommy hit the floor so hard he broke off three of his front teeth. When he woke up he was in solitary, and confined to same for a week, riding a boxcar on Sam Norton's famous grain and drain train. Plus a black mark on his report card.

That was in early February in 1963, and Tommy Williams went around to six or seven other long-timers after he got out of solitary and got pretty much the same story. I know; I was one of them. But when I asked him why he wanted it, he just clammed up.

Then one day he went to the library and spilled one helluva big budget of information to Andy Dufresne. And for the first and last time, at least since he had approached me about the Rita Hayworth poster like a kid buying his first pack of Trojans, Andy lost his cool . . . only this time he blew it entirely.

I saw him later that day, and he looked like a man who has stepped on the business end of a rake and given himself a good one, whap between the eyes. His hands were trembling, and when I spoke to him, he didn't answer. Before that afternoon was out he had caught up with Billy Hanlon, who was the head screw, and set up an appointment with Warden Norton for the following day. He told me later that he didn't sleep a wink all that night; he just listened to a cold winter wind howling outside, watched the searchlights go around and around, putting long, moving shadows on the cement walls of the cage he had called home since Harry Truman was President, and tried to think it all out. He said it was as if Tommy had produced a key which fitted a cage in the back of his mind, a cage like his own cell. Only instead of holding a man, that cage held a tiger, and that tiger's name was Hope. Williams had produced the key that unlocked the cage and the tiger was out, willy-nilly, to roam his brain.

Four years before, Tommy Williams had been arrested in Rhode Island, driving a stolen car that was full of stolen merchandise. Tommy turned in his accomplice, the DA played ball, and he got a lighter sentence . . . two to four, with time served. Eleven months after beginning his term, his old cell-mate got a ticket out and Tommy got a new one, a man named Elwood Blatch. Blatch had been busted for burglary with a weapon and was serving six to twelve.

'I never seen such a high-strung guy,' Tommy said. 'A man like that should never want to be a burglar, specially not with a gun. The slightest little noise, he'd go three feet into the air . . . and come down shooting, more likely than not. One night he almost strangled me because some guy down the hall was whopping on his cell bars with a tin cup.

'I did seven months with him, until they let me walk free. I got time served and time off, you understand. I can't say we talked because you didn't, you know, exactly hold a conversation with El Blatch. *He* held a conversation with *you*. He talked all the time. Never shut up. If you tried to get a word in, he'd shake his fist at you and roll his eyes. It gave me the cold chills whenever he done that. Big tall guy he was, mostly bald, with these green eyes set way down deep in the sockets. Jeez, I hope I never see him again.

'It was like a talkin' jag every night. Where he grew up, the orphanages he run away from, the jobs he done, the women he fucked, the crap games he cleaned out. I just let him run on. My face ain't much, but I didn't want it, you know, rearranged for me.

'According to him, he'd burgled over two hundred joints. It was hard for me to believe, a guy like him who went off like a firecracker every time someone cut a loud fart, but he swore it was true. Now . . . listen to me, Red. I know guys sometimes make things up after they know a thing, but even before I knew about this golf pro guy, Quentin, I remember thinking that if El Blatch ever burgled *my* house, and I found out about it later, I'd have to count myself just about the luckiest motherfucker going still to be alive. Can you imagine him in some lady's bedroom, sifting through her jool'ry box, and she coughs in her sleep or turns over quick? It gives me the cold chills just to think of something like that, I swear on my mother's name it does.

'He said he'd killed people, too. People that gave him shit. At least that's what he said. And I believed him. He sure looked like a man that could do some killing. He was just so fucking high-strung! Like a pistol with a sawed-off firing pin. I knew a guy who had a Smith & Wesson Police Special with a sawed-off firing pin. It wasn't no good for nothing, except maybe for something to jaw about. The pull on that gun was so light that it would fire if this guy, Johnny Callahan, his name was, if he turned his record-player on full volume and put it on top of one of the speakers. That's how El Blatch was. I can't explain it any better. I just never doubted that he had greased some people.

'So one night, just for something to say, I go: "Who'd you kill?" Like a joke, you know. So he laughs and says, "There's one guy doing time up-Maine for these two people I killed. It was this guy and the wife of the slob who's doing time. I was creeping their place and the guy started to give me some shit."

'I can't remember if he ever told me the woman's name or not,' Tommy went on. 'Maybe he did. But in New England, Dufresne's like Smith or Jones in the rest of the country, because there's so many Frogs up here. Dufresne, Lavesque, Ouelette, Poulin, who can remember Frog names? But he told me the guy's name. He said the guy was Glenn Quentin and he was a prick, a big rich prick, a golf pro. El said he thought the guy might have cash in the house, maybe as much as five thousand dollars. That was a lot of money back then, he says to me. So I go, "When was that?" And he goes, "After the war. Just after the war."

'So he went in and he did the joint and they woke up and the guy gave him some trouble. That's what *El* said. Maybe the guy just started to snore, that's what *I* say. Anyway, El said Quentin was in the sack with some hotshot lawyer's wife and they sent the lawyer up to Shawshank State Prison. Then he laughs this big laugh. Holy Christ, I was never so glad of anything as I was when I got my walking papers from that place.'

I guess you can see why Andy went a little wonky when Tommy told him that story, and why he wanted to see the warden right away. Elwood Blatch had been serving a six-to-twelve rap when Tommy knew him four years before. By the time Andy heard all of this, in 1963, he might be on the verge of getting out . . . or already out. So those were the two prongs of the spit Andy was roasting on – the idea that Blatch might still be in on one hand, and the very real possibility that he might be gone like the wind on the other.

There were inconsistencies in Tommy's story, but aren't there always in real life? Blatch told Tommy the man who got sent up was a hotshot lawyer, and Andy was a banker, but those are two professions that people who aren't very educated could easily get mixed up. And don't forget that twelve years had gone by between the time Blatch was reading the clippings about the trial and the time he told the tale to Tommy Williams. He also told Tommy he got better than a thousand dollars from a footlocker Quentin had in his closet, but the police said at Andy's trial that there had been no sign of burglary. I have a few ideas about that. First, if you take the cash and the man it belonged to is dead, how are you going to know anything was stolen, unless someone else can tell you it was there to start with? Second, who's to say Blatch wasn't lying about that part of it? Maybe he didn't want to admit killing two people for nothing. Third, maybe there were signs of burglary and the cops either overlooked them – cops can be pretty dumb – or deliberately covered them up so they wouldn't screw the DA's case. The guy was running for public office, remember, and he needed a conviction to run on. An unsolved burglary-murder would have done him no good at all.

But of the three, I like the middle one best. I've known a few Elwood Blatches in my time at Shawshank – the trigger-pullers with the crazy eyes. Such fellows want you to think they got away with the equivalent of the Hope Diamond on every caper, even if they got caught with a two-dollar Timex and nine bucks on the one they're doing time for.

And there was one thing in Tommy's story that convinced Andy beyond a shadow of a doubt. Blatch hadn't hit Quentin at random. He had called Quentin 'a big rich prick', and he had *known* Quentin was a golf pro. Well, Andy and his wife had been going out to that country club for drinks and dinner once or twice a week for a couple of years, and Andy had done a considerable amount of drinking there once he found out about his wife's affair. There was a marina with the country club, and for a while in 1947 there had been a part-time grease-and-gas jockey working there who matched Tommy's description of Elwood Blatch. A big tall man, mostly bald, with deep-set green eyes. A man who had an unpleasant way of looking at you, as though he was sizing you up. He wasn't there long, Andy said. Either he quit or Briggs, the fellow in charge of the marina, fired him. But he wasn't a man you forgot. He was too striking for that.

So Andy went to see Warden Norton on a rainy, windy day with big grey clouds scudding across the sky above the grey walls, a day when the last of the snow was starting to melt away and show lifeless patches of last year's grass in the fields beyond the prison.

The warden has a good-sized office in the administration wing, and behind the warden's desk there's a door which connects with the assistant warden's office. The assistant warden was out that day, but a trustee was there. He was a half-lame fellow whose real name I have forgotten; all the inmates, me included, called him Chester, after Marshall Dillon's sidekick. Chester was supposed to be watering the plants and dusting and waxing the floor. My guess is that the plants went thirsty that day and the only waxing that was done happened because of Chester's dirty ear polishing the keyhole plate of that connecting door.

He heard the warden's main door open and close and then Norton saying, 'Good morning, Dufresne, how can I help you?'

'Warden,' Andy began, and old Chester told us that he could hardly recognize Andy's voice it was so changed. 'Warden . . . there's something . . . something's happened to me that's . . . that's so . . . so . . . I hardly know where to begin.'

'Well, why don't you just begin at the beginning?' the warden said, probably in his sweetest let's-all-turn-to-the-23rd-psalm-and-read-in-unison voice. 'That usually works the best.'

And so Andy did. He began by refreshing Norton of the details of the crime he had been imprisoned for. Then he told the warden exactly what Tommy Williams had told him. He also gave out Tommy's name, which you may think wasn't so wise in light of later developments, but I'd just ask you what else he could have done, if his story was to have any credibility at all.

When he had finished, Norton was completely silent for some time. I can just see him, probably tipped back in his office chair under the picture of Governor Reed hanging on the wall, his fingers steepled, his liver lips pursed, his brow wrinkled into ladder rungs halfway to the crown of his head, his thirty-year pin gleaming mellowly.

'Yes,' he said finally. 'That's the damnedest story I ever heard. But I'll tell you what surprises me most about it, Dufresne.'

'What's that, sir?'

'That you were taken in by it.'

'Sir? I don't understand what you mean.' And Chester said that Andy Dufresne, who had faced down Byron Hadley on the plate-shop roof thirteen years before, was almost floundering for words.

'Well now,' Norton said. 'It's pretty obvious to me that this young fellow Williams is impressed with you. Quite taken with you, as a matter of fact. He hears your tale of woe, and it's quite natural of him to want to . . . cheer you up, let's say. Quite natural. He's a young man, not terribly bright. Not surprising he didn't realize what a state it would put you into. Now what I suggest is —'

'Don't you think I thought of that?' Andy asked. 'But I'd never told Tommy about the man working down at the marina. I never told *anyone* that — it never even crossed my mind! But Tommy's description of his cellmate and that man . . . they're *identical*!'

'Well now, you may be indulging in a little selective perception there,' Norton said with a chuckle. Phrases like that, selective perception, are required learning for people in the penalogy and corrections business, and they use them all they can.

'That's not it at all. Sir.'

'That's your slant on it,' Norton said, 'but mine differs. And let's remember that I have only your word that there *was* such a man working at the Falmouth Country Club back then.'

'No, sir,' Andy broke in again. 'No, that isn't true. Because —'

'Anyway,' Norton overrode him, expansive and loud, 'let's just look at it from the other end of the telescope, shall we? Suppose — just suppose, now — that there really *was* a fellow named Elwood Blotch.'

'Blatch,' Andy said tightly.

'Blatch, by all means. And let's say he *was* Thomas Williams's cellmate in Rhode Island. The chances are excellent that he has been released by now. *Excellent.* Why, we don't even know how much time he might have done there before he ended up with Williams, do we? Only that he was doing a six-to-twelve.'

'No. We don't know how much time he'd done. But Tommy said he was a bad actor, a cut-up. I think there's a fair chance that he may still be in. Even if he's been released, the prison will have a record of his last known address, the names of his relatives —'

'And both would almost certainly be dead ends.'

Andy was silent for a moment, and then he burst out: 'Well, it's a *chance*, isn't it?'

'Yes, of course it is. So just for a moment, Dufresne, let's assume that Blatch exists and that he is still safely ensconced in the Rhode Island State Penitentiary. Now what is he going to say if we bring this kettle of fish to him in a bucket? Is he going to fall down on his knees, roll his eyes, and say "I did it! I did it! By all means add a life term onto my burglary charge!"?'

'How can you be so obtuse?' Andy said, so low that Chester could barely hear. But he heard the warden just fine.

'What? What did you call me?'

'*Obtuse!*' Andy cried. 'Is it deliberate?'

'Dufresne, you've taken five minutes of my time – no, seven – and I have a very busy schedule today. So I believe we'll just declare this little meeting closed and –'

'The country club will have all the old time-cards, don't you realize that?' Andy shouted. 'They'll have tax-forms and W-2s and unemployment compensation forms, all with his name on them! There will be employees there now that were there then, maybe Briggs himself! It's been fifteen years, not forever! They'll remember him! *They will remember Blatch!* If I've got Tommy to testify to what Blatch told him, and Briggs to testify that Blatch was there, actually *working* at the country club, I can get a new trial! I can –'

'Guard! *Guard!* Take this man away!'

'What's the *matter* with you?' Andy said, and Chester told me he was very nearly screaming by then. 'It's my life, my chance to get out, don't you see that? And you won't make a single long-distance call to at least verify Tommy's story? Listen, I'll pay for the call! I'll pay for –'

Then there was a sound of thrashing as the guards grabbed him and started to drag him out.

'Solitary,' Warden Norton said dryly. He was probably fingering his thirty-year pin as he said it. 'Bread and water.'

And so they dragged Andy away, totally out of control now, still screaming at the warden; Chester said you could hear him even after the door was shut: '*It's my life! It's my life, don't you understand it's my life?*'

Twenty days on the grain and drain train for Andy down there in solitary. It was his second jolt in solitary, and his dust-up with Norton was his first real black mark since he had joined our happy little family.

I'll tell you a little bit about Shawshank's solitary while we're on the subject. It's something of a throwback to those hardy pioneer days of the early-to-mid-1700s in Maine. In those days no one wasted much time with such things as 'penalogy' and 'rehabilitation' and 'selective perception'. In those days, you were taken care of in terms of absolute black and white. You were either guilty or innocent. If you were guilty, you were either hung or put in gaol. And if you were sentenced to gaol, you did not go to an institution. No, you dug your own gaol with a spade provided to you by the Province of Maine. You dug it as wide and as deep as you could during the period between sunup and sundown. Then they gave you a couple of skins and a bucket, and down you went. Once down, the gaoler would bar the top of your hole, throw down some grain or maybe a piece of maggoty meat once or twice a week, and maybe there would be a dipperful of barley soup on Sunday night. You pissed in the bucket, and you held up the same bucket for water when the gaoler came around at six in the morning. When it rained, you used the bucket to bail out your gaol-cell . . . unless, that is, you wanted to drown like a rat in a rainbarrel.

No one spent a long time 'in the hole', as it was called; thirty months was an unusually long term, and so far as I've been able to tell, the longest term ever spent from which an inmate actually emerged alive was served by the so-called 'Durham Boy', a fourteen-year-old psychopath who castrated a schoolmate with a piece of rusty metal. He did seven years, but of course he went in young and strong.

You have to remember that for a crime that was more serious than petty theft or blasphemy or forgetting to put a snotrag in your pocket when out of doors on the Sabbath, you were hung. For low crimes such as those just mentioned and for others like them, you'd do your three or six or nine months in the hole and come out fishbelly white, cringing from the wide-open spaces, your eyes half-blind, your teeth more than likely rocking and rolling in their sockets from the scurvy, your feet crawling with fungus. Jolly old Province of Maine. Yo-ho-ho and a bottle of rum.

Shawshank's Solitary Wing was nowhere as bad as that . . . I guess. Things come in three major degrees in the human experience, I think. There's good, bad, and terrible. And as you go down into progressive darkness towards terrible, it gets harder and harder to make subdivisions.

To get to Solitary Wing you were led down twenty-three steps to a basement level where the only sound was the drip of water. The only light was supplied by a series of dangling sixty-watt bulbs. The cells were keg-shaped, like those wall-safes rich people sometimes hide behind a picture. Like a safe, the round doorways were hinged, and solid instead of barred. You get ventilation from above, but no light except for your own sixty-watt bulb, which was turned off from a master-switch promptly at eight p.m., an hour before lights-out in the rest of the prison. The wire wasn't in a wire mesh cage or anything like that. The feeling was that if you wanted to exist down there in the dark, you were welcome to it. Not many did . . . but after eight, of course, you had no choice. You had a bunk bolted to the wall and a can with no toilet seat. You had three ways to spend your time: sitting, shitting, or sleeping. Big choice. Twenty days could get to seem like a year. Thirty days could seem like two, and forty days like ten. Sometimes you could hear rats in the ventilation system. In a situation like that, subdivisions of terrible tend to get lost.

If anything at all can be said in favour of solitary, it's just that you get time to think. Andy had twenty days in which to think while he enjoyed his grain and drain, and when he got out he requested another meeting with the warden. Request denied. Such a meeting, the warden told him, would be 'counter-productive'. That's another of those phrases you have to master before you can go to work in the prisons and corrections field.

Patiently, Andy renewed his request. And renewed it. And renewed it. He had changed, had Andy Dufresne. Suddenly, as that spring of 1963 bloomed around us, there were lines in his face and sprigs of grey showing in his hair. He had lost that little trace of a smile that always seemed to linger around his mouth. His eyes stared out into space more often, and you get to know that when a man stares that way, he is counting up the years served, the months, the weeks, the days.

He renewed his request and renewed it. He was patient. He had nothing but time. It got to be summer. In Washington, President Kennedy was promising a fresh assault on poverty and on civil rights inequalities, not knowing he had only half a year to live. In Liverpool, a musical group called The Beatles was emerging as a force to be reckoned with in British music, but I guess that no one Stateside had yet heard of them. The Boston Red Sox, still four years away from what New England folks call The Miracle of '67, were languishing in the cellar of the American League. All of those things were going on out in a larger world where people walked free.

Norton saw him near the end of June, and this conversation I heard about from Andy himself some seven years later.

'If it's the money, you don't have to worry,' Andy told Norton in a low voice. 'Do you think I'd talk that up? I'd be cutting my own throat. I'd be just as indictable as —'

'That's enough,' Norton interrupted. His face was as long and cold as a slate gravestone. He leaned back in his office chair until the back of his head almost touched the sampler reading HIS JUDGMENT COMETH AND THAT RIGHT EARLY.

'But —'

'Don't you ever mention money to me again,' Norton said. 'Not in this office, not anywhere. Not unless you want to see that library turned back into a storage room and paint-locker again. Do you understand?'

'I was trying to set your mind at ease, that's all.'

'Well now, when I need a sorry son of a bitch like you to set my mind at ease, I'll retire. I agreed to this appointment because I got tired of being pestered, Dufresne. I want it to stop. If you want to buy this particular Brooklyn Bridge, that's your affair. Don't make it mine. I could hear crazy stories like yours twice a week if I wanted to lay myself open to them. Every sinner in this place would be using me for a crying towel. I had more respect for you. But this is the end. The end. Have we got an understanding?'

'Yes,' Andy said. 'But I'll be hiring a lawyer, you know.'

'What in God's name for?'

'I think we can put it together,' Andy said. 'With Tommy Williams and with my testimony and corroborative testimony from records and employees at the country club, I think we can put it together.'

'Tommy Williams is no longer an inmate of this facility.'

'*What?*'

'He's been transferred.'

'Transferred *where?*'

'Cashman.'

At that, Andy fell silent. He was an intelligent man, but it would have taken an extraordinarily stupid man not to smell *deal* all over that. Cashman was a minimum-security prison far up north in Aroostook County. The inmates pick a lot of potatoes, and that's hard work, but they are paid a decent wage for their labour and they can attend classes at CVI, a pretty decent vocational-technical institute, if they so desire. More important to a fellow like Tommy, a fellow with a young wife and a child, Cashman had a furlough programme . . . which meant a chance to live like a normal man, at least on the weekends. A chance to build a model plane with his kid, have sex with his wife, maybe go on a picnic.

Norton had almost surely dangled all of that under

Tommy's nose with only one string attached: not one more word about Elwood Blatch, not now, not ever. Or you'll end up doing hard time in Thomaston down there on scenic Route 1 with the real hard guys, and instead of having sex with your wife you'll be having it with some old bull queer.

'But why?' Andy said. 'Why would –'

'As a favour to you,' Norton said calmly, 'I checked with Rhode Island. They did have an inmate named Elwood Blatch. He was given what they call a PP – provisional parole, another one of these crazy liberal programmes to put criminals out on the streets. He's since disappeared.'

Andy said: 'The warden down there . . . is he a friend of yours?'

Sam Norton gave Andy a smile as cold as a deacon's watchchain. 'We are acquainted,' he said.

'*Why?*' Andy repeated. 'Can't you tell me why you did it? You knew I wasn't going to talk about . . . about anything you might have had going. You *knew* that. So *why?*'

'Because people like you make me sick,' Norton said deliberately. 'I like you right where you are, Mr Dufresne, and as long as I am warden here at Shawshank, you are going to be right here. You see, you used to think that you were better than anyone else. I have gotten pretty good at seeing that on a man's face. I marked it on yours the first time I walked into the library. It might as well have been written on your forehead in capital letters. That look is gone now, and I like that just fine. It is not just that you are a useful vessel, never think that. It is simply that men like you need to learn humility. Why, you used to walk around that exercise yard as if it was a living room and you were at one of those cocktail parties where the hellbound walk around coveting each others' wives and husbands and getting swin-ishly drunk. But you don't walk around that way anymore. And I'll be watching to see if you should start to walk that way again. Over a period of years, I'll be watching you with great pleasure. Now get the hell out of here.'

'Okay. But all the extracurricular activities stop now, Norton. The investment counselling, the scams, the free tax advice. It all stops. Get H & R Block to tell you how to declare your extortionate income.'

Warden Norton's face first went brick-red . . . and then all the colour fell out of it. 'You're going back into soli-tary for that. Thirty days. Bread and water. Another black mark. And while you're in, think about this: if *anything* that's been going on should stop, the library goes. I will make it my personal business to see that it goes back to what it was before you came here. And I will make your life . . . very hard. Very difficult. You'll do the hardest time it's possible to do. You'll lose that one-bunk Hilton down in Cellblock 5, for starters, and you'll lose those rocks on the windowsill, and you'll lose any protection the guards have given you against the sodomites. You will . . . lose everything. Clear?'

I guess it was clear enough.

Time continued to pass – the oldest trick in the world, and maybe the only one that really is magic. But Andy Dufresne had changed. He had grown harder. That's the only way I can think of to put it. He went on doing Warden Norton's dirty work and he held onto the library, so outwardly things were about the same. He continued to have his birthday drinks and his New Year's Eve drinks; he continued to share out the rest of each bottle. I got him fresh rock-polishing cloths from time to time, and in 1967 I got him a new rock-hammer – the one I'd gotten him nineteen years ago had plumb worn out. *Nineteen years!* When you say it sudden like that, those three syllables sound like the thud and double-locking of a tomb door. The rock-hammer, which had been a ten-dollar item back then, went for twenty-two by '67. He and I had a sad little grin over that.

Andy continued to shape and polish the rocks he found in the exercise yard, but the yard was smaller by then; half of what had been there in 1950 had been asphalted over in 1962. Nonetheless, he found enough to keep him occupied, I guess. When he had finished with each rock he would put it carefully on his window ledge, which faced east. He told me he liked to look at them in the sun, the pieces of the planet he had taken up from the dirt and shaped. Schists, quartzes, granites. Funny little mica sculptures that were held together with airplane glue. Various sedimentary conglomerates that were polished and cut in such a way that you could see why Andy called them 'millennium sandwiches' – the layers of different material that had built up over a period of decades and centuries.

Andy would give his stones and his rock-sculptures away from time to time in order to make room for new ones. He gave me the greatest number, I think – counting the stones that looked like matched cufflinks, I had five. There was one of the mica sculptures I told you about, carefully crafted to look like a man throwing a javelin, and two of the sedimentary conglomerates, all the levels showing in smoothly polished cross-section. I've still got them, and I take them down every so often and think about what a man can do, if he has time enough and the will to use it, a drop at a time.

So, on the outside, at least, things were about the same. If Norton had wanted to break Andy as badly as he had said, he would have had to look below the surface to see the change. But if he *had* seen how different Andy had become, I think Norton would have been well-satisfied with the four years following his clash with Andy.

He had told Andy that Andy walked around the exercise yard as if he were at a cocktail party. That isn't the way I would have put it, but I know what he meant. It goes back to what I said about Andy wearing his freedom like an invisible coat, about how he never really developed a prison mentality. His eyes never got that dull look. He never developed the walk that men get when the day is over and they are going back to their cells for another endless night – that flat-footed, hump-shouldered walk. Andy walked with his shoulders squared and his step was always light, as if he was heading home to a good home-cooked meal and a good woman instead of to a tasteless mess of soggy vegetables, lumpy mashed potato, and a slice or two of that fatty, gristly stuff most of the cons called mystery meat . . . that, and a picture of Raquel Welch on the wall.

But for those four years, although he never became *exactly* like the others, he did become silent, introspective, and brooding. Who could blame him? So maybe it was Warden Norton who was pleased . . . at least, for a while.

His dark mood broke around the time of the 1967 World Series. That was the dream year, the year the Red Sox won the pennant instead of placing ninth, as the Las Vegas bookies had predicted. When it happened – when they won the American League pennant – a kind of ebullience engulfed the whole prison. There was a goofy sort of feeling that if the Dead Sox could come to life, then maybe *anybody* could do it. I can't explain that feeling now, any more than an ex-Beatlemaniac could explain *that* madness, I suppose. But it was real. Every radio in the place was tuned to the games as the Red Sox pounded down the stretch. There was gloom when the Sox dropped a pair in Cleveland near the end, and a nearly riotous joy when Rico Petrocelli put away the pop fly that clinched it. And then there was the gloom that came when Lonborg was beaten in the seventh game of the Series to end the dream just short of complete fruition. It probably pleased Norton to no end, the son of a bitch. He liked his prison wearing sackcloth and ashes.

But for Andy, there was no tumble back down into gloom. He wasn't much of a baseball fan anyway, and maybe that was why. Nevertheless, he seemed to have caught the current of good feeling, and for him it didn't peter out again after the last game of the Series. He had taken that invisible coat out of the closet and put it on again.

I remember one bright-gold fall day in very late October, a couple of weeks after the World Series had ended. It must have been a Sunday, because the exercise yard was full of men 'walking off the week' – tossing a Frisbee or two, passing around a football, bartering what they had to barter. Others would be at the long table in the Visitors' Hall, under the watchful eyes of the screws, talking with their relatives, smoking cigarettes, telling sincere lies, receiving their picked-over care packages.

Andy was squatting Indian-fashion against the wall, chunking two small rocks together in his hands, his face turned up into the sunlight. It was surprisingly warm, that sun, for a day so late in the year.

'Hello, Red,' he called. 'Come on and sit a spell.'

I did.

'You want this?' he asked, and handed me one of the two carefully polished 'millennium sandwiches' I just told you about.

'I sure do,' I said. 'It's very pretty. Thank you.'

He shrugged and changed the subject. 'Big anniversary coming up for you next year.'

I nodded. Next year would make me a thirty-year man. Sixty per cent of my life spent in Shawshank Prison.

'Think you'll ever get out?'

'Sure. When I have a long white beard and just about three marbles left rolling around upstairs.'

He smiled a little and then turned his face up into the sun again, his eyes closed. 'Feels good.'

'I think it always does when you know the damn winter's almost right on top of you.'

He nodded, and we were silent for a while.

'When I get out of here,' Andy said finally, 'I'm going where it's warm all the time.' He spoke with such calm assurance you would have thought he had only a month or so left to serve. 'You know where I'm goin', Red?'

'Nope.'

'Zihuatanejo,' he said, rolling the word softly from his tongue like music. 'Down in Mexico. It's a little place maybe twenty miles from Playa Azul and Mexico Highway 37. It's a hundred miles north-west of Acapulco on the Pacific Ocean. You know what the Mexicans say about the Pacific?'

I told him I didn't.

'They say it has no memory. And that's where I want to finish out my life, Red. In a warm place that has no memory.'

He had picked up a handful of pebbles as he spoke; now he tossed them, one by one, and watched them bounce and roll across the baseball diamond's dirt infield, which would be under a foot of snow before long.

'Zihuatanejo. I'm going to have a little hotel down there. Six cabanas along the beach, and six more set further back, for the highway trade. I'll have a guy who'll take my guests out charter fishing. There'll be a trophy for the guy who catches the biggest marlin of the season, and I'll put his picture up in the lobby. It won't be a family place. It'll be a place for people on their honeymoons . . . first or second varieties.'

'And where are you going to get the money to buy this fabulous place?' I asked. 'Your stock account?'

He looked at me and smiled. 'That's not so far wrong,' he said. 'Sometimes you startle me, Red.'

'What are you talking about?'

'There are really only two types of men in the world when it comes to bad trouble,' Andy said, cupping a match between his hands and lighting a cigarette. 'Suppose there was a house full of rare paintings and sculptures and fine old antiques, Red? And suppose the guy who owned the house heard that there was a monster of a hurricane headed right at it. One of those two kinds of men just hopes for the best. The hurricane will change course, he says to himself. No right-thinking hurricane would ever dare wipe out all these Rembrandts, my two Degas horses, my Jackson Pollocks and my Paul Klees. Furthermore, God wouldn't allow it. And if

87

worst comes to worst, they're insured. That's one sort of man. The other sort just assumes that hurricane is going to tear right through the middle of his house. If the weather bureau says the hurricane just changed course, this guy assumes it'll change back in order to put his house on ground zero again. This second type of guy knows there's no harm in hoping for the best as long as you're prepared for the worst.'

I lit a cigarette of my own. 'Are you saying you prepared for the eventuality?'

'Yes. I prepared for the *hurricane*. I knew how bad it looked. I didn't have much time, but in the time I had, I operated. I had a friend – just about the only person who stood by me – who worked for an investment company in Portland. He died about six years ago.'

'Sorry.'

'Yeah.' Andy tossed his butt away. 'Linda and I had about fourteen thousand dollars. Not a big bundle, but hell, we were young. We had our whole lives ahead of us.' He grimaced a little, then laughed. 'When the shit hit the fan, I started lugging my Rembrandts out of the path of the hurricane. I sold my stocks and paid the capital gains tax just like a good little boy. Declared everything. Didn't cut any corners.'

'Didn't they freeze your estate?'

'I was charged with murder, Red, not dead! You can't freeze the assets of an innocent man – thank God. And it was a while before they even got brave enough to charge me with the crime. Jim – my friend – and I, we had some time. I got hit pretty good, just dumping everything like that. Got my nose skinned. But at the time I had worse things to worry about than a small skinning on the stock market.'

'Yeah, I'd say you did.'

'But when I came to Shawshank it was all safe. It's still safe. Outside these walls, Red, there's a man that no living soul has ever seen face to face. He has a Social Security card and a Maine driver's license. He's got a birth certificate. Name of Peter Stevens. Nice, anonymous name, huh?'

'Who is he?' I asked. I thought I knew what he was going to say, but I couldn't believe it.

'Me.'

'You're not going to tell me that you had time to set up a false identity while the bulls were sweating you,' I said, 'or that you finished the job while you were on trial for —'

'No, I'm not going to tell you that. My friend Jim was the one who set up the false identity. He started after my appeal was turned down, and the major pieces of identification were in his hands by the spring of 1950.'

'He must have been a pretty close friend,' I said. I was not sure how much of this I believed — a little, a lot, or none. But the day was warm and the sun was out, and it was one hell of a good story. 'All of that's one hundred per cent illegal, setting up a false ID like that.'

'He was a close friend,' Andy said. 'We were in the war together. France, Germany, the occupation. He was a good friend. He knew it was illegal, but he also knew that setting up a false identity in this country is very easy and very safe. He took my money — my money with all the taxes on it paid so the IRS wouldn't get too interested — and invested it for Peter Stevens. He did that in 1950 and 1951. Today it amounts to three hundred and seventy thousand dollars, plus change.'

I guess my jaw made a thump when it dropped against my chest, because he smiled.

'Think of all the things people wish they'd invested in since 1950 or so, and two or three of them will be things Peter Stevens was into. If I hadn't ended up in here, I'd probably be worth seven or eight million bucks by now. I'd have a Rolls . . . and probably an ulcer as big as a portable radio.'

His hands went to the dirt and began sifting out more pebbles. They moved gracefully, restlessly.

'I was hoping for the best and expecting the worst – nothing but that. The false name was just to keep what little capital I had untainted. It was lugging the paintings out of the path of the hurricane. But I had no idea that the hurricane . . . that it could go on as long as it has.'

I didn't say anything for a while. I guess I was trying to absorb the idea that this small, spare man in prison grey next to me could be worth more money than Warden Norton would make in the rest of his miserable life, even with the scams thrown in.

'When you said you could get a lawyer, you sure weren't kidding,' I said at last. 'For that kind of dough you could have hired Clarence Darrow, or whoever's passing for him these days. Why didn't you, Andy? Christ! You could have been out of here like a rocket.'

He smiled. It was the same smile that had been on his face when he'd told me he and his wife had had their whole lives ahead of them. 'No,' he said.

'A good lawyer would have sprung the Williams kid from Cashman whether he wanted to go or not,' I said. I was getting carried away now. 'You could have gotten your new trial, hired private detectives to look for that guy Blatch, and blown Norton out of the water to boot. Why not, Andy?'

'Because I outsmarted myself. If I ever try to put my hands on Peter Stevens's money from inside here, I'd lose every cent of it. My friend Jim could have arranged it, but Jim's dead. You see the problem?'

I saw it. For all the good the money could do Andy, it might as well have really belonged to another person. In a way, it did. And if the stuff it was invested in suddenly turned bad, all Andy could do would be to watch the plunge, to trace it day after day on the stocks-and-bonds page of the *Press-Herald*. It's a tough life if you don't weaken, I guess.

'I'll tell you how it is, Red. There's a big hayfield in the town of Buxton. You know where Buxton is at, don't you?'

I said I did. It lies right next door to Scarborough.

'That's right. And at the north end of this particular hayfield there's a rock wall, right out of a Robert Frost poem. And somewhere along the base of that wall is a rock that has no business in a Maine hayfield. It's a piece of volcanic glass, and until 1947 it was a paperweight on my office desk. My friend Jim put it in that wall. There's a key underneath it. The key opens a safe deposit box in the Portland branch of the Casco Bank.'

'I guess you're in a pack of trouble,' I said. 'When your friend Jim died, the IRS must have opened all of his safety deposit boxes. Along with the executor of his will, of course.'

Andy smiled and tapped the side of my head. 'Not bad. There's more up there than marshmallows, I guess. But we took care of the possibility that Jim might die while I was in the slam. The box is in the Peter Stevens name, and once a year the firm of lawyers that served as Jim's executors sends a check to the Casco to cover the rental of the Stevens box.

'Peter Stevens is inside that box, just waiting to get out.

His birth certificate, his S.S. card, and his driver's licence. The licence is six years out of date because Jim died six years ago, true, but it's still perfectly renewable for a five-dollar fee. His stock certificates are there, the tax-free municipals, and about eighteen bearer bonds in the amount of ten thousand dollars each.'

I whistled.

'Peter Stevens is locked in a safe deposit box at the Casco Bank in Portland and Andy Dufresne is locked in a safe deposit box at Shawshank,' he said. 'Tit for tat. And the key that unlocks the box and the money and the new life is under a hunk of black glass in a Buxton hayfield. Told you this much, so I'll tell you something else, Red – for the last twenty years, give or take, I have been watching the papers with a more than usual interest for news of any construction projects in Buxton. I keep thinking that someday soon I'm going to read that they're putting a highway through there, or erecting a new community hospital, or building a shopping centre. Burying my new life under ten feet of concrete, or spitting it into a swamp somewhere with a big load of fill.'

I blurted, 'Jesus Christ, Andy, if all of this is true, how do you keep from going crazy?'

He smiled. 'So far, all quiet on the Western front.'

'But it could be years –'

'It will be. But maybe not as many as the state and Warden Norton think it's going to be. I just can't afford to wait that long. I keep thinking about Zihuatanejo and that small hotel. That's all I want from my life now, Red, and I don't think that's too much to want. I didn't kill Glenn Quentin and I didn't kill my wife, and that hotel . . . it's not too much to want. To swim and get a tan and sleep in a room with open windows and *space* . . . that's not too much to want.'

He slung the stones away.

'You know, Red,' he said in an offhand voice, 'a place like that . . . I'd have to have a man who knows how to get things.'

I thought about it for a long time. And the biggest drawback in my mind wasn't even that we were talking pipedreams in a shitty little prison exercise yard with armed guards looking down at us from their sentry posts. 'I couldn't do it,' I said. 'I couldn't get along on the outside. I'm what they call an institutional man now. In here I'm the man who can get it for you, yeah. But out there, anyone can get it for you. Out there, if you want posters or rock-hammers or one particular record or a boat-in-a-bottle model kit, you can use the fucking Yellow Pages. In here, *I'm* the fucking Yellow Pages. I wouldn't know how to begin. Or where.'

'You underestimate yourself,' he said. 'You're a self-educated man, a self-made man. A rather remarkable man, I think.'

'Hell, I don't even have a high school diploma.'

'I know that,' he said. 'But it isn't just a piece of paper that makes a man. And it isn't just prison that breaks one, either.'

'I couldn't hack it outside, Andy. I know that.'

He got up. 'You think it over,' he said casually, just as the inside whistle blew. And he strolled off, as if he was a free man who had just made another free man a proposition. And for a while just that was enough to make me *feel* free. Andy could do that. He could make me forget for a time that we were both lifers, at the mercy of a hard-ass parole board and a psalm-singing warden who liked Andy Dufresne right where he was. After all, Andy was a lap-dog who could do tax-returns. What a wonderful animal!

But by that night in my cell I felt like a prisoner again. The whole idea seemed absurd, and that mental image of blue water and white beaches seemed more cruel than foolish – it dragged at my brain like a fishhook. I just couldn't wear that invisible coat the way Andy did. I fell asleep that night and dreamed of a great glassy black stone in the middle of a hayfield; a stone shaped like a giant blacksmith's anvil. I was trying to rock the stone up so I could get the key that was underneath. It wouldn't budge; it was just too damned big.

And in the background, but getting closer, I could hear the baying of bloodhounds.

Which leads us, I guess, to the subject of jailbreaks.

Sure, they happen from time to time in our happy little family. You don't go over the wall, though, not at Shawshank, not if you're smart. The searchlight beams go all night, probing long white fingers across the open fields that surround the prison on three sides and the stinking marshland on the fourth. Cons do go over the wall from time to time, and the searchlights almost always catch them. If not, they get picked up trying to thumb a ride on Highway 6 or Highway 99. If they try to cut across country, some farmer sees them and just phones the location in to the prison. Cons who go over the wall are stupid cons. Shawshank is no Canon City, but in a rural area a man humping his ass across country in a grey pyjama suit sticks out like a cockroach on a wedding cake.

Over the years, the guys who have done the best – maybe

oddly, maybe not so oddly – are the guys who did it on the spur of the moment. Some of them have gone out in the middle of a cartful of sheets; a convict sandwich on white, you could say. There was a lot of that when I first came in here, but over the years they have more or less closed that loophole.

Warden Norton's famous 'Inside-Out' programme produced its share of escapees, too. They were the guys who decided they liked what lay to the right of the hyphen better than what lay to the left. And again, in most cases it was a very casual kind of thing. Drop your blueberry rake and stroll into the bushes while one of the screws is having a glass of water at the truck or when a couple of them get too involved in arguing over yards passing or rushing on the old Boston Patriots.

In 1969, the Inside-Outers were picking potatoes in Sabbatus. It was the third of November and the work was almost done. There was a guard named Henry Pugh – and he is no longer a member of our happy little family, believe me – sitting on the back bumper of one of the potato trucks and having his lunch with his carbine across his knees when a beautiful (or so it was told to me, but sometimes these things get exaggerated) ten-point buck strolled out of the cold early afternoon mist. Pugh went after it with visions of just how that trophy would look mounted in his rec room, and while he was doing it, three of his charges just walked away. Two were recaptured in a Lisbon Falls pinball parlour. The third has not been found to this day.

I suppose the most famous case of all was that of Sid Nedeau. This goes back to 1958, and I guess it will never be topped. Sid was out lining the ball-field for a Saturday intramural baseball game when the three o'clock inside whistle blew, signalling the shiftchange for the guards. The parking lot is just beyond the exercise yard, on the other side of the electrically-operated main gate. At three the gate opens and the guards coming on duty and those going off mingle. There's a lot of back-slapping and bullyragging, comparison of league bowling scores and the usual number of tired old ethnic jokes.

Sid just trundled his lining machine right out through the gate, leaving a three-inch baseline all the way from third base in the exercise yard to the ditch on the far side of Route 6, where they found the machine overturned in a pile of lime. Don't ask me how he did it. He was dressed in his prison uniform, he stood six-feet-two, and he was billowing clouds of lime-dust behind him. All I can figure is that, it being Friday afternoon and all, the guards going off were so happy to be going off, and the guards coming on were so down-hearted to be coming on, that the members of the former group never got their heads out of the clouds and those in the latter never got their noses off their shoetops . . . and old Sid Nedeau just sort of slipped out between the two.

So far as I know, Sid is still at large. Over the years, Andy Dufresne and I had a good many laughs over Sid Nedeau's great escape, and when we heard about that airline hijacking for ransom, the one where the guy parachuted from the back door of the airplane, Andy swore up and down that D B Cooper's real name was Sid Nedeau.

'And he probably had a pocketful of baseline lime in his pocket for good luck,' Andy said. 'That lucky son of a bitch.'

But you should understand that a case like Sid Nedeau, or the fellow who got away clean from the Sabbatus potato-field crew, guys like that are winning the prison version of the Irish Sweepstakes. Purely a case of six different kinds of luck somehow jelling together all at the same moment. A stiff like Andy could wait ninety years and not get a similar break.

Maybe you remember, a ways back, I mentioned a guy named Henley Backus, the washroom foreman in the laundry. He came to Shawshank in 1922 and died in the prison infirmary thirty-one years later. Escapes and escape attempts were a hobby of his, maybe because he never quite dared to take the plunge himself. He could tell you a hundred different schemes, all of them crackpot, and all of them had been tried in the Shank at one time or another. My favourite was the tale of Beaver Morrison, a b & e convict who tried to build a glider from scratch in the plate-factory basement. The plans he was working from were in a circa-1900 book called *The Modern Boy's Guide to Fun and Adventure*. Beaver got it built without being discovered, or so the story goes, only to discover there was no door from the basement big enough to get the damned thing out. When Henley told that story, you could bust a gut laughing, and he knew a dozen – no, two dozen – just as funny.

When it came to detailing Shawshank bust-outs, Henley had it down chapter and verse. He told me once that during his time there had been better than four hundred escape attempts *that he knew of*. Really think about that for a moment before you just nod your head and read on. Four *hundred* escape attempts! That comes out to 12.9 escape attempts for every year Henley Backus was in Shawshank and keeping track of them. The Escape Attempt of the Month Club. Of course most of them were pretty slipshod affairs, the sort of thing that ends up with a guard grabbing some poor, sidling slob's arm and growling, 'Where do you think *you're* going, you happy asshole?'

Henley said he'd class maybe sixty of them as more serious attempts, and he included the 'prison break' of 1937, the year before I arrived at the Shank. The new administration wing was under construction then and fourteen cons got out, using construction equipment in a poorly locked shed. The whole of southern Maine got into a panic over those fourteen 'hardened criminals', most of whom were scared to death and had no more idea of where they should go than a jackrabbit does when it's headlight-pinned to the highway with a big truck bearing down on it. Not one of those fourteen got away. Two of them were shot dead – by civilians, not police officers or prison personnel – but none got away.

How many *had* gotten away between 1938, when I came here, and that day in October when Andy first mentioned Zihuatanejo to me? Putting my information and Henley's together, I'd say ten. Ten that got away clean. And although it isn't the kind of thing you can know for sure, I'd guess that at least half of those ten are doing time in other institutions of lower learning like the Shank. Because you *do* get institutionalized. When you take away a man's freedom and teach him to live in a cell, he seems to lose his ability to think in dimensions. He's like that jackrabbit I mentioned, frozen in the oncoming lights of the truck that is bound to kill it. More often than not a con who's just out will pull some dumb job that hasn't a chance in hell of succeeding . . . and why? Because it'll get him back inside. Back where he understands how things work.

Andy wasn't that way, but I was. The idea of seeing the

Pacific *sounded* good, but I was afraid that actually being there would scare me to death – the bigness of it.

Anyhow, the day of that conversation about Mexico, and about Mr Peter Stevens . . . that was the day I began to believe that Andy had some idea of doing a disappearing act. I hoped to God he would be careful if he did, and still, I wouldn't have bet money on his chances of succeeding. Warden Norton, you see, was watching Andy with a special close eye. Andy wasn't just another deadhead with a number to Norton; they had a working relationship, you might say. Also, he had brains and he had heart. Norton was determined to use the one and crush the other.

As there are honest politicians on the outside – ones who stay bought – there are honest prison guards, and if you are a good judge of character and if you have some loot to spread around, I suppose it's possible that you could buy enough look-the-other-way to make a break. I'm not the man to tell you such a thing has never been done, but Andy Dufresne wasn't the man who could do it. Because, as I've said, Norton was watching. Andy knew it, and the screws knew it, too.

Nobody was going to nominate Andy for the Inside-Out programme, not as long as Warden Norton was evaluating the nominations. And Andy was not the kind of man to try a casual Sid Nedeau type of escape.

If I had been him, the thought of that key would have tormented me endlessly. I would have been lucky to get two hours' worth of honest shuteye a night. Buxton was less than thirty miles from Shawshank. So near and yet so far.

I still thought his best chance was to engage a lawyer and try for the retrial. Anything to get out from under

Norton's thumb. Maybe Tommy Williams could be shut up by nothing more than a cushy furlough programme, but I wasn't entirely sure. Maybe a good old Mississippi hardass lawyer could crack him . . . and maybe that lawyer wouldn't even have to work that hard. Williams had honestly liked Andy. Every now and then I'd bring these points up to Andy, who would only smile, his eyes far away, and say he was thinking about it.

Apparently he'd been thinking about a lot of other things, as well.

In 1975, Andy Dufresne escaped from Shawshank. He hasn't been recaptured, and I don't think he ever will be. In fact, I don't think Andy Dufresne even exists anymore. But I think there's a man down in Zihuatanejo, Mexico named Peter Stevens. Probably running a very new small hotel in this year of our Lord 1977.

I'll tell you what I know and what I think; that's about all I can do, isn't it?

On 12 March 1975, the cell doors in Cellblock 5 opened at 6.30 a.m., as they do every morning around here except Sunday. And as they do every day except Sunday, the inmates of those cells stepped forward into the corridor and formed two lines as the cell doors slammed shut behind them. They walked up to the main cellblock gate, where they were counted off by two guards before being sent on down to the cafeteria for a breakfast of oatmeal, scrambled eggs, and fatty bacon.

All of this went according to routine until the count at the cellblock gate. There should have been twenty-nine.

Instead, there were twenty-eight. After a call to the Captain of the Guards, Cellblock 5 was allowed to go to breakfast.

The Captain of the Guards, a not half-bad fellow named Richard Gonyar, and his assistant, a jolly prick named Dave Burkes, came down to Cellblock 5 right away. Gonyar reopened the cell doors and he and Burkes went down the corridor together, dragging their sticks over the bars, their guns out. In a case like that what you usually have is someone who has been taken sick in the night, so sick he can't even step out of his cell in the morning. More rarely, someone had died . . . or committed suicide.

But this time, they found a mystery instead of a sick man or a dead man. They found no man at all. There were fourteen cells in Cellblock 5, seven to a side, all fairly neat – restriction of visiting privileges is the penalty for a sloppy cell at Shawshank – and all very empty.

Gonyar's first assumption was that there had been a miscount or a practical joke. So instead of going off to work after breakfast, the inmates of Cellblock 5 were sent back to their cells, joking and happy. Any break in the routine was always welcome.

Cell doors opened; prisoners stepped in; cell doors closed. Some clown shouting, 'I want my lawyer, I want my lawyer, you guys run this place just like a frigging prison.'

Burkes: 'Shut up in there, or I'll rank you.'

The clown: 'I ranked your wife, Burkie.'

Gonyar: 'Shut up, all of you, or you'll spend the day in there.'

He and Burkes went up the line again, counting noses. They didn't have to go far.

'Who belongs in this cell?' Gonyar asked the rightside night guard.

'Andrew Dufresne,' the rightside answered, and that was all it took. Everything stopped being routine right then. The balloon went up.

In all the prison movies I've seen, this wailing horn goes off when there's been a break. That never happens at Shawshank. The first thing Gonyar did was to get in touch with the warden. The second thing was to get a search of the prison going. The third was to alert the State Police in Scarborough to the possibility of a breakout.

That was the routine. It didn't call for them to search the suspected escapee's cell, and so no one did. Not then. Why would they? It was a case of what you see is what you get. It was a small square room, bars on the window and bars on the sliding door. There was a toilet and an empty cot. Some pretty rocks on the windowsill.

And the poster, of course. It was Linda Ronstadt by then. The poster was right over his bunk. There had been a poster there, in that exact same place, for twenty-six years. And when someone – it was Warden Norton himself, as it turned out, poetic justice if there ever was any – looked behind it, they got one hell of a shock.

But that didn't happen until 6.30 that night, almost twelve hours after Andy had been reported missing, prob-ably twenty hours after he had actually made his escape.

Norton hit the roof.

I have it on good authority – Chester, the trustee, who was waxing the hall floor in the Admin Wing that day. He didn't have to polish any keyplates with his ear that day; he said you could hear the warden clear down to Records & Files as he chewed on Rich Gonyar's ass.

'What do you mean, you're "satisfied he's not on the prison grounds"? What does that mean? It means you didn't find him! You better find him! You better! Because I want him! Do you hear me? I want him!'

Gonyar said something.

'Didn't happen on your shift? That's what *you* say. So far as *I* can tell, no one knows *when* it happened. Or how. Or if it really did. Now, I want him in my office by three o'clock this afternoon, or some heads are going to roll. I can promise you that, and I *always* keep my promises.'

Something else from Gonyar, something that seemed to provoke Norton to even greater rage.

'No? Then look at this! *Look at this!* You recognize it? Last night's tally for Cellblock 5. Every prisoner accounted for! Dufresne was locked up last night at nine and it is impossible for him to be gone now! *It is impossible! Now you find him!*'

But at six that evening Andy was still among the missing. Norton himself stormed down to Cellblock 5, where the rest of us had been locked up all of that day. Had we been questioned? We had spent most of that long day being questioned by harried screws who were feeling the breath of the dragon on the backs of their necks. We all said the same thing: we had seen nothing, heard nothing. And so far as I know, we were all telling the truth. I know that I was. All we could say was that Andy had indeed been in his cell at the time of the lock-in, and at lights-out an hour later.

One wit suggested that Andy had poured himself out through the keyhole. The suggestion earned the guy four days in solitary. They were uptight.

So Norton came down – stalked down – glaring at us with blue eyes nearly hot enough to strike sparks from the tempered steel bars of our cages. He looked at us as if he believed we were all in on it. Probably he did believe it.

He went into Andy's cell and looked around. It was just as Andy had left it, the sheets of his bunk turned back but without looking slept-in. Rocks on the windowsill . . . but not all of them. The ones he liked best he took with him.

'Rocks,' Norton hissed, and swept them off the window-ledge with a clatter. Gonyar, already four hours overtime, winced but said nothing.

Norton's eyes fell on the Linda Ronstadt poster. Linda was looking back over her shoulder, her hands tucked into the back pockets of a very tight pair of fawn-coloured slacks. She was wearing a halter and she had a deep California tan. It must have offended the hell out of Norton's Baptist sensibilities, that poster. Watching him glare at it, I remembered what Andy had once said about feeling he could almost step through the picture and be with the girl.

In a very real way, that was exactly what he did – as Norton was only seconds from discovering.

'Wretched thing!' he grunted, and ripped the poster from the wall with a single swipe of his hand.

And revealed the gaping, crumbled hole in the concrete behind it.

Gonyar wouldn't go in.

Norton ordered him – God, they must have heard Norton ordering Rich Gonyar to go in there all over the prison – and Gonyar just refused him, point-blank.

'I'll have your job for this!' Norton screamed. He was as

hysterical as a woman having a hot-flush. He had utterly blown his cool. His neck had turned a rich, dark red, and two veins stood out, throbbing, on his forehead. 'You can count on it, you . . . you Frenchman! I'll have your job and I'll see to it that you never get another one in any prison system in New England!'

Gonyar silently held out his service pistol to Norton, butt first. He'd had enough. He was four hours overtime, going on five, and he'd just had enough. It was as if Andy's defection from our happy little family had driven Norton right over the edge of some private irrationality that had been there for a long time . . . certainly he was crazy that night.

I don't know what that private irrationality might have been, of course. But I do know that there were twenty-eight cons listening to Norton's little dust-up with Rich Gonyar that evening as the last of the light faded from a dull late-winter sky, all of us hard-timers and long-line riders who had seen the administrators come and go, the hard-asses and the candy-asses alike, and we all knew that Warden Samuel Norton had just passed what the engineers like to call 'the breaking strain'.

And by God, it almost seemed to me that somewhere I could hear Andy Dufresne laughing.

Norton finally got a skinny drink of water on the night shift to go into that hole that had been behind Andy's poster of Linda Ronstadt. The skinny guard's name was Rory Tremont, and he was not exactly a ball of fire in the brains department. Maybe he thought he was going to win a Bronze Star or something. As it turned out, it was fortunate that Norton got someone of Andy's approximate height and build to go in there; if they had sent a big-assed fellow – as most prison guards seem to be – the guy would have stuck in there as sure as God made green grass . . . and he might be there still.

Tremont went in with a nylon filament rope, which someone had found in the trunk of his car, tied around his waist and a big six-battery flashlight in one hand. By then Gonyar, who had changed his mind about quitting and who seemed to be the only one there still able to think clearly, had dug out a set of blueprints. I knew well enough what they showed him – a wall which looked, in cross-section, like a sandwich. The entire wall was ten feet thick. The inner and outer sections were each about four feet thick. In the centre was two feet of pipe-space, and you want to believe that was the meat of the thing . . . in more ways than one.

Tremont's voice came out of the hole, sounding hollow and dead. 'Something smells awful in here, Warden.'

'Never mind that! Keep going.'

Tremont's lower legs disappeared into the hole. A moment later his feet were gone, too. His light flashed dimly back and forth.

'Warden, it smells pretty damn bad.'

'Never *mind*, I said!' Norton cried.

Dolorously, Tremont's voice floated back: 'Smells like shit. Oh God, that's what it is, it's *shit*, oh my God lemme outta here I'm gonna blow my groceries oh shit it's shit oh my *Gawwwwwd* –' And then came the unmistakable sound of Rory Tremont losing his last couple of meals.

Well, that was it for me. I couldn't help myself. The whole day – hell no, the last thirty *years* – all came up on me at once and I started laughing fit to split, a laugh such as I'd never had since I was a free man, the kind of laugh I never expected to have inside these grey walls. And oh dear *God* didn't it feel good!

'Get that man out of here!' Warden Norton was screaming, and I was laughing so hard I didn't know if he meant me or Tremont. I just went on laughing and kicking my feet and holding onto my belly. I couldn't have stopped if Norton had threatened to shoot me dead-bang on the spot. '*Get him OUT!*'

Well, friends and neighbours, I was the one who went. Straight down to solitary, and there I stayed for fifteen days. A long shot. But every now and then I'd think about poor old not-too-bright Rory Tremont bellowing *oh shit it's shit*, and then I'd think about Andy Dufresne heading south in his own car, dressed in a nice suit, and I'd just have to laugh. I did that fifteen days in solitary practically standing on my head. Maybe because half of me was with Andy Dufresne, Andy Dufresne who had waded in shit and came out clean on the other side, Andy Dufresne, headed for the Pacific.

I heard the rest of what went on that night from half a dozen sources. There wasn't all that much, anyway. I guess that Rory Tremont decided he didn't have much left to lose after he'd lost his lunch and dinner, because he did go on. There was no danger of falling down the pipe-shaft between the inner and outer segments of the cellblock wall; it was so narrow that Tremont actually had to wedge himself down. He said later that he could only take half-breaths and that he knew what it would be like to be buried alive.

What he found at the bottom of the shaft was a master sewer-pipe which served the fourteen toilets in Cellblock 5, a porcelain pipe that had been laid thirty-three years before. It had been broken into. Beside the jagged hole in the pipe, Tremont found Andy's rock-hammer.

Andy had gotten free, but it hadn't been easy.

The pipe was even narrower than the shaft Tremont had just descended; it had a two-foot bore. Rory Tremont didn't go in, and so far as I know, no one else did, either. It must have been damn near unspeakable. A rat jumped out of the pipe as Tremont was examining the hole and the rock-hammer, and he swore later that it was nearly as big as a cocker spaniel pup. He went back up the crawlspace to Andy's cell like a monkey on a stick.

Andy had gone into that pipe. Maybe he knew that it emptied into a stream five hundred yards beyond the prison on the marshy western side. I think he did. The prison blueprints were around, and Andy would have found a way to look at them. He was a methodical cuss. He would have known or found out that the sewerpipe running out of Cellblock 5 was the last one in Shawshank not hooked into the new waste-treatment plant, and he would have known it was do it by mid-1975 or do it never, because in August they were going to switch us over to the new waste-treatment plant, too.

Five hundred yards. The length of five football fields. Just shy of a mile. He crawled that distance, maybe with one of those small Penlites in his hand, maybe with nothing but a couple of books of matches. He crawled through foulness that I either can't imagine or don't want to imagine. Maybe the rats scattered in front of him, or maybe they went for him the way such animals sometimes will when they've had a chance to grow bold in the dark. He must have had just enough clearance at the shoulders to keep moving, and he probably had to shove himself through the places where the lengths of pipe were joined. If it had been me, the claustrophobia would have driven me mad a dozen times over. But he did it.

At the far end of the pipe they found a set of muddy footprints leading out of the sluggish, polluted creek the pipe fed into. Two miles from there a search party found his prison uniform – that was a day later.

The story broke big in the papers, as you might guess, but no one within a fifteen-mile radius of the prison stepped forward to report a stolen car, stolen clothes, or a naked man in the moonlight. There was not so much as a barking dog in a farmyard. He came out of the sewerpipe and he disappeared like smoke.

But I am betting he disappeared in the direction of Buxton.

Three months after that memorable day, Warden Norton resigned. He was a broken man, it gives me great pleasure to report. The spring was gone from his step. On his last day he shuffled out with his head down like an old con shuffling down to the infirmary for his codeine pills. It was Gonyar who took over, and to Norton that must have seemed like the unkindest cut of all. For all I know, Sam Norton is down there in Eliot now, attending services at the Baptist church every Sunday, and wondering how the hell Andy Dufresne ever could have gotten the better of him.

I could have told him; the answer to the question is simplicity itself. Some have got it, Sam. And some don't, and never will.

★　　★　　★

STEPHEN KING

That's what I know; now I'm going to tell you what I think.
I may have it wrong on some of the specifics, but I'd be
willing to bet my watch and chain that I've got the general
outline down pretty well. Because, with Andy being the sort
of man that he was, there's only one or two ways that it
could have been. And every now and then, when I think it
out, I think of Normaden, that half-crazy Indian. 'Nice fella,'
Normaden had said after celling with Andy for six or eight
months. 'I was glad to go, me. All the time cold. He don't
let nobody touch his things. That's okay. Nice man, never
make fun. But big draught.' Poor crazy Normaden. He knew
more than all the rest of us, and he knew it sooner. And it
was eight long months before Andy could get him out of
there and have the cell to himself again. If it hadn't been
for the eight months Normaden had spent with him after
Warden Norton first came in, I do believe that Andy would
have been free before Nixon resigned.

I believe now that it began in 1949, way back then – not
with the rock-hammer, but with the Rita Hayworth poster.
I told you how nervous he seemed when he asked for that,
nervous and filled with suppressed excitement. At the time
I thought it was just embarrassment, that Andy was the sort
of guy who'd never want someone else to know that he had
feet of clay and wanted a woman . . . even if it was only a
fantasy-woman. But I think now that I was wrong. I think
now that Andy's excitement came from something else altogether.

What was responsible for the hole that Warden Norton
eventually found behind the poster of a girl that hadn't even
been born when that photo of Rita Hayworth was taken?
Andy Dufresne's perseverance and hard work, yeah – I don't

take any of that away from him. But there were two other elements in the equation: a lot of luck, and WPA concrete.

You don't need me to explain the luck, I guess. The WPA concrete I checked out for myself. I invested some time and a couple of stamps and wrote first to the University of Maine History Department and then to a fellow whose address they were able to give me. This fellow had been foreman of the WPA project that built the Shawshank Max Security Wing.

The wing, which contains Cellblocks 3, 4, and 5, was built in the years 1934–37. Now, most people don't think of cement and concrete as 'technological developments', the way we think of cars and oil furnaces and rocket-ships, but they really are. There was no modern cement until 1870 or so, and no modern concrete until after the turn of the century. Mixing concrete is as delicate a business as making bread. You can get it too watery or not watery enough. You can get the sand-mix too thick or too thin, and the same is true of the gravel-mix. And back in 1934, the science of mixing the stuff was a lot less sophisticated than it is today.

The walls of Cellblock 5 were solid enough, but they weren't exactly dry and toasty. As a matter of fact, they were and are pretty damned dank. After a long wet spell they would sweat and sometimes even drip. Cracks had a way of appearing, some an inch deep, and were routinely mortared over.

Now here comes Andy Dufresne into Cellblock 5. He's a man who graduated from the University of Maine's school of business, but he's also a man who took two or three geology courses along the way. Geology had, in fact, become his chief hobby. I imagine it appealed to his patient, meticulous nature.

A ten-thousand-year ice age here. A million years of mountain-building there. Tectonic plates grinding against each other deep under the earth's skin over the millennia. *Pressure.* Andy told me once that all of geology is the study of pressure.

And time, of course.

He had time to study those walls. Plenty of time. When the cell door slams and the lights go out, there's nothing else to look at.

First-timers usually had a hard time adjusting to the confinement of prison life. They get screw-fever. Sometimes they have to be hauled down to the infirmary and sedated a couple of times before they get on the beam. It's not unusual to hear some new member of our happy little family banging on the bars of his cell and screaming to be let out . . . and before the cries have gone on for long, the chant starts up along the cellblock: 'Fresh *fish*, hey little fishie, fresh *fish*, fresh *fish*, got fresh *fish* today!'

Andy didn't flip out like that when he came to the Shank in 1948, but that's not to say that he didn't feel many of the same things. He may have come close to madness; some do, and some go sailing right over the edge. Old life blown away in the wink of an eye, indeterminate nightmare stretching out ahead, a long season in hell.

So what did he do, I ask you? He searched almost desperately for something to divert his restless mind. Oh, there are all sorts of ways to divert yourself, even in prison; it seems like the human mind is full of an infinite number of possibilities when it comes to diversion. I told you about the sculptor and his Three Ages of Jesus. There were coin collectors who were always losing their collections to thieves, stamp collectors, one fellow who had postcards from thirty-five different countries – and let me tell you, he would have turned out your lights if he'd caught you diddling with his postcards.

Andy got interested in rocks. And the walls of his cell.

I think that his initial intention might have been to do no more than to carve his initials into the wall where the poster of Rita Hayworth would soon be hanging. His initials, or maybe a few lines from some poem. Instead, what he found was that interestingly weak concrete. Maybe he started to carve his initials and a big chunk of the wall fell out. I can see him, lying there on his bunk, looking at that broken chunk of concrete, turning it over in his hands. Never mind the wreck of your whole life, never mind that you got rail-roaded into this place by a whole trainload of bad luck. Let's forget all that and look at this piece of concrete.

Some months further along he might have decided it would be fun to see how much of that wall he could take out. But you can't just start digging into your wall and then, when the weekly inspection (or one of the surprise inspections that are always turning up interesting caches of booze, drugs, dirty pictures, and weapons) comes around, say to the guard: 'This? Just excavating a little hole in my cell wall. Not to worry, my good man.'

No, he couldn't have that. So he came to me and asked if I could get him a Rita Hayworth poster. Not a little one but a big one.

And, of course, he had the rock-hammer. I remember thinking when I got him that gadget back in '48 that it would take a man six hundred years to burrow through the wall with it. True enough. But Andy went right *through* the wall – even with the soft concrete, it took him two rock-hammers and twenty-seven years to hack a hole big enough to get his slim body through four feet of it.

Of course he lost most of one of those years to Normaden, and he could only work at night, preferably late at night, when almost everybody is asleep – including the guards who work the night shift. But I suspect the thing which slowed him down the most was getting rid of the wall as he took it out. He could muffle the sound of his work by wrapping the head of his hammer in rock-polishing cloths, but what to do with the pulverized concrete and the occasional chunks that came out whole?

I think he must have broken up the chunks into pebbles and . . .

I remembered the Sunday after I had gotten him the rock-hammer. I remember watching him walk across the exercise yard, his face puffy from his latest go-round with the sisters. I saw him stoop, pick up a pebble . . . and it disappeared up his sleeve. That inside sleeve-pocket is an old prison trick. Up your sleeve or just inside the cuff of your pants. And I have another memory, very strong but unfocused, maybe something I saw more than once. This memory is of Andy Dufresne walking across the exercise yard on a hot summer day when the air was utterly still. Still, yeah . . . except for the little breeze that seemed to be blowing sand around Andy Dufresne's feet.

So maybe he had a couple of cheaters in his pants below the knees. You loaded the cheaters up with fill and then just strolled around, your hands in your pockets, and when you feel safe and unobserved, you gave the pockets a little twitch. The pockets, of course, are attached by string or strong thread to the cheaters. The fill goes cascading out of your pantslegs as you walk. The World War II POWS who were trying to tunnel out used the dodge.

The years went past and Andy brought his wall out to the exercise yard cupful by cupful. He played the game with administrator after administrator, and they thought it was because he wanted to keep the library growing. I have no doubt that was part of it, but the main thing Andy wanted was to keep cell 14 in Cellblock 5 a single occupancy.

I doubt if he had any real plans or hopes of breaking out, at least not at first. He probably assumed the wall was ten feet of solid concrete, and that if he succeeded in boring all the way through it, he'd come out thirty feet over the exercise yard. But like I say, I don't think he was worried overmuch about breaking through. His assumption could have run this way: I'm only making a foot of progress every seven years or so; therefore, it would take me seventy years to break through; that would make me one hundred and seven years old.

Here's a second assumption I would have made, had I been Andy: that eventually I would be caught and get a lot of solitary time, not to mention a very large black mark on my record. After all, there was the regular weekly inspection and a surprise toss – which usually came at night – every second week or so. He must have decided that things couldn't go on for long. Sooner or later, some screw was going to peek behind Rita Hayworth just to make sure Andy didn't have a sharpened spoon-handle or some marijuana reefers Scotch-taped to the wall.

And his response to that second assumption must have been *to hell with it*. Maybe he even made a game out of it. How far in can I get before they find out? Prison is a goddam boring place, and the chance of being surprised by an unscheduled inspection in the middle of the night while he had his poster unstuck probably added some spice to his life during the early years.

And I do believe it would have been impossible for him to get away just on dumb luck. Not for twenty-seven years. Nevertheless, I have to believe that for the first two years – until mid-May of 1950, when he helped Byron Hadley get around the tax on his windfall inheritance – that's exactly what he did get by on.

Or maybe he had something more than dumb luck going for him even back then. He had money, and he might have been slipping someone a little squeeze every week to take it easy on him. Most guards will go along with that if the price is right; it's money in their pockets and the prisoner gets to keep his whack-off pictures or his tailormade cigarettes. Also, Andy was a model prisoner – quiet, well-spoken, respectful, non-violent. It's the crazies and the stampeders that get their cells turned upside-down at least once every six months, their mattresses unzipped, their pillows taken away and cut open, the outflow pipe from their toilets carefully probed.

Then, in 1950, Andy became something more than a model prisoner. In 1950, he became a valuable commodity, a murderer who did tax returns as well as H & R Block. He gave gratis estate-planning advice, set up tax-shelters, filled out loan applications (sometimes creatively). I can remember him sitting behind his desk in the library, patiently going over a car-loan agreement paragraph by paragraph with a screwhead who wanted to buy a used DeSoto, telling the guy what was good about the agreement and what was bad about it, explaining to him that it was possible to shop for a loan and not get hit quite so bad, steering him away from the finance companies which in those days were sometimes little better than legal loan-sharks. When he'd finished, the screwhead started to put out his hand . . . and then drew it back to himself quickly. He'd forgotten for a moment, you see, that he was dealing with a mascot, not a man.

Andy kept up on the tax laws and the changes in the stock market, and so his usefulness didn't end after he'd been in cold storage for a while, as it might have done. He began to get his library money, his running war with the sisters had ended, and nobody tossed his cell very hard. He was a good nigger.

Then one day, very late in the going – perhaps around October of 1967 – the long-time hobby suddenly turned into something else. One night while he was in the hole up to his waist with Raquel Welch hanging down over his ass, the pick end of his rock-hammer must have suddenly sunk into concrete past the hilt.

He would have dragged some chunks of concrete back, but maybe he heard others falling down into that shaft, bouncing back and forth, clinking off that standpipe. Did he know by then that he was going to come upon that shaft, or was he totally surprised? I don't know. He might have seen the prison blueprints by then or he might not have. If not, you can be damned sure he found a way to look at them not long after.

All at once he must have realized that, instead of just playing a game, he was playing for high stakes . . . in terms of his own life and his own future, the highest. Even then he couldn't have known for sure, but he must have had a pretty good idea because it was right around then that he talked to me about Zihuatanejo for the first time. All of a sudden, instead of just being a toy, that stupid hole in the wall became his master – if he knew about the sewer-pipe at the bottom, and that it led under the outer wall, it did, anyway.

He'd had the key under the rock in Buxton to worry about for years. Now he had to worry that some eager-beaver new guard would look behind his poster and expose the whole thing, or that he would get another cellmate, or that he would, after all those years, suddenly be transferred. He had all those things on his mind for the next seven years. All I can say is that he must have been one of the coolest men who ever lived. I would have gone completely nuts after a while, living with all that uncertainty. But Andy just went on playing the game.

He had to carry the possibility of discovery for another eight years – the *probability* of it, you might say, because no matter how carefully he stacked the cards in his favour, as an inmate of a state prison, he just didn't have that many to stack . . . and the gods had been kind to him for a very long time; some eighteen years.

The most ghastly irony I can think of would have been if he had been offered a parole. Can you imagine it? Three days before the parolee is actually released, he is transferred into the light security wing to undergo a complete phys-ical and a battery of vocational tests. While he's there, his old cell is completely cleaned out. Instead of getting his parole, Andy would have gotten a long turn downstairs in solitary, followed by some more time upstairs . . . but in a different cell.

If he broke into the shaft in 1967, how come he didn't escape until 1975?

I don't know for sure – but I can advance some pretty good guesses.

First, he would have become more careful than ever. He was too smart to just push ahead at flank speed and try to get out in eight months, or even in eighteen. He must have gone on widening the opening on the crawlspace a little at a time. A hole as big as a teacup by the time he took his New Year's Eve drink that year. A hole as big as a dinner-plate by the time he took his birthday drink in 1968. As big as a serving-tray by the time the 1969 baseball season opened.

For a time I thought it should have gone much faster than it apparently did – after he broke through, I mean. It seemed to me that, instead of having to pulverize the crap and take it out of his cell in the cheater gadgets I have described, he could simply let it drop down the shaft. The length of time he took makes me believe that he didn't dare do that. He might have decided that the noise would arouse someone's suspicions. Or, if he knew about the sewer-pipe, as I believe he must have, he would have been afraid that a falling chunk of concrete would break it before he was ready, screwing up the cellblock sewage system and leading to an investigation. And an investigation, needless to say, would lead to ruin.

Still and all, I'd guess that, by the time Nixon was sworn in for his second term, the hole would have been wide enough for him to wriggle through . . . and probably sooner than that. Andy was a small guy.

Why didn't he go then?

That's where my educated guesses run out, folks; from this point they become progressively wilder. One possibility is that the crawlspace itself was clogged with crap and he had to clear it out. But that wouldn't account for all the time. So what was it?

I think that maybe Andy got scared.

I've told you as well as I can how it is to be an institutional man. At first you can't stand those four walls, then you get so you can abide them, then you get so you accept them . . . and then, as your body and your mind and your spirit adjust to life on an HO scale, you get to love them. You are told when to eat, when you can write letters, when you can smoke. If you're at work in the laundry or the plate-shop, you're assigned five minutes of each hour when you can go to the bathroom. For thirty-five years, my time was twenty-five minutes after the hour, and after thirty-five years, that's the only time I ever felt the need to take a piss or have a crap: twenty-five minutes past the hour. And if for some reason I couldn't go, the need would pass at thirty after, and come back at twenty-five past the next hour.

I think Andy may have been wrestling with that tiger – that institutional syndrome – and also with the bulking fears that all of it might have been for nothing.

How many nights must he have lain awake under his poster, thinking about that sewer line, knowing that the one chance was all he'd ever get? The blueprints might have told him how big the pipe's bore was, but a blueprint couldn't tell him what it would be like inside that pipe – if he would be able to breathe without choking, if the rats were big enough and mean enough to fight instead of retreating . . . and a blueprint couldn't've told him what he'd find at the end of the pipe, when and if he got there. Here's a joke even funnier than the parole would have been: Andy breaks into the sewer line, crawls through five hundred yards of choking, shit-smelling darkness, and comes up against a heavy-gauge mesh screen at the end of it all. Ha, ha, very funny.

That would have been on his mind. And if the long shot actually came in and he was able to get out, would he be able to get some civilian clothes and get away from the vicinity of the prison undetected? Last of all, suppose he got out of the pipe, got away from Shawshank before the alarm was raised, got to Buxton, overturned the right rock . . . and found nothing beneath? Not necessarily something so dramatic as arriving at the right field and discovering that a high-rise apartment building had been erected on the spot, or that it had turned into a supermarket parking lot. It could have been that some little kid who liked rocks noticed that piece of volcanic glass, turned it over, saw the deposit-box key, and took both it and the rock back to his room as souvenirs. Maybe a November hunter kicked the rock, left the key exposed, and a squirrel or a crow with a liking for bright shiny things had taken it away. Maybe there had been spring floods one year, breaching the wall, washing the key away. Maybe anything.

So I think – wild guess or not – that Andy just froze in place for a while. After all, you can't lose if you don't bet. What did he have to lose, you ask? His library, for one thing. The poison peace of institutional life, for another. Any future chance to grab his safe identity.

But he finally did it, just as I have told you. He tried . . . and, my! Didn't he succeed in spectacular fashion? You tell me!

But *did* he get away, you ask? What happened after? What happened when he got to that meadow and turned over the rock . . . always assuming the rock was still there?

I can't describe that scene for you, because this institutional man is still in this institution, and expects to be for years to come.

But I'll tell you this. Very late in the summer of 1975, on 15 September to be exact, I got a postcard which had been mailed from the tiny town of McNary, Texas. That town is on the American side of the border, directly across from El Porvenir. The message side of the card was totally blank. But I know. I know it in my heart as surely as I know that we're all going to die someday.

McNary was where he crossed. McNary, Texas.

So that's my story, Jack. I never believed how long it would take to write it all down, or how many pages it would take. I started writing just after I got that postcard, and here I am finishing up on 14 January 1976. I've used three pencils right down to knuckle-stubs, and a whole tablet of paper. I've kept the pages carefully hidden . . . not that many could read my hen-tracks, anyway.

It stirred up more memories than I ever would have believed. Writing about yourself seems to be a lot like sticking a branch into clear river-water and roiling up the muddy bottom.

Well, you weren't writing about yourself, I hear someone in the peanut-gallery saying. *You were writing about Andy Dufresne.*

You're nothing but a minor character in your own story. But you know, that's just not so. It's *all* about me, every damned word of it. Andy was the part of me they could never lock up, the part of me that will rejoice when the gates finally open for me and I walk out in my cheap suit with my twenty dollars of mad-money in my pocket. That part of me will rejoice no matter how old and broken and scared the rest of me is. I guess it's just that Andy had more of that part than me, and used it better.

There are others here like me, others who remember Andy. We're glad he's gone, but a little sad, too. Some birds are not meant to be caged, that's all. Their feathers are too bright, their songs too sweet and wild. So you let them go, or when you open the cage to feed them they somehow fly out past you. And the part of you that knows it was wrong to imprison them in the first place rejoices, but still, the place where you live is that much more drab and empty for their departure.

That's the story and I'm glad I told it, even if it is a bit inconclusive and even though some of the memories the pencil prodded up (like that branch poking up the river-mud) made me feel a little sad and even older than I am. Thank you for listening. And Andy: If you're really down there, as I believe you are, look at the stars for me just after sunset, and touch the sand, and wade in the water, and feel free.

I never expected to take up this narrative again, but here I am with the dog-eared, folded pages open on the desk in front of me. Here I am adding another three or four pages, writing in a brand-new tablet. A tablet I bought in a store – I just walked into a store on Portland's Congress Street and bought it.

I thought I had put finish to my story in a Shawshank prison cell on a bleak January day in 1976. Now it's late June of 1977 and I am sitting in a small, cheap room of the Brewster Hotel in Portland, adding to it.

The window is open, and the sound of the traffic floating in seems huge, exciting, and intimidating. I have to look constantly over at the window and reassure myself that there are no bars on it. I sleep poorly at night because the bed in this room, as cheap as the room is, seems much too big and luxurious. I snap awake every morning promptly at six-thirty, feeling disorientated and frightened. My dreams are bad. I have a crazy feeling of free fall. The sensation is as terrifying as it is exhilarating.

What has happened in my life? Can't you guess? I was paroled. After thirty-eight years of routine hearings and routine details (in the course of those thirty-eight years, three lawyers died on me), my parole was granted. I suppose they decided that, at the age of fifty-eight, I was finally used up enough to be deemed safe.

I came very close to burning the document you have just read. They search outgoing parolees just as carefully as they search incoming 'new fish'. And beyond containing enough dynamite to assure me of a quick turnaround and another six or eight years inside, my 'memoirs' contained something else: the name of the town where I believe Andy Dufresne to be. Mexican police gladly cooperate with the American police, and I didn't want my freedom – or my unwilling-ness to give up the story I'd worked so long and hard to write – to cost Andy his.

Then I remembered how Andy had brought in his five hundred dollars back in 1948, and I took out my story of him the same way. Just to be on the safe side, I carefully rewrote each page which mentioned Zihuatanejo. If the papers had been found during my 'outside search', as they call it at the Shank, I would have gone back in on turn-around . . . but the cops would have been looking for Andy in a Peruvian seacoast town named Las Intrudres.

The Parole Committee got me a job as a 'stock-room assistant' at the big FoodWay Market at the Spruce Mall in South Portland – which means I became just one more ageing bag-boy. There's only two kinds of bag-boys, you know; the old ones and the young ones. No one ever looks at either kind. If you shop at the Spruce Mall FoodWay, I may have even taken your groceries out to your car . . . but you'd have had to have shopped there between March and April of 1977, because that's as long as I worked there.

At first I didn't think I was going to be able to make it on the outside at all. I've described prison society as a scaled-down model of your outside world, but I had no idea of how *fast* things moved on the outside; the *raw speed* people move at. They even talk faster. And louder.

It was the toughest adjustment I've ever had to make, and I haven't finished making it yet . . . not by a long way. Women, for instance. After hardly knowing that they were half of the human race for forty years, I was suddenly working in a store filled with them. Old women, pregnant women wearing T-shirt with arrows pointing downward and the printed motto reading BABY HERE, skinny women with their nipples poking out of their shirts – a woman wearing something like that when I went in would have gotten arrested and then had a sanity hearing – women of every shape and size. I found myself going around with a semi-hard almost all the time and cursing myself for being a dirty old man.

Going to the bathroom, that was another thing. When I had to go (and the urge always came on me at twenty-five past the hour), I had to fight the almost overwhelming need to check it with my boss. Knowing that was something I could just go and do in this too-bright outside world was one thing; adjusting my inner self to that knowledge after all those years of checking it with the nearest screwhead or facing two days in solitary for the oversight . . . that was something else.

My boss didn't like me. He was a young guy, twenty-six or -seven, and I could see that I sort of disgusted him, the way a cringing, servile old dog that crawls up to you on its belly to be petted will disgust a man. Christ, I disgusted myself. But . . . I couldn't make myself stop. I wanted to tell him, That's what a whole life in prison does for you, young man. It turns everyone in a position of authority into a master, and you into every master's dog. Maybe you know you've become a dog, even in prison, but since everyone else in grey is a dog, too, it doesn't seem to matter so much. Outside, it does. But I couldn't tell a young guy like him. He would never understand. Neither would my P.O., a big, bluff ex-Navy man with a huge red beard and a large stock of Polish jokes. He saw me for about five minutes every week. 'Are you staying out of the bars, Red?' he'd ask when he'd run out of Polish jokes. I'd say yeah, and that would be the end of it until next week.

Music on the radio. When I went in, the big bands were just getting up a good head of steam. Now every song sounds like it's about fucking. So many cars. At first I felt like I was taking my life into my hands every time I crossed the street.

There was more – *everything* was strange and frightening – but maybe you get the idea, or can at least grasp a corner of it. I began to think about doing something to get back in. When you're on parole, almost anything will serve. I'm ashamed to say it, but I began to think about stealing some money or shoplifting stuff from the FoodWay, anything, to get back in where it was quiet and you knew everything that was going to come up in the course of the day.

If I had never known Andy, I probably would have done that. But I kept thinking of him, spending all those years chipping patiently away at the cement with his rock-hammer so he could be free. I thought of that and it made me ashamed and I'd drop the idea again. Oh, you can say he had more reason to be free than I did – he had a new identity and a lot of money. But that's not really true, you know. Because he didn't know for sure that the new identity was still there, and without the new identity, the money would always be out of reach. No, what he needed was just to be free, and if I kicked away what I had, it would be like spitting in the face of everything he had worked so hard to win back.

So what I started to do on my time off was to hitchhike a ride down to the little town of Buxton. This was in the early April of 1977, the snow just starting to melt off the fields, the air just beginning to be warm, the baseball teams coming north to start a new season playing the only game I'm sure God approves of. When I went on these trips, I carried a Silva compass in my pocket.

There's a big hayfield in Buxton, Andy had said, *and at the north end of that hayfield there's a rock wall, right out of a Robert*

Frost poem. And somewhere along the base of that wall is a rock that has no earthly business in a Maine hayfield.

A fool's errand, you say. How many hayfields are there in a small rural town like Buxton? Fifty? A hundred? Speaking from personal experience, I'd put it at even higher than that, if you add in the fields now cultivated which might have been haygrass when Andy went in. And if I did find the right one, I might never know it. Because I might overlook that black piece of volcanic glass, or, much more likely, Andy put it into his pocket and took it with him.

So I'd agree with you. A fool's errand, no doubt about it. Worse, a dangerous one for a man on parole, because some of those fields were clearly marked with NO TRESPASSING signs. And, as I've said, they're more than happy to slam your ass back inside if you get out of line. A fool's errand . . . but so is chipping at a blank concrete wall for twenty-eight years. And when you're no longer the man who can get it for you and just an old bag-boy, it's nice to have a hobby to take your mind off your new life. My hobby was looking for Andy's rock.

So I'd hitchhike to Buxton and walk the roads. I'd listen to the birds, to the spring runoff in the culverts, examine the bottles the retreating snows had revealed – all useless non-returnables, I am sorry to say; the world seems to have gotten awfully spendthrift since I went into the slam – and looking for hayfields.

Most of them could be eliminated right off. No rock walls. Others had rock walls, but my compass told me they were facing the wrong direction. I walked these wrong ones anyway. It was a comfortable thing to be doing, and on those outings I really *felt* free, at peace. An old dog walked with me one Saturday. And one day I saw a winter-skinny deer.

Then came 23 April, a day I'll not forget even if I live another fifty-eight years. It was a balmy Saturday afternoon, and I was walking up what a little boy fishing from a bridge told me was called The Old Smith Road. I had taken a lunch in a brown FoodWay bag, and had eaten it sitting on a rock by the road. When I was done I carefully buried my leavings, as my dad had taught me before he died, when I was a sprat no older than the fisherman who had named the road for me.

Around two o'clock I came to a big field on my left. There was a stone wall at the far end of it, running roughly north-west. I walked back to it, squelching over the wet ground, and began to walk the wall. A squirrel scolded me from an oak tree.

Three-quarters of the way to the end, I saw the rock. No mistake. Black glass and as smooth as silk. A rock with no earthly business in a Maine hayfield. For a long time I just looked at it, feeling that I might cry, for whatever reason. The squirrel had followed me, and it was still chattering away. My heart was beating madly.

When I felt I had myself under control, I went to the rock, squatted beside it – the joints in my knees went off like a double-barrelled shotgun – and let my hand touch it. It was real. I didn't pick it up because I thought there would be anything under it; I could just as easily have walked away without finding what was beneath. I certainly had no plans to take it away with me, because I didn't feel it was mine to take – I had a feeling that taking that rock from the field would have been the worst kind of theft. No, I only picked it up to feel it better, to get the heft of the thing, and, I suppose, to prove its reality by feeling its satiny texture against my skin.

I had to look at what was underneath for a long time. My eyes saw it, but it took a while for my mind to catch up. It was an envelope, carefully wrapped in a plastic bag to keep away the damp. My name was written across the front in Andy's clear script.

I took the envelope and left the rock where Andy had left it, and Andy's friend before him.

> *Dear Red,*
>
> *If you're reading this, then you're out. One way or another, you're out. And if you've followed along this far, you might be willing to come a little further. I think you remember the name of the town, don't you? I could use a good man to help me get my project on wheels.*
>
> *Meantime, have a drink on me – and do think it over. I will be keeping an eye out for you. Remember that hope is a good thing, Red, maybe the best of things, and no good thing ever dies. I will be hoping that this letter finds you, and finds you well.*
>
> *Your friend,*
> *Peter Stevens*

I didn't read that letter in the field. A kind of terror had come over me, a need to get away from there before I was seen. To make what may be an appropriate pun, I was in terror of being apprehended.

I went back to my room and read it there, with the smell of old men's dinners drifting up the stairwell to me – Beefaroni,

Ricearoni, Noodleroni. You can bet that whatever the old folks of America, the ones on fixed incomes, are eating tonight, it almost certainly ends in roni.

I opened the envelope and read the letter and then I put my head in my arms and cried. With the letter there were twenty new fifty-dollar bills.

And here I am in the Brewster Hotel, technically a fugitive from justice again – parole violation is my crime. No one's going to throw up any roadblocks to catch a criminal wanted on that charge, I guess – wondering what I should do now.

I have this manuscript. I have a small piece of luggage about the size of a doctor's bag that holds everything I own. I have nineteen fifties, four tens, a five, three ones, and assorted change. I broke one of the fifties to buy this tablet of paper and a deck of smokes.

Wondering what I should do.

But there's really no question. It always comes down to just two choices. Get busy living or get busy dying.

First I'm going to put this manuscript back in my bag. Then I'm going to buckle it up, grab my coat, go downstairs, and check out of this fleabag. Then I'm going to walk uptown to a bar and put that five dollar bill down in front of the bartender and ask him to bring me two straight shots of Jack Daniels – one for me and one for Andy Dufresne. Other than a beer or two, they'll be the first drinks I've taken as a free man since 1938. Then I am going to tip the bartender a dollar and thank him kindly. I will leave the bar and walk up Spring Street to the Greyhound terminal there and buy a bus ticket to El Paso by way of New York City. When I get to El Paso, I'm going to buy a ticket to McNary.

And when I get to McNary, I guess I'll have a chance to find out if an old crook like me can find a way to float across the border and into Mexico.

Sure I remember the name. Zihuatanejo. A name like that is just too pretty to forget.

I find I am excited, so excited I can hardly hold the pencil in my trembling hand. I think it is the excitement that only a free man can feel, a free man starting a long journey whose conclusion is uncertain.

I hope Andy is down there.

I hope I can make it across the border.

I hope to see my friend and shake his hand.

I hope the Pacific is as blue as it has been in my dreams.

I *hope*.

Summer of Corruption

APT PUPIL

For Elaine Koster and Herbert Schnall

1

He looked like the total all-American kid as he pedalled his twenty-six-inch Schwinn with the ape-hanger handlebars up the residential suburban street, and that's just what he was: Todd Bowden, thirteen years old, five-feet-eight and a healthy one hundred and forty pounds, hair the colour of ripe corn, blue eyes, white even teeth, lightly tanned skin marred by not even the first shadow of adolescent acne.

He was smiling a summer vacation smile as he pedalled through the sun and shade three blocks from his own house. He looked like the kind of kid who might have a paper route, and as a matter of fact, he did – he delivered the Santa Donato *Clarion*. He also looked like the kind of kid who might sell greeting cards for premiums, and he had done that, too. They were the kind that come with your name printed inside – JACK AND MARY BURKE, or DON AND SALLY, or THE MURCHISONS. He looked like the sort of boy who might whistle while he worked, and he often did so. He whistled quite prettily, in fact. His dad was an architectural engineer who made $40,000 a year. His mom was a housewife and a secretarial school graduate (she had met Todd's father one day when he needed a secretary from the pool) who typed manuscripts in her spare time. She had kept all of Todd's old school report cards in a folder. Her favourite was his final fourth-grade card, on which Mrs Upshaw had scratched: 'Todd is an extremely apt pupil.' He was, too. Straight As and Bs all the way up the line. If he'd done any better – straight As, for example – his friends might have begun to think he was weird.

Now he brought his bike to a halt in front of 963 Claremont Street and stepped off it. The house was a small bungalow set discreetly back on its lot. It was white with green shutters and green trim. A hedge ran around the front. The hedge was well-watered and well-clipped.

Todd brushed his blond hair out of his eyes and walked the Schwinn up the cement path to the steps. He was still smiling, and his smile was open and expectant and beautiful, a marvel of modern dentistry and fluoridated water. He pushed down the bike's kickstand with the toe of one Nike running-shoe and then picked the folded newspaper off the bottom step. It wasn't the *Clarion*; it was the LA *Times*. He put it under his arm and mounted the steps. At the top was a heavy wooden door with no window inside of a latched screen door. There was a doorbell on the right-hand doorframe, and below the bell were two small signs, each neatly screwed into the wood and covered with protective plastic so they wouldn't yellow or waterspot. German efficiency, Todd thought, and his smile widened a little. It was an adult thought, and he always mentally congratulated himself when he had one of those.

The top sign said ARTHUR DENKER.

The bottom one said NO SOLICITORS, NO PEDDLERS, NO SALESMEN.

Smiling still, Todd rang the bell.

He could barely hear its muted burring, somewhere far off inside the small house. He took his finger off the bell and cocked his head a little, listening for footsteps. There were none. He looked at his Timex watch (one of the premiums he had gotten for selling personalized greeting cards) and saw that it was twelve past ten. The guy should be up by now. Todd himself was always up by seven-thirty at the latest, even during summer vacation. The early bird catches the worm.

He listened for another thirty seconds and when the house remained silent he leaned on the bell, watching the sweep second hand on his Timex as he did so. He had been pressing the doorbell for exactly seventy-one seconds when he finally heard shuffling footsteps. Slippers, he deduced from the soft *wish-wish* sound. Todd was into deductions. His current ambition was to become a private detective when he grew up.

'All right! All right!' the man who was pretending to be Arthur Denker called querulously. 'I'm coming! Let it go! I'm coming!'

Todd stopped pushing the doorbell button. He looked at the tip of his forefinger. There was a small red circle there.

A chain and bolt rattled on the far side of the window-less inner door. Then it was pulled open.

An old man, hunched inside a bathrobe, stood looking out through the screen. A cigarette smouldered between his fingers. Todd thought the man looked like a cross between Albert Einstein and Boris Karloff. His hair was long and white but beginning to yellow in an unpleasant way that was more nico-tine than ivory. His face was wrinkled and pouched and puffy with sleep, and Todd saw with some distaste that he hadn't bothered shaving for the last couple of days. Todd's father was fond of saying, 'A shave puts a shine on the morning.' Todd's father shaved every day, whether he had to work or not.

The eyes looking out at Todd were watchful but deeply sunken, laced with snaps of red. Todd felt an instant of deep disappointment. The guy *did* look a little bit like Albert

Einstein, and he *did* look a little bit like Boris Karloff, but what he looked like more than anything else was one of the seedy old winos that hung around down by the railroad yard.

But of course, Todd reminded himself, the man had just gotten up. Todd had seen Denker many times before today (although he had been very careful to make sure that Denker hadn't seen *him*, no *way*, Jose), and on his public occasions, Denker looked very natty, every inch an officer in retirement, you might say, even though he was seventy-six if the articles Todd had read at the library had his birth-date right. On the days when Todd had shadowed him to the Shoprite where Denker did his shopping or to one of the three movie theatres on the bus line – Denker had no car – he was always dressed in one of four neatly kept suits, no matter how warm the weather. If the weather looked threatening he carried a furled umbrella under one arm like a swagger stick. He sometimes wore a trilby hat. And on the occasions when Denker went out, he was always neatly shaved and his white moustache (worn to conceal an imperfectly corrected harelip) was carefully trimmed.

'A boy,' he said now. His voice was thick and sleepy. Todd saw with new disappointment that his robe was faded and tacky. One rounded collar point stood up at a drunken angle to poke at his wattled neck. There was a splotch of something that might have been chili or possibly A-1 Steak Sauce on the left lapel, and he smelled of cigarettes and stale booze.

'A boy,' he repeated. 'I don't need anything, boy. Read the sign. You can read, can't you? Of course you can. All American boys can read. Don't be a nuisance, boy. Good day.'

The door began to close.

He might have dropped it right there, Todd thought much

later on one of the nights when sleep was hard to find. His disappointment at seeing the man for the first time at close range, seeing him with his street-face put away – hanging in the closet, you might say, along with his umbrella and his trilby – might have done it. It could have ended in that moment, the tiny, unimportant snicking sound of the latch cutting off everything that happened later as neatly as a pair of shears. But, as the man himself had observed, he was an American boy, and he had been taught that persistence is a virtue.

'Don't forget your paper, Mr Dussander,' Todd said, holding the *Times* out politely.

The door stopped dead in its swing still inches from the jamb. A tight and watchful expression flitted across Kurt Dussander's face and was gone at once. There might have been fear in that expression. It was good, the way he had made that expression disappear, but Todd was disappointed for the third time. He hadn't expected Dussander to be good; he had expected Dussander to be *great*.

Boy, Todd thought with real disgust. *Boy oh boy*.

He pulled the door open again. One hand, bunched with arthritis, unlatched the screen door. The hand pushed the screen door open just enough to wriggle through like a spider and close over the edge of the paper Todd was holding out. The boy saw with distaste that the old man's fingernails were long and yellow and horny. It was a hand that had spent most of its waking hours holding one cigarette after another. Todd thought smoking was a filthy dangerous habit, one he himself would never take up. It really was a wonder that Dussander had lived as long as he had.

The old man tugged. 'Give me my paper.'

'Sure thing, Mr Dussander.' Todd released his hold on the paper. The spider-hand yanked it inside. The screen closed.

'My name is Denker,' the old man said. 'Not this Doo-Zander. Apparently you cannot read. What a pity. Good day.'

The door started to close again. Todd spoke rapidly into the narrowing gap. 'Bergen-Belsen, January 1943 to June 1943, Auschwitz, June 1943 to June of 1944, *Unterkommandant*. Patin —'

The door stopped again. The old man's pouched and pallid face hung in the gap like a wrinkled, half-deflated balloon. Todd smiled.

'You left Patin just ahead of the Russians. You got to Buenos Aires. Some people say you got rich there, investing the gold you took out of Germany in the drug trade. Whatever, you were in Mexico City from 1950 to 1952. Then —'

'Boy, you are crazy like a cuckoo bird.' One of the arthritic fingers twirled circles around a misshapen ear. But the toothless mouth was quivering in an infirm, panicky way.

'From 1952 until 1958, I don't know,' Todd said, smiling more widely still. 'No one does, I guess, or at least they're not telling. But an Israeli agent spotted you in Cuba, working as the *concierge* in a big hotel just before Castro took over. They lost you when the rebels came into Havana. You popped up in West Berlin in 1965. They almost got you.' He pronounced the last two words as one: *gotcha*. At the same time he squeezed all of his fingers together into one large, wriggling fist. Dussander's eyes dropped to those well-made and well-nourished American hands, hands that were made for building soapbox racers and Aurora models. Todd had done both. In fact, the year before, he and his dad had built a model of the *Titanic*. It had taken almost four months, and Todd's father kept it in his office.

'I don't know what you are talking about,' Dussander said. Without his false teeth, his words had a mushy sound Todd didn't like. It didn't sound . . . well, authentic. Colonel Klink on *Hogan's Heroes* sounded more like a Nazi than Dussander did. But in his time he must have been a real whiz. In an article on the death-camps in *Men's Action*, the writer had called him The Blood-Fiend of Patin. 'Get out of here, boy. Before I call the police.'

'Gee, I guess you better call them, Mr Dussander. Or Herr Dussander, if you like that better.' He continued to smile, showing perfect teeth that had been fluoridated since the beginning of his life and bathed thrice a day in Crest toothpaste for almost as long. 'After 1965, no one saw you again . . . until I did, two months ago, on the downtown bus.'

'You're insane.'

'So if you want to call the police,' Todd said, smiling, 'you go right ahead. I'll wait on the stoop. But if you don't want to call them right away, why don't I come in? We'll talk.'

There was a long moment while the old man looked at the smiling boy. Birds twitted in the trees. On the next block a power mower was running, and far off, on busier streets, horns honked out their own rhythm of life and commerce.

In spite of everything, Todd felt the onset of doubt. He couldn't be wrong, could he? Was there some mistake on his part? He didn't think so, but this was no schoolroom exercise. It was real life. So he felt a surge of relief (*mild* relief, he assured himself later) when Dussander said: 'You may come in for a moment, if you like. But only because I do not wish to make trouble for you, you understand?'

'Sure, Mr Dussander,' Todd said. He opened the screen and came into the hall. Dussander closed the door behind them, shutting off the morning.

The house smelled stale and slightly malty. It smelled the way Todd's own house smelled sometimes the morning after his folks had thrown a party and before his mother had had a chance to air it out. But this smell was worse. It was lived-in and ground-in. It was liquor, fried food, sweat, old clothes, and some stinky medicinal smell like Vicks or Mentholatum. It was dark in the hallway, and Dussander was standing too close, his head hunched into the collar of his robe like the head of a vulture waiting for some hurt animal to give up the ghost. In that instant, despite the stubble and the loosely hanging flesh, Todd could see the man who had stood inside the black SS uniform more clearly than he had ever seen him on the street. And he felt a sudden lancet of fear slide into his belly. *Mild* fear, he amended later.

'I should tell you that if anything happens to me –' he began, and then Dussander shuffled past him and into the living room, his slippers *wish-wishing* on the floor. He flapped a contemptuous hand at Todd, and Todd felt a flush of hot blood mount into his throat and cheeks.

Todd followed him, his smile wavering for the first time. He had not pictured it happening quite like this. But it would work out. Things would come into focus. Of course they would. Things always did. He began to smile again as he stepped into the living room.

It was another disappointment – and how! – but one he supposed he should have been prepared for. There was of course no oil portrait of Hitler with his forelock dangling and eyes that followed you. No medals in cases, no ceremonial sword mounted on the wall, no Luger or PPK Walther on the mantle (there was, in fact, no mantle). Of course, Todd told himself, the guy would have to be crazy to put any of those things out where people could see them. Still, it was hard to put everything you saw in the movies or on TV out of your head. It looked like the living room of any old man living alone on a slightly frayed pension. The fake fireplace was faced with fake bricks. A Westclox hung over it. There was a black and white Motorola TV on a stand; the tips of the rabbit ears had been wrapped in aluminium foil to improve reception. The floor was covered with a grey rug; its nap was balding. The magazine rack by the sofa held copies of *National Geographic, Reader's Digest,* and the LA *Times*. Instead of Hitler or a ceremonial sword hung on the wall, there was a framed certificate of citizenship and a picture of a woman in a funny hat. Dussander later told him that sort of hat was called a cloche, and they had been popular in the twenties and thirties.

'My wife,' Dussander said sentimentally. 'She died in 1955 of a lung disease. At that time I was a draughtsman at the Menschler Motor Works in Essen. I was heartbroken.'

Todd continued to smile. He crossed the room as if to get a better look at the woman in the picture. Instead of looking at the picture, he fingered the shade on a small table-lamp.

'*Stop that!*' Dussander barked harshly. Todd jumped back a little.

'That was good,' he said sincerely. 'Really commanding. It was Ilse Koch who had the lampshades made out of human skin, wasn't it? And she was the one who had the trick with the little glass tubes.'

'I don't know what you're talking about,' Dussander said. There was a package of Kools, the kind with no filter, on top of the TV. He offered them to Todd. 'Cigarette?' he asked, and grinned. His grin was hideous.

'No. They give you lung cancer. My dad used to smoke, but he gave it up. He went to SmokeEnders.'

'Did he?' Dussander produced a wooden match from the pocket of his robe and scratched it indifferently on the plastic case of the Motorola. Puffing, he said: 'Can you give me one reason why I shouldn't call the police and tell them of the monstrous accusations you've just made? One reason? Speak quickly, boy. The telephone is just down the hall. Your father would spank you, I think. You would sit for dinner on a cushion for a week or so, eh?'

'My parents don't believe in spanking. Corporal punishment causes more problems than it cures.' Todd's eyes suddenly gleamed. 'Did you spank any of them? The women? Did you take off their clothes and —'

With a muffled exclamation, Dussander started for the phone.

Todd said coldly: 'You better not do that.'

Dussander turned. In measured tones that were spoiled only slightly by the fact that his false teeth were not in, he said: 'I tell you this once, boy, and once only. My name is Arthur Denker. It has never been anything else; it has not even been Americanized. I was in fact named Arthur by my father, who greatly admired the stories of Arthur Conan Doyle. It has never been Doo-Zander, nor Himmler, nor Father Christmas. I was a reserve lieutenant in the war. I never joined the Nazi party. In the battle of Berlin I fought for three years. I will admit that in the late thirties, when I was first married, I supported Hitler. He ended the depression and returned some of the pride we had lost in the aftermath of the sickening and unfair Treaty of Versailles. I suppose I supported him mostly because I got a job and there was tobacco again, and I didn't need to hunt through the gutters when I needed to smoke. I thought, in the late thirties, that he was a great man. In his own way, perhaps he was. But at the end he was mad, directing phantom armies at the whim of an astrologer. He even gave Blondi, his dog, a death-capsule. The act of a madman; by the end they were all madmen, singing the Horst Wessel Song as they fed poison to their children. On 2 May 1945, my regiment gave up to the Americans. I remember that a private soldier named Hackermeyer gave me a chocolate bar. I wept. There was no reason to fight on; the war was over, and really had been since February. I was interned at Essen and was treated very well. We listened to the Nuremberg trials on the radio and when Goering committed suicide, I traded fourteen American cigarettes for half a bottle of schnapps and got drunk. I was released in January of 1946. At the Essen Motor Works I put wheels on cars until 1963, when I retired and emigrated to the United States. To come here was a lifelong ambition. In 1967 I became a citizen. I am an American. I vote. No Buenos Aires. No drug dealing. No Berlin. No Cuba.' He pronounced it *Koo-ba*. 'And now, unless you leave, I make my telephone call.'

He watched Todd do nothing. Then he went down the hall and picked up the telephone. Still Todd stood in the living room, beside the table with the small lamp on it.

Dussander began to dial. Todd watched him, his heart speeding up until it was drumming in his chest. After the

145

fourth number, Dussander turned and looked at him. His shoulders sagged. He put the phone down.

'A boy,' he breathed. 'A *boy*.'

Todd smiled widely but rather modestly.

'How did you find out?'

'One piece of luck and a lot of hard work,' Todd said. 'There's this friend of mine, Harold Pegler his name is, only all the kids call him Foxy. He plays second base for our team. And his dad's got all these magazines out in his garage. Great big stacks of them. War magazines. They're old. I looked for some new ones, but the guy who runs the newsstand across from the school says most of them went out of business. In most of them there's pictures of Krauts – German soldiers, I mean – and Japs torturing these women. And articles about the concentration camps. I really groove on all that concentration camp stuff.'

'You . . . groove on it.' Dussander was staring at him, one hand rubbing up and down on his cheek, producing a very small sandpapery sound.

'Groove. You know. I get off on it. I'm interested.'

He remembered that day in Foxy's garage as clearly as anything in his life – more clearly, he suspected. He remembered in the fourth grade, before Careers Day, how Mrs Anderson (all the kids called her Bugs because of her big front teeth) had talked to them about what she called finding YOUR GREAT INTEREST.

'It comes all at once,' Bugs Anderson had rhapsodized. 'You see something for the first time, and right away you know you have found YOUR GREAT INTEREST. It's like a key turning in a lock. Or falling in love for the first time. That's why Careers Day is so important, children – it may

be the day on which you find YOUR GREAT INTEREST.'
And she had gone on to tell them about her own GREAT
INTEREST, which turned out not to be teaching the fourth
grade but collecting nineteenth-century postcards.

Todd had thought Mrs Anderson was full of bullspit at
the time, but that day in Foxy's garage, he remembered what
she had said and wondered if maybe she hadn't been right
after all.

The Santa Anas had been blowing that day, and to the
east there were brush-fires. He remembered the smell of
burning, hot and greasy. He remembered Foxy's crewcut,
and the flakes of Butch Wax clinging to the front of it. He
remembered *everything*.

'I know there's comics here someplace,' Foxy had said. His
mother had a hangover and had kicked them out of the house
for making too much noise. 'Neat ones. They're Westerns,
mostly, but there's some *Turok, Son of Stones* and –'

'What are those?' Todd asked, pointing at the bulging
cardboard cartons under the stairs.

'Ah, they're no good,' Foxy said. 'True war stories, mostly.
Boring.'

'Can I look at some?'

'Sure. I'll find the comics.'

But by the time fat Foxy Pegler found them, Todd no
longer wanted to read comics. He was lost. Utterly lost.

*It's like a key turning in a lock. Or falling in love for the first
time.*

It *had* been like that. He had known about the war, of
course – not the stupid one going on now, where the
Americans had gotten the shit kicked out of them by a
bunch of gooks in black pyjamas – but World War II. He

knew that the Americans wore round helmets with net on them and the Krauts wore sort of square ones. He knew that the Americans won most of the battles and that the Germans had invented rockets near the end and shot them from Germany onto London. He had even known something about the concentration camps.

The difference between all of that and what he found in the magazines under the stairs in Foxy's garage was like the difference between being *told* about germs and then actually *seeing* them in a microscope, squirming around and alive.

Here was Ilse Koch. Here were crematoriums with their doors standing open on their soot-clotted hinges. Here were officers in SS uniforms and prisoners in striped uniforms. The smell of the old pulp magazines was like the smell of the brush-fires burning out of control on the east of Santo Donato, and he could feel the old paper crumbling against the pads of his fingers, and he turned the pages, no longer in Foxy's garage but caught somewhere crosswise in time, trying to cope with the idea that *they had really done those things*, that *somebody had really done those things*, and that *somebody had let them do those things*, and his head began to ache with a mixture of revulsion and excitement, and his eyes were hot and strained, but he read on, and from a column of print beneath a picture of tangled bodies at a place called Dachau, this figure jumped out at him:

6,000,000

And he thought: *Somebody goofed there, somebody added a zero or two, that's three times as many people as there are in LA!* But then, in another magazine (the cover of this one showed a

148

woman chained to a wall while a guy in a Nazi uniform approached her with a poker in his hand and a grin on his face), he saw it again:

6,000,000

His headache got worse. His mouth went dry. Dimly, from some distance, he heard Foxy saying he had to go in for supper. Todd asked Foxy if he could stay out here in the garage and read while Foxy ate. Foxy gave him a look of mild puzzlement, shrugged, and said sure. And Todd read, hunched over the boxes of the old true war magazines, until his mother called and asked if he was *ever* going to go home.

Like a key turning in a lock.

All the magazines said it was bad, what had happened. But all the stories were continued at the back of the book, and when you turned to those pages, the words saying it was bad were surrounded by ads, and these ads sold German knives and belts and helmets as well as Magic Trusses and Guaranteed Hair Restorer. These ads sold German flags emblazoned with swastikas and Nazi Lugers and a game called Panzer Attack as well as correspondence lessons and offers to make you rich selling elevator shoes to short men. They said it was bad, but it seemed like a lot of people must not mind.

Like falling in love.

Oh yes, he remembered that day very well. He remembered everything about it – a yellowing pin-up calendar for a defunct year on the back wall, the oil-stain on the cement floor, the way the magazines had been tied together with orange twine. He remembered how his headache had gotten a little worse each time he thought of that incredible number,

6,000,000

He remembered thinking: *I want to know about everything that happened in those places. Everything. And I want to know which is more true — the words, or the ads they put beside the words.*

He remembered Bugs Anderson as he at last pushed the boxes back under the stairs and thought: *She was right. I've found my GREAT INTEREST.*

Dussander looked at Todd for a long time. Then he crossed the living room and sat down heavily in a rocking chair. He looked at Todd again, unable to analyze the slightly dreamy, slightly nostalgic expression on the boy's face.

'Yeah. It was the magazines that got me interested, but I figured a lot of what they said was just, you know, bullspit. So I went to the library and found out a lot more stuff. Some of it was even neater. At first the crummy librarian didn't want me to look at any of it because it was in the adult section of the library, but I told her it was for school. If it's for school they have to let you have it. She called my dad, though.' Todd's eyes turned up scornfully. 'Like she thought dad didn't know what I was doing, if you can dig that.'

'He did know?'

'Sure. My dad thinks kids should find out about life as soon as they can — the bad as well as the good. Then they'll be ready for it. He says life is a tiger you have to grab by the tail, and if you don't know the nature of the beast it will eat you up.'

'Mmmmm,' Dussander said.

'My mom thinks the same way.'

'Mmmmm.' Dussander looked dazed, not quite sure where he was.

'Anyhow,' Todd said, 'the library stuff was real good. They must have had a hundred books with stuff in them about the Nazi concentration camps, just here in the Santa Donato library. A *lot* of people must like to read about that stuff. There weren't as many pictures as in Foxy's dad's magazines, but the other stuff was real gooshy. Chairs with spikes sticking up through the seats. Pulling out gold teeth with pliers. Poison gas that came out of the showers.' Todd shook his head. 'You guys just went overboard, you know that? You really did.'

'Gooshy,' Dussander said heavily.

'I really *did* do a research paper, and you know what I got on it? An A Plus. Of course I had to be careful. You have to write that stuff in a certain way. You got to be careful.'

'Do you?' Dussander asked. He took another cigarette with a hand that trembled.

'Oh yeah. All those library books, they read a certain way. Like the guys who wrote them got puking sick over what they were writing about.' Todd was frowning, wrestling with the thought, trying to bring it out. The fact that *tone*, as that word is applied to writing, wasn't yet in his vocabulary, made it more difficult. 'They all write like they lost a lot of sleep over it. How we've got to be careful so nothing like that ever happens again. I made my paper like that, and I guess the teacher gave me an A just 'cause I read the source material without losing my lunch.' Once more, Todd smiled winningly.

Dussander dragged heavily on his unfiltered Kool. The tip trembled slightly. As he feathered smoke out of his nostrils, he coughed an old man's dank, hollow cough. 'I can hardly believe this conversation is taking place,' he said. He leaned forward and peered closely at Todd. 'Boy, do you know the word "existentialism"?'

Todd ignored the question. 'Did you ever meet Ilse Koch?'

'Ilse Koch?' Almost inaudibly, Dussander said: 'Yes. I met her.'

'Was she beautiful?' Todd asked eagerly. 'I mean . . .' His hands described an hourglass in the air.

'Surely you have seen her photograph?' Dussander asked. 'An aficionado such as yourself?'

'What's an af . . . aff . . .'

'An aficionado,' Dussander said, 'is one who grooves. One who . . . gets off on something.'

'Yeah? Cool.' Todd's grin, puzzled and weak for a moment, shone out triumphantly again. 'Sure, I've seen her picture. But you know how they are in those books.' He spoke as if Dussander had them all. 'Black and white, fuzzy . . . just snapshots. None of those guys knew they were taking pictures for, you know, *history*. Was she really stacked?'

'She was fat and dumpy and she had bad skin,' Dussander said shortly. He crushed his cigarette out half-smoked in a Table Talk pie dish filled with dead butts.

'Oh. Golly.' Todd's face fell.

'Just luck,' Dussander mused, looking at Todd. 'You saw my picture in a war-adventures magazine and happened to ride next to me on the bus. *Tcha!*' He brought a fist down on the arm of his easy chair, but without much force.

'No sir, Mr Dussander. There was more to it than that. A *lot*,' Todd added earnestly, leaning forward.

'Oh? Really?' The bushy eyebrows rose, signalling polite disbelief.

'Sure. I mean, the pictures of you in my scrapbook were all thirty years old, at least. I mean, it *is* 1974.'

'You keep a . . . a scrapbook?'

'Oh, yes, sir! It's a good one. Hundreds of pictures. I'll show it to you sometime. You'll go ape.'

Dussander's face pulled into a revolted grimace, but he said nothing.

'The first couple of times I saw you, I wasn't sure at all. And then you got on the bus one day when it was raining, and you had this shiny black slicker on —'

'That,' Dussander breathed.

'Sure. There was a picture of you in a coat like that in one of the magazines out in Foxy's garage. Also, a photo of you in your SS greatcoat in one of the library books. And when I saw you that day, I just said to myself, "It's for sure. That's Kurt Dussander." So I started to shadow you —'

'You did *what*?'

'Shadow you. Follow you. My ambition is to be a private detective like Sam Spade in the books, or Mannix on TV. Anyway, I was super careful. I didn't want you to get wise. Want to look at some pictures?'

Todd took a folded-over manilla envelope from his back pocket. Sweat had stuck the flap down. He peeled it back carefully. His eyes were sparkling like a boy thinking about his birthday, or Christmas, or the firecrackers he will shoot off on the Fourth of July.

'You took pictures of me?'

'Oh, you bet. I got this little camera. A Kodak. It's thin and flat and fits right into your hand. Once you get the hang of it, you can take pictures of the subject just by holding the camera in your hand and spreading your fingers enough to let the lens peek through. Then you hit the button with your thumb.' Todd laughed modestly. 'I got the hang of it, but I took a lot of pictures of my fingers while I did. I hung

153

right in there, though. I think a person can do anything if they try hard enough, you know it? It's corny but true.'

Kurt Dussander had begun to look white and ill, shrunken inside his robe. 'Did you have these pictures finished by a commercial developer, boy?'

'Huh?' Todd looked shocked and startled, then contemptuous. 'No! What do you think I am, stupid? My dad's got a darkroom. I've been developing my own pictures since I was nine.'

Dussander said nothing, but he relaxed a little and some colour came back into his face.

Todd handed him several glossy prints, the rough edges confirming that they had been home-developed. Dussander went through them, silently grim. Here he was sitting erect in a window-seat of the downtown bus, with a copy of the latest James Michener, *Centennial*, in his hands. Here he was at the Devon Avenue bus stop, his umbrella cocked under his arm and his head cocked back at an angle which suggested De Gaulle at his most imperial. Here he was standing in line just under the marquee of the Majestic Theatre, erect and silent, conspicuous among the leaning teenagers and blank-faced housewives in curlers by his height and his bearing. Finally, here he was peering into his own mailbox.

'I was scared you might see me on that one,' Todd said. 'It was a calculated risk. I was right across the street. Boy oh boy, I wish I could afford a Minolta with a telephoto lens. Someday . . .' Todd looked wistful.

'No doubt you had a story ready, just in case.'

'I was going to ask you if you'd seen my dog. Anyway, after I developed the pix, I compared them to these.'

He handed Dussander three Xeroxed photographs. He

had seen them all before, many times. The first showed him in his office at the Patin resettlement camp; it had been cropped so nothing showed but him and the Nazi flag on its stand by his desk. The second was a picture that had been taken on the day of his enlistment. The last showed him shaking hands with Heinrich Glücks, who had been sub-ordinate only to Himmler himself.

'I was pretty sure then, but I couldn't see if you had the harelip because of your goshdamn moustache. But I had to be sure, so I got this.'

He handed over the last sheet from his envelope. It had been folded over many times. Dirt was grimed into the creases. The corners were lopped and milled – the way papers get when they spend a long time in the pockets of young boys who have no shortage of things to do and places to go. It was a copy of the Israeli want-sheet on Kurt Dussander. Holding it in his hands, Dussander reflected on corpses that were unquiet and refused to stay buried.

'I took your fingerprints,' Todd said, smiling. 'And then I did the compares to the one on the sheet.'

Dussander gaped at him and then uttered the German word for shit. 'You did not!'

'Sure I did. My mom and dad gave me a fingerprint set for Christmas last year. A real one, not just a toy. It had the powder and three brushes for three different surfaces and special paper for lifting them. My folks know I want to be a PI when I grow up. Of course, they think I'll grow out of it.' He dismissed this idea with a disinterested lift and drop of his shoulders. 'The book explained all about whorls and lands and points of similarity. They're called *compares*. You need eight compares for a fingerprint to get accepted in court.

'So anyway, one day when you were at the movies, I came here and dusted your mailbox and doorknob and lifted all the prints I could. Pretty smart, huh?'

Dussander said nothing. He was clutching the arms of his chair, and his toothless, deflated mouth was trembling. Todd didn't like that. It made him look like he was on the verge of tears. That, of course, was ridiculous. The Blood Fiend of Patin in tears? You might as well expect Chevrolet to go bankrupt or McDonald's to give up burgers and start selling caviar and truffles.

'I got two sets of prints,' Todd said. 'One of them didn't look anything like the ones on the wanted poster. I figured those were the postman's. The rest were yours. I found more than eight compares. I found fourteen good ones.' He grinned. 'And that's how I did it.'

'You are a little *bastard*,' Dussander said, and for a moment his eyes shone dangerously. Todd felt a tingling little thrill, as he had in the hall. Then Dussander slumped back again.

'Who have you told?'

'No one.'

'Not even this friend? This Cony Pegler?'

'Foxy. Foxy Pegler. Nah, he's a blabbermouth. I haven't told anybody. There's nobody I trust that much.'

'What do you want? Money? There is none, I'm afraid. In South America there was, although it was nothing as romantic or dangerous as the drug trade. There is – there *was* – a kind of "old boy network" in Brazil and Paraguay and Santo Domingo. Fugitives from the war. I became part of their circle and made a fortune in minerals and ores – tin, copper, bauxite. Then the changes came. Nationalism, anti-Americanism. I might have ridden out the changes, but then Weisenthal's men caught my scent. Bad luck follows bad luck, boy, like dogs after a bitch in heat. Twice they almost had me; once I heard the Jew-bastards in the next room.

'They hung Eichmann,' he whispered. One hand went to his neck, and his eyes had become as round as the eyes of a child listening to the darkest passage of a scary tale – *Hansel and Gretel*, perhaps, or *Bluebeard*. 'He was an old man, of no danger to anyone. He was apolitical. Still, they hung him.'

Todd nodded.

'At last, I went to the only people who could help me. They had helped others, and I could run no more.'

'You went to the Odessa?' Todd asked eagerly.

'To the Sicilians,' Dussander said dryly, and Todd's face fell again. 'It was arranged. False papers, false past. Would you care for a drink, boy?'

'Sure. You got a Coke?'

'No Coke.' He pronounced it *Kök*.

'Milk?'

'Milk.' Dussander went through the archway and into the kitchen. A fluorescent bar buzzed into life. 'I live now on stock dividends,' his voice came back. 'Stocks I picked up after the war under yet another name. Through a bank in the State of Maine, if you please. The banker who bought them for me went to jail for murdering his wife a year after I bought them . . . life is sometimes strange, boy, *hein*?'

A refrigerator door opened and closed.

'The Sicilian jackals didn't know about those stocks,' he said. 'Today they are everywhere, but in those days, Boston was as far north as they could be found. If they had known, they would have had those as well. They would have picked

STEPHEN KING

me clean and sent me to America to starve on welfare and food stamps.'

Todd heard a cupboard door open; he heard liquid poured into a glass.

'A little General Motors, a little American Telephone and Telegraph, a hundred and fifty shares of Revlon. All this banker's choices. Dufresne, his name was – I remember, because it sounds a little like mine. It seems he was not so smart at wife-killing as he was at picking growth stocks. The *crime passionnel*, boy. It only proves that all men are donkeys who can read.'

He came back into the room, slippers whispering. He held two green plastic glasses that looked like the premiums they sometimes give out at gas station openings. When you filled your tank, you got a free glass. Dussander thrust a glass at Todd.

'I lived adequately on the stock portfolio this Dufresne had set up for me for the first five years. But then I sold my Diamond Match stock in order to buy this house and a small cottage not far from Big Sur. Then, inflation. Recession. I sold the cottage and one by one I sold the stocks, many of them at fantastic profits. I wish to God I had bought more. But I thought I was well-protected in other directions; the stocks were, as you Americans say, a "flier" . . .' He made a toothless hissing sound and snapped his fingers.

Todd was bored. He had not come here to listen to Dussander whine about his money or mutter about his stocks. The thought of blackmailing Dussander had never crossed Todd's mind. Money? What would he do with it? He had his allowance; he had his paper route. If his monetary needs went higher than what these could provide during any given week, there was always someone who needed his lawn mowed.

Todd lifted his milk to his lips and then hesitated. His

smile shone out again . . . an admiring smile. He extended the gas-station premium glass to Dussander.

'*You* have some of it,' he said slyly.

Dussander stared at him for a moment, uncomprehending, and then rolled his bloodshot eyes. '*Gruss Gott!*' He took the glass, swallowed twice, and handed it back. 'No gasping for breath. No clawing at the throat. No smell of bitter almonds. It is milk, boy. *Milk*. From the Dairylea Farms. On the carton is a picture of a smiling cow.'

Todd watched him warily for a moment, then took a small sip. Yes, it *tasted* like milk, sure did, but somehow he didn't feel very thirsty anymore. He put the glass down. Dussander shrugged, raised his own glass – it contained a large knock of whiskey – and took a swallow. He smacked his lips over it.

'Schnapps?' Todd asked.

'Bourbon. Ancient Age. Very nice. And cheap.'

Todd fiddled his fingers along the seams of his jeans.

'So,' Dussander said, 'if you have decided to have a "flier" of your own, you should be aware that you have picked a worthless stock.'

'Huh?'

'Blackmail,' Dussander said. 'Isn't that what they call it on *Mannix* and *Hawaii Five-O* and *Barnaby Jones*? Extortion. If that was what –'

But Todd was laughing – hearty, boyish laughter. He shook his head, tried to speak, could not, and went on laughing.

'No,' Dussander said, and suddenly he looked grey and more frightened than he had since he and Todd had begun to speak. He took another large swallow of his drink, grimaced, and shuddered. 'I see that is not it . . . at least, not the extortion of money. But, though you laugh, I smell extortion in it somewhere. What is it? Why do you come here and disturb an old man! Perhaps, as you say, I was once a Nazi. Gestapo, even. Now I am only old, and to have a bowel movement I have to use a suppository. So what do you want?'

Todd had sobered again. He stared at Dussander with an open and appealing frankness. 'Why . . . I want to hear about it. That's all. That's all I want. Really.'

'*Hear* about it?' Dussander echoed. He looked utterly perplexed.

Todd leaned forward, tanned elbows on bluejeaned knees. 'Sure. The firing squads. The gas chambers. The ovens. The guys who had to dig their own graves and then stand on the ends so they'd fall into them. The . . .' His tongue came out and wetted his lips. 'The examinations. The experiments. Everything. All the gooshy stuff.'

Dussander stared at him with a certain amazed detachment, the way a veterinarian might stare at a cat who was giving birth to a succession of two-headed kittens. 'You are a monster,' he said softly.

Todd sniffed. 'According to the books I read for my report, *you're* the monster, Mr Dussander. Not me. You sent them to the ovens, not me. Two thousand a day at Patin before you came, three thousand after, thirty-five-hundred before the Russians came and made you stop. Himmler called you an efficiency expert and gave you a medal. So you call me a monster. Oh *boy*.'

'All of that is a filthy American lie,' Dussander said, stung. He set his glass down with a bang, slopping bourbon onto his hands and the table. 'The problem was not of my making, nor was the solution. I was given orders and directives, which I followed.'

Todd's smile widened; it was now almost a smirk.

'Oh, I know how the Americans have distorted that,' Dussander muttered. 'But your own politicians make our Dr Goebbels look like a child playing with picture books in a kindergarten. They speak of morality while they douse screaming children and old women in burning napalm. Your draft-resisters are called cowards and "peaceniks". For refusing to follow orders they are either put in jails or scourged from the country. Those who demonstrate against this country's unfortunate Asian adventure are clubbed down in the streets. The GI soldiers who kill the innocent are decorated by Presidents, welcomed home from the bayoneting of children and the burning of hospitals with parades and bunting. They are given dinners, Keys to the City, free tickets to pro football games.' He toasted his glass in Todd's direction. 'Only those who lose are tried as war criminals for following orders and directives.' He drank and then had a coughing fit that brought thin colour to his cheeks.

Through most of this Todd fidgeted the way he did when his parents discussed whatever had been on the news that night – good old Walter Klondike, his dad called him. He didn't care about Dussander's politics any more than he cared about Dussander's stocks. His idea was that people made up politics so they could do things. Like when he wanted to feel around under Sharon Ackerman's dress last year. Sharon said it was bad for him to want to do that, even though he could tell from her tone of voice that the idea sort of excited her. So he told her he wanted to be a doctor when he grew up and then she let him. That was politics. He wanted to hear about German doctors trying to mate women with dogs, putting identical twins into refrigerators to see whether they would die at the same time or if one of them would last

161

longer, and electroshock therapy, and operations without anaesthetic, and German soldiers raping all the women they wanted. The rest was just so much tired bullshit to cover up the gooshy stuff after someone came along and put a stop to it.

'If I hadn't followed orders, I would have been dead.' Dussander was breathing hard, his upper body rocking back and forth in the chair, making the springs squeak. A little cloud of liquor-smell hung around him. 'There was always the Russian front, *nicht wahr*? Our leaders were madmen, granted, but does one argue with madmen . . . especially when the maddest of them all has the luck of Satan? He escaped a brilliant assassination attempt by inches. Those who conspired were strangled with piano-wire, strangled slowly. Their death-agonies were filmed for the edification of the elite —'

'Yeah! Neat!' Todd cried impulsively. 'Did you see that movie?'

'Yes. I saw. We all saw what happened to those unwilling or unable to run before the wind and wait for the storm to end. What we did then was the right thing. For that time and that place, it was the right thing. I would do it again. But . . .'

His eyes dropped to his glass. It was empty.

'. . . but I don't wish to speak of it, or even think of it. What we did was motivated only by survival, and nothing about survival is pretty. I had dreams . . .' He slowly took a cigarette from the box on the TV. 'Yes. For years I had them. Blackness, and sounds in the blackness. Tractor engines. Bulldozer engines. Gunbutts thudding against what might have been frozen earth, or human skulls. Whistles, sirens, pistol-shots, screams. The doors of cattle-cars rumbling open on cold winter afternoons.

'Then, in my dreams, all sounds would stop — and eyes would open in the dark, gleaming like the eyes of animals in a rainforest. For many years I lived on the edge of the jungle, and I suppose that is why it is always the jungle I smelled and felt in those dreams. When I woke from them I would be drenched with sweat, my heart thundering in my chest, my hand stuffed into my mouth to stifle the screams. And I would think: *the dream is the truth*. Brazil, Paraguay, Cuba . . . those places are the dream. In the reality I am still at Patin. The Russians are closer today than yesterday. Some of them are remembering that in1943 they had to eat frozen German corpses to stay alive. Now they long to drink hot German blood. There were rumours, boy, that some of them did just that when they crossed into Germany: cut the throats of some prisoners and drank their blood out of a boot. I would wake up and think: *The work must go on, if only so there is no evidence of what we did here, or so little that the world, which doesn't want to believe it, won't have to*. I would think: *The work must go on if we are to survive.'*

Unlike what had gone before, Todd listened to this with close attention and great interest. This was pretty good, but he was sure there would be better stuff in the days ahead. All Dussander needed was a little prodding. Heck, he was lucky. Lots of men his age were senile.

Dussander dragged deeply on his cigarette. 'Later, after the dreams went away, there were days when I would think I had seen someone from Patin. Never guards or fellow officers, always inmates. I remember one afternoon in West Germany, ten years ago. There was an accident on the autobahn. Traffic was frozen in every lane. I sat in my Morris, listening to the radio, waiting for the traffic to move. I looked to my right. There was a very old Simca in the next lane, and the man behind the wheel was looking at me. He was perhaps fifty, and he looked ill. There was a scar on his cheek.

His hair was white, short, cut badly. I looked away. The minutes passed and still the traffic didn't move. I began snatching glances at the man in the Simca. Every time I did, he was looking at me, his face as still as death, his eyes sunken in their sockets. I became convinced he had been at Patin. He had been there and he had recognized me.'

Dussander wiped a hand across his eyes.

'It was winter. The man was wearing an overcoat. But I was convinced that if I got out of my car and went to him, made him take off his coat and push up his shirtsleeves, I would see the number on his arm.

'At last the traffic began to move again. I pulled away from the Simca. If the jam had lasted another ten minutes, I believe I would have gotten out of my car and pulled the old man out of his. I would have beaten him, number or no number. I would have beaten him for looking at me that way.

'Shortly after that, I left Germany forever.'

'Lucky for you,' Todd said.

Dussander shrugged. 'It was the same everywhere. Havana, Mexico City, Rome. I was in Rome for three years, you know. I would see a man looking at me over his *cappuccino* in a cafe . . . a woman in a hotel lobby who seemed more interested in me than in her magazine . . . a waiter in a restaurant who would keep glancing at me no matter who he was serving. I would become convinced that these people were studying me, and that night the dream would come — the sounds, the jungle, the eyes.

'But when I came to America I put it out of my mind. I go to movies. I eat out once a week, always at one of those fast-food places that are so clean and so well-lighted by fluorescent bars. Here at my house I do jigsaw puzzles and I read novels – most of them bad ones – and watch TV. At night I drink until I'm sleepy. The dreams don't come anymore. When I see someone looking at me in the supermarket or the library or the tobacconist's, I think it must be because I look like their grandfather . . . or an old teacher . . . or a neighbour in a town they left some years ago.' He shook his head at Todd. 'Whatever happened at Patin, it happened to another man. Not to me.'

'Great!' Todd said. 'I want to hear all about it.'

Dussander's eyes squeezed closed, and then opened slowly. 'You don't understand. I do not wish to speak of it.'

'You will, though. If you don't, I'll tell everyone who you are.'

Dussander stared at him, grey-faced. 'I knew,' he said, 'that I would find the extortion sooner or later.'

'Today I want to hear about the gas ovens,' Todd said. 'How you baked the Jews.' His smile beamed out, rich and radiant. 'But put your teeth in before you start. You look better with your teeth in.'

Dussander did as he was told. He talked to Todd about the gas ovens until Todd had to go home for lunch. Every time he tried to slip over into generalities, Todd would frown severely and ask him specific questions to get him back on the track. Dussander drank a great deal as he talked. He didn't smile. Todd smiled. Todd smiled enough for both of them.

2

August, 1974.

They sat on Dussander's back porch under a cloudless, smiling sky. Todd was wearing jeans, Keds, and his Little

League shirt. Dussander was wearing a baggy grey shirt and shapeless khaki pants held up with suspenders – wino-pants, Todd thought with private contempt; they looked like they had come straight from a box in the back of the Salvation Army store downtown. He was really going to have to do something about the way Dussander dressed when he was at home. It spoiled some of the fun.

The two of them were eating Big Macs that Todd had brought in his bike basket, pedalling fast so they wouldn't get cold. Todd was sipping a Coke through a plastic straw. Dussander had a glass of bourbon.

His old man's voice rose and fell, papery, hesitant, some-times nearly inaudible. His faded blue eyes, threaded with the usual snaps of red, were never still. An observer might have thought them grandfather and grandson, the latter perhaps attending some rite of passage, a handing down.

'And that's all I remember,' Dussander finished presently, and took a large bite of his sandwich. McDonald's Secret Sauce dribbled down his chin.

'You can do better than that,' Todd said softly.

Dussander took a large swallow from his glass. 'The uniforms were made of paper,' he said finally, almost snarling. 'When one inmate died, the uniform was passed on if it could still be worn. Sometimes one paper uniform could dress as many as forty inmates. I received high marks for my frugality.'

'From Glücks?'

'From Himmler.'

'But there was a clothing factory in Patin. You told me that just last week. Why didn't you have the uniforms made there? The inmates themselves could have made them.'

'The job of the factory in Patin was to make uniforms

for German soldiers. And as for us . . .' Dussander's voice faltered for a moment, and then he forced himself to go on. 'We were not in the business of rehabilitation,' he finished.

Todd smiled his broad smile.

'Enough for today? Please? My throat is sore.'

'You shouldn't smoke so much, then,' Todd said, continuing to smile. 'Tell me some more about the uniforms.'

'Which? Inmate or SS?' Dussander's voice was resigned.

Smiling, Todd said: 'Both.'

3

September, 1974.

Todd was in the kitchen of his house, making himself a peanut butter and jelly sandwich. You got to the kitchen by going up half a dozen redwood steps to a raised area that gleamed with chrome and Formica. His mother's electric typewriter had been going steadily ever since Todd had gotten home from school. She was typing a master's thesis for a grad student. The grad student had short hair, wore thick glasses, and looked like a creature from outer space, in Todd's humble opinion. The thesis was on the effect of fruitflies in the Salinas Valley after World War II, or some good shit like that. Now her typewriter stopped and she came out of her office.

'Todd-baby,' she greeted him.

'Monica-baby,' he hailed back, amiably enough.

His mother wasn't a bad-looking chick for thirty-six, Todd thought; blonde hair that was streaked ash in a couple of places, tall, shapely, now dressed in dark red shorts and a sheer blouse of a warm whiskey colour – the blouse was casually knotted below her breasts, putting her flat, unlined midriff on show. A typewriter eraser was tucked into her hair, which had been pinned carelessly back with a turquoise clip.

'So how's school?' she asked him, coming up the steps into the kitchen. She brushed his lips casually with hers and then slid onto one of the stools in front of the breakfast counter.

'School's cool.'

'Going to be on the honour roll again?'

'Sure.' Actually, he thought his grades might slip a notch this first quarter. He had been spending a lot of time with Dussander, and when he wasn't actually with the old Kraut, he was thinking about the things Dussander had told him. Once or twice he had dreamed about the things Dussander had told him. But it was nothing he couldn't handle.

'Apt pupil,' she said, ruffling his shaggy blond hair. 'How's that sandwich?'

'Good,' he said.

'Would you make me one and bring it into my office?'

'Can't,' he said, getting up. 'I promised Mr Denker I'd come over and read to him for an hour or so.'

'Are you still on *Robinson Crusoe*?'

'Nope.' He showed her the spine of a thick book he had bought in a junk shop for twenty cents. '*Tom Jones*.'

'Ye gods and little fishes! It'll take you the whole school-year to get through that, Todd-baby. Couldn't you at least find an abridged edition, like with *Crusoe*?'

'Probably, but he wanted to hear all of this one. He said so.'

'Oh.' She looked at him for a moment, then hugged him. It was rare for her to be so demonstrative, and it made Todd a little uneasy. 'You're a peach to be taking so much of your spare time to read to him. Your father and I think it's just . . . just exceptional.'

Todd cast his eyes down modestly.

'And to not want to tell anybody,' she said. 'Hiding your light under a bushel.'

'Oh, the kids I hang around with – they'd probably think I was some kind of weirdo,' Todd said, smiling modestly down at the floor. 'All that good shit.'

'Don't say that,' she admonished absently. Then: 'Do you think Mr Denker would like to come over and have dinner with us some night?'

'Maybe,' Todd said vaguely. 'Listen, I gotta put an egg in my shoe and beat it.'

'Okay. Supper at six-thirty. Don't forget.'

'I won't.'

'Your father's got to work late so it'll just be me and thee again, okay?'

'Crazy, baby.'

She watched him go with a fond smile, hoping there was nothing in *Tom Jones* he shouldn't be reading; he was only thirteen. She didn't suppose there was. He was growing up in a society where magazines like *Penthouse* were available to anyone with a dollar and a quarter, or to any kid who could reach up to the top shelf of the magazine rack and grab a quick peek before the clerk could shout for him to put that up and get lost. In a society that seemed to believe most of all in the creed of hump thy neighbour, she didn't think there could be much in a book two hundred years old to screw up Todd's head – although she supposed the old man might get off on it a little. And as Richard liked to say, for a kid the whole world's a laboratory. You have to

let them poke around in it. And if the kid in question has
a healthy home life and loving parents, he'll be all the stronger
for having knocked around a few strange corners.

And there went the healthiest kid she knew, pedalling up
the street on his Schwinn. *We did okay by the lad*, she thought,
turning to make her sandwich. *Damned if we didn't do okay.*

4

October, 1974.

Dussander had lost weight. They sat in the kitchen, the
shopworn copy of *Tom Jones* between them on the oilcloth-
covered table (Todd, who tried never to miss a trick, had
purchased the Cliff's Notes on the book with part of his
allowance and had carefully read the entire summary against
the possibility that his mother or father might ask him questions about the plot). Todd was eating a Ring-Ding he had
bought at the market. He had bought one for Dussander, but
Dussander hadn't touched it. He only looked at it
morosely from time to time as he drank his bourbon. Todd
hated to see anything as tasty as Ring-Dings go to waste. If
he didn't eat it pretty quick, Todd was going to ask him if
he could have it.

'So how did the stuff get to Patin?' he asked Dussander.

'In railroad cars,' Dussander said. 'In railroad cars labelled
MEDICAL SUPPLIES. It came in long crates that looked
like coffins. Fitting, I suppose. The inmates off-loaded the
crates and stacked them in the infirmary. Later, our own
men stacked them in the storage sheds. They did it at night.
The storage sheds were behind the showers.'

'Was it always Zyklon-B?'

'No, from time to time we would be sent something else. Experimental gases. The High Command was always interested in improving efficiency. Once they sent us a gas code-named PEGASUS. A nerve-gas. Thank God they never sent it again. It —' Dussander saw Todd lean forward, saw those eyes sharpen, and he suddenly stopped and gestured casually with his gas-station-premium glass. 'It didn't work very well,' he said. 'It was . . . quite boring.'

But Todd was not fooled, not in the least. 'What did it do?'

'It killed them — what do you think it did, made them walk on water? It killed them, that's all.'

'Tell me.'

'No,' Dussander said, now unable to hide the horror he felt. He hadn't thought of PEGASUS in . . . how long? Ten years? Twenty? 'I won't tell you! I refuse!'

'Tell me,' Todd repeated, licking chocolate icing from his fingers. 'Tell me or you know what.'

Yes, Dussander thought. I know what. Indeed I do, you putrid little monster.

'It made them dance,' he said reluctantly.

'Dance?'

'Like the Zyklon-B, it came in through the shower-heads. And they . . . they began to vomit, and to . . . to defecate helplessly.'

'Wow,' Todd said. 'Shit themselves, huh?' He pointed at the Ring-Ding on Dussander's plate. He had finished his own. 'You going to eat that?'

Dussander didn't reply. His eyes were hazed with memory. His face was far away and cold, like the dark side of a planet which does not rotate. Inside his mind he felt the *queerest* combination of revulsion and — could it be? — *nostalgia*?

'They began to twitch all over and to make high, strange sounds in their throats. My men . . . they called PEGASUS the Yodelling Gas. At last they all collapsed and just lay there on the floor in their own filth, they lay there, yes, they lay there on the concrete, screaming and yodelling, with bloody noses. But I lied, boy. The gas didn't kill them, either because it wasn't strong enough or because we couldn't bring ourselves to wait long enough. I suppose it was that. Men and women like that could not have lived long. Finally I sent in five men with rifles to end their agonies. It would have looked bad on my record if it had shown up, I've no doubt of that – it would have looked like a waste of cartridges at a time when the Führer had declared every cartridge a national resource. But those five men I trusted. There were times, boy, when I thought I would never forget the sound they made. The yodelling sound. The laughing.'

'Yeah, I bet,' Todd said. He finished Dussander's Ring-Ding in two bites. Waste not, want not, Todd's mother said on the rare occasions when Todd complained about left-overs. 'That was a good story, Mr Dussander. You always tell them good. Once I get you going.'

Todd smiled at him. And incredibly – certainly not because he wanted to – Dussander found himself smiling back.

5

November, 1974.

Dick Bowden, Todd's father, looked remarkably like a movie and TV actor named Lloyd Bochner. He – Bowden, not Bochner – was thirty-eight. He was a thin, narrow man who liked to dress in Ivy League style shirts and solid-colour suits, usually dark. When he was on a construction site, he wore khakis and a hard-hat that was a souvenir of his Peace Corps days, when he had helped to design and build two dams in Africa. When he was working in his study at home, he wore half-glasses that had a way of slipping down to the end of his nose and making him look like a college dean. He was wearing these glasses now as he tapped his son's first-quarter report card against his desk's gleaming glass top.

'One B. Four Cs. One D. A *D*, for Christ's sake! Todd, your mother's not showing it, but she's really upset.'

Todd dropped his eyes. He didn't smile. When his dad swore, that wasn't exactly the best of news.

'My God, you've *never* gotten a report like this. A *D* in Beginning Algebra? What *is* this?'

'I don't know, Dad.' He looked humbly at his knees.

'Your mother and I think that maybe you've been spending a little too much time with Mr Denker. Not hitting the books enough. We think you ought to cut it down to weekends, slugger. At least until we see where you're going academically . . .'

Todd looked up, and for a single second Bowden thought he saw a wild, pallid anger in his son's eyes. His own eyes widened, his fingers clenched on Todd's buff-coloured report card . . . and then it was just Todd, looking at him openly if rather unhappily. Had that anger really been there? Surely not. But the moment had unsettled him, made it hard for him to know exactly how to proceed. Todd hadn't been mad, and Dick Bowden didn't want to *make* him mad. He and his son were friends, always had been friends, and Dick wanted things to stay that way. They had no secrets from each other, none at all (except for the fact that Dick Bowden was sometimes unfaithful with his secretary, but that wasn't exactly the sort of thing you told your thirteen-year-old son, was it? . . . and besides, that had absolutely no bearing on his home life, his *family* life). That was the way it was supposed to be, the way it *had* to be in a cockamamie world where murderers went unpunished, high-school kids skin-popped heroin, and junior high schoolers – kids Todd's age – turned up with VD.

'No, Dad, please don't do that. I mean, don't punish Mr Denker for something that's my fault. I mean, he'd be lost without me. I'll do better. Really. That algebra . . . it just threw me to start with. But I went over to Ben Tremaine's, and after we studied together for a few days, I started to get it. It just . . . I dunno, I sorta choked at first.'

'I think you're spending too much time with him,' Bowden said, but he was weakening. It was hard to refuse Todd, hard to disappoint him, and what he said about punishing the old man for Todd's falling-off . . . goddammit, it made sense. The old man looked forward to his visits so much.

'That Mr Storrman, the algebra teacher, is really hard,' Todd said. 'Lots of kids got Ds. Three or four got Fs.'

Bowden nodded thoughtfully.

'I won't go Wednesdays anymore. Not until I bring my grades up.' He had read his father's eyes. 'And instead of going out for anything at school, I'll stay after every day and study. I promise.'

'You really like the old guy that much?'

'He's really neat,' Todd said sincerely.

'Well . . . okay. We'll try it your way, slugger. But I want to see a big improvement in your marks come January, you understand me? I'm thinking of your future. You may think junior high's too soon to start thinking about that, but it's not. Not by a long chalk.' As his mother liked to say *Waste not, want not,* so Dick Bowden liked to say *Not by a long chalk.*

'I understand, Dad,' Todd said gravely. Man to man stuff.

'Get out of here and give those books a workout then.' He pushed his half-glasses up on his nose and clapped Todd on the shoulder.

Todd's smile, broad and bright, broke across his face. 'Right on, Dad!'

Bowden watched Todd go with a prideful smile of his own. One in a million. And that hadn't been anger on Todd's face. For sure. Pique, maybe . . . but not that high-voltage emotion he had at first thought he'd seen there. If Todd was that mad, he would have known; he could read his son like a book. It had always been that way.

Whistling, his fatherly duty discharged, Dick Bowden unrolled a blueprint and bent over it.

6

December, 1974.

The face that came in answer to Todd's insistent finger on the bell was haggard and yellowed. The hair, which had been lush in July, had now begun to recede from the bony brow; it looked lustreless and brittle. Dussander's body, thin to begin with, was now gaunt . . . although, Todd thought, he was nowhere near as gaunt as the inmates who had once been delivered into his hands.

Todd's left hand had been behind his back when Dussander came to the door. Now he brought it out and handed a wrapped package to Dussander. 'Merry Christmas!' he yelled.

Dussander had cringed from the box; now he took it

with no expression of pleasure or surprise. He handled it gingerly, as if it might contain explosive. Beyond the porch, it was raining. It had been raining off and on for almost a week, and Todd had carried the box inside his coat. It was wrapped in gay foil and ribbon.

'What is it?' Dussander asked without enthusiasm as they went to the kitchen.

'Open it and see.'

Todd took a can of Coke from his jacket pocket and put it on the red and white checked oilcloth that covered the kitchen table. 'Better pull down the shades,' he said confidentially.

Distrust immediately leaked onto Dussander's face. 'Oh? Why?'

'Well . . . you can never tell who's looking,' Todd said, smiling. 'Isn't that how you got along all those years? By seeing the people who might be looking before they saw you?'

Dussander pulled down the kitchen shades. Then he poured himself a glass of bourbon. Then he pulled the bow off the package. Todd had wrapped it the way boys so often wrap Christmas packages – boys who have more important things on their minds, things like football and street hockey and the Friday Nite Creature Feature you'll watch with a friend who's sleeping over, the two of you wrapped in a blanket and crammed together on one end of the couch, laughing. There were a lot of ragged corners, a lot of uneven seams, a lot of Scotch tape. It spoke of impatience with such a womanly thing.

Dussander was a little touched in spite of himself. And later, when the horror had receded a little, he thought: *I should have known.*

It was a uniform. An SS uniform. Complete with jackboots.

He looked numbly from the contents of the box to its cardboard cover: PETER'S QUALITY COSTUME CLOTHIERS – AT THE SAME LOCATION SINCE 1951!

'No,' he said softly. 'I won't put it on. This is where it ends, boy. I'll die before I put it on.'

'Remember what they did to Eichmann,' Todd said solemnly. 'He was an old man and he had no politics. Isn't that what you said? Besides, I saved the whole fall for it. It cost over eighty bucks, with the boots thrown in. You didn't mind wearing it in 1944, either. Not at all.'

'You little *bastard*!' Dussander raised one fist over his head. Todd didn't flinch at all. He stood his ground, eyes shining.

'Yeah,' he said soflty. 'Go ahead and touch me. You just touch me *once*.'

Dussander lowered the hand. His lips were quivering. 'You are a fiend from hell,' he muttered.

'Put it on,' Todd invited.

Dussander's hands went to the tie of his robe and paused there. His eyes, sheeplike and begging, looked into Todd's. 'Please,' he said. 'I am an old man. No more.'

Todd shook his head slowly but firmly. His eyes were still shining. He liked it when Dussander begged. The way they must have begged him once. The inmates at Patin.

Dussander let the robe fall to the floor and stood naked except for his slippers and his boxer shorts. His chest was sunken, his belly slightly bloated. His arms were scrawny old man's arms. But the uniform, Todd thought. The uniform will make a difference.

Slowly, Dussander took the tunic out of the box and began to put it on.

Ten minutes later he stood fully dressed in the SS uniform. The cap was slightly askew, the shoulders slumped, but still the death's-head insignia stood out clearly. Dussander had a dark dignity — at least in Todd's eyes — that he had not possessed earlier. In spite of his slump, in spite of the cock-eyed angle of his feet, Todd was pleased. For the first time Dussander looked to Todd as Todd believed he should look. Older, yes. Defeated, certainly. But in uniform again. Not an old man spinning away his sunset years watching Lawrence Welk on a cruddy black and white TV with tinfoil on the rabbit-ears, but Kurt Dussander, the Blood Fiend of Patin.

As for Dussander, he felt disgust, discomfort . . . and a mild, sneaking sense of relief. He partly despised this latter emotion, recognizing it as the truest indicator yet of the psychological domination the boy had established over him. He was the boy's prisoner, and every time he found he could live through yet another indignity, every time he felt that mild relief, the boy's power grew. And yet he *was* relieved. It was only cloth and buttons and snaps . . . and it was a sham at that. The fly was a zipper; it should have been buttons. The insignia was wrong, the tailoring sloppy, the boots a cheap grade of imitation leather. It was only a trumpery uniform after all, and it wasn't exactly *killing* him, was it? No. It —

'Straighten your cap!' Todd said loudly.

Dussander blinked at him, startled.

'*Straighten your cap, soldier!*'

Dussander did so, unconsciously giving it that final small

178

insolent twist that had been the trademark of his *Oberleutnants* – and, sadly wrong as it was, this was an *Oberleutnant's* uniform.

'Get those feet together!'

He did so, bringing the heels together with a smart rap, doing the correct thing with hardly a thought, doing it as if the intervening years had slipped off along with his bathrobe.

'*Achtung!*'

He snapped to attention, and for a moment Todd was scared – really scared. He felt like the sorcerer's apprentice, who had brought the brooms to life but who had not possessed enough skill to stop them once they got started. The old man living on his pension was gone. Dussander was here.

Then his fear was replaced by a tingling sense of power.

'*About face!*'

Dussander pivoted neatly, the bourbon forgotten, the torment of the last three months forgotten. He heard his heels click together again as he faced the grease-splattered stove. Beyond it, he could see the dusty parade ground of the military academy where he had learned his soldier's trade.

'*About face!*'

He whirled again, this time not executing the order as well, losing his balance a little. Once it would have been ten demerits and the butt of a swagger-stick in his belly, sending his breath out in a hot and agonized gust. Inwardly he smiled a little. The boy didn't know all the tricks. No indeed.

'Now *march!*' Todd cried. His eyes were hot, glowing.

The iron went out of Dussander's shoulders; he slumped forward again. 'No,' he said. 'Please –'

'*March! March! March, I said!*'

With a strangled sound, Dussander began to goose-step across the faded linoleum of his kitchen floor. He right-faced to avoid the table; right-faced again as he approached the wall. His face was uptilted slightly, expressionless. His legs rammed out before him, then crashed down, making the cheap china rattle in the cabinet over the sink. His arms moved in short arcs.

The image of the walking brooms recurred to Todd, and his fright recurred with it. It suddenly struck him that he didn't want Dussander to be enjoying any part of this, and that perhaps – just perhaps – he had wanted to make Dussander appear ludicrous even more than he had wanted to make him appear authentic. But somehow, despite the man's age and the cheap dime-store furnishings of the kitchen, he didn't look ludicrous in the least. He looked frightening. For the first time the corpses in the ditches and the crematoriums seemed to take on their own reality for Todd. The photographs of the tangled arms and legs and torsos, fishbelly white in the cold spring rains of Germany, were not something staged like a scene in a horror film – a pile of bodies created from department store dummies, say, to be picked up by the grips and propmen when the scene was done – but simply a real fact, stupendous and inexplicable and evil. For a moment it seemed to him that he could smell the bland and slightly smoky odour of decomposition.

Terror gathered him in.

'Stop!' he shouted.

Dussander continued to goose-step, his eyes blank and far away. His head had come up even more, pulling the scrawny chicken-tendons of his throat tight, tilting his chin at an arrogant angle. His nose, blade-thin, jutted obscenely.

Todd felt sweat in his armpits. '*Halt!*' he cried out.

Dussander halted, right foot forward, left coming up

and then down beside the right with a single pistonlike stamp. For a moment the cold lack of expression held on his face – robotic, mindless – and then it was replaced by confusion. Confusion was followed by defeat. He slumped.

Todd let out a silent breath of relief and for a moment he was furious with himself. *Who's in charge here, anyway?* Then his self-confidence flooded back in. *I am, that's who. And he better not forget it.*

He began to smile again. 'Pretty good. But with a little practice, I think you'll be a lot better.'

Dussander stood mute, his head hanging.

'You can take it off now,' Todd added generously . . . and couldn't help wondering if he really wanted Dussander to put it on again. For a few seconds there –

7

January, 1975.

Todd left school by himself after the last bell, got his bike, and pedalled down to the park. He found a deserted bench, set his Schwinn up on its kickstand, and took his report card out of his hip pocket. He took a look around to see if there was anyone in the area he knew, but the only other people in sight were two high school kids making out by the pond and a pair of gross-looking winos passing a paper bag back and forth. Dirty fucking winos, he thought, but it wasn't the winos that had upset him. He opened his card.

English: C. American History: C. Earth Science: D. Your Community and You: B. Primary French: F. Beginning Algebra: F.

He stared at the grades, unbelieving. He had known it was going to be bad, but this was disaster.

Maybe that's best, an inner voice spoke up suddenly. *Maybe you even did it on purpose, because a part of you wants it to end. Needs for it to end. Before something bad happens.*

He shoved the thought roughly aside. Nothing bad was going to happen. Dussander was under his thumb. Totally under his thumb. The old man thought one of Todd's friends had a letter, but he didn't know which friend. If anything happened to Todd – *anything* – that letter would go to the police. Once he supposed Dussander might have tried it anyway. Now he was too old to run, even with a head start.

'He's under control, dammit,' Todd whispered, and then pounded his thigh hard enough to make the muscle knot. Talking to yourself was bad shit – crazy people talked to themselves. He had picked up the habit over the last six weeks or so, and didn't seem to be able to break it. He'd caught several people looking at him strangely because of it. A couple of them had been teachers. And that asshole Bernie Everson had come right out and asked him if he was going fruitcrackers. Todd had come very, very close to punching the little pansy in the mouth, and that sort of stuff – brawls, scuffles, punch-outs – was no good. That sort of stuff got you noticed in all the wrong ways. Talking to yourself was bad, right, okay, but –

'The dreams are bad, too,' he whispered. He didn't catch himself that time.

Just lately the dreams had been very bad. In the dreams he was always in uniform and he was standing in line with hundreds of gaunt men; the smell of burning was in the air and he could hear the choppy roar of bulldozer engines. Then Dussander would come up the line, pointing out this one or that one. They were left. The others were marched away towards the crematoriums. Some of them kicked and struggled, but most were too undernourished, too exhausted. Then Dussander was standing in front of Todd. Their eyes met for a long, paralyzing moment, and then Dussander levelled a faded umbrella at Todd.

'Take this one to the laboratories,' Dussander said in the dream. His lip curled back to reveal his false teeth. 'Take this American *boy*.'

In another dream he wore an SS uniform. His jackboots were shined to a mirror-reflecting surface. The death's head insignia and the lightning bolts glittered. But he was standing in the middle of Santa Donato Boulevard and everyone was looking at him. They began to point. Some of them began to laugh. Others looked shocked, angry, or revolted. In this dream an old car came to a squealing, creaky halt and Dussander peered out at him, a Dussander who looked two hundred years old and nearly mummified, his skin a yellowed scroll.

'I know you!' the dream-Dussander proclaimed shrilly. He looked around at the spectators and then back to Todd. 'You were in charge at Patin! Look, everybody! This is the Blood-Fiend of Patin! Himmler's "Efficiency Expert"! I denounce you, murderer! I denounce you, butcher! I denounce you, killer of infants! I denounce you!'

In yet another dream, he wore a striped convict's uniform and was being led down a stone-walled corridor by two guards who looked like his parents. Both wore conspicuous yellow armbands with the Star of David on them. Walking behind them was a minister, reading from the Book of Deuteronomy. Todd looked back over his shoulder and saw that the minister was Dussander, and he was wearing the black cloak of an SS officer.

At the end of the stone corridor, double doors opened on an octagonal room with glass walls. There was a scaffold in the centre of it. Behind the glass walls stood ranks of emaciated men and women, all naked, all watching with the same dark, flat expression. On each arm was a blue number.

'It's all right,' Todd whispered to himself. 'It's okay, really, everything's under control.'

The couple that had been making out glanced over at him. Todd stared at them fiercely, daring them to say anything. At last they looked back the other way. Had the boy been grinning?

Todd got up, jammed his report card into his hip pocket, and mounted his bike. He pedalled down to a drugstore two blocks away. There he bought a bottle of ink eradicator and a fine-point pen that dispensed blue ink. He went back to the park (the make-out couple was gone, but the winos were still there, stinking the place up) and changed his English grade to a B, American History to A, Earth Science to B, Primary French to C, and Beginning Algebra to B. Your Community and You he eradicated and then simply wrote in again, so the card would have a uniform look.

Uniforms, right.

'Never mind,' he whispered to himself. 'That'll hold them. That'll hold them, all right.'

One night late in the month, sometime after two o'clock, Kurt Dussander awoke struggling with the bedclothes, gasping and moaning, into a darkness that seemed close and terrifying. He felt half-suffocated, paralyzed with fear. It was as if a heavy stone lay on his chest, and he wondered if he could be having a heart attack. He clawed in the darkness for the bedside lamp and almost knocked it off the nightstand turning it on.

I'm in my own room, he thought, my own bedroom, here in Santa Donato, here in California, here in America. See, the same brown drapes pulled across the same window, the same bookshelves filled with dime paperbacks from the bookshop on Soren Street, same grey rug, same blue wallpaper. No heart attack. No jungle. No eyes.

But the terror still clung to him like a stinking pelt, and his heart went on racing. The dream had come back. He had known that it would, sooner or later, if the boy kept on. The cursed boy. He thought the boy's letter of protection was only a bluff, and not a very good one at that; something he had picked up from the TV detective programmes. What friend would the boy trust not to open such a momentous letter? No friend, that was who. Or so he thought. If he could be *sure* –

His hands closed with an arthritic, painful snap and then opened slowly.

He took the packet of cigarettes from the table and lit one, scratching the wooden match indifferently on the bedpost. The clock's hands stood at 2.41. There would be no more sleep for him this night. He inhaled smoke and then coughed it out in a series of wracking spasms. No more sleep unless he wanted to go downstairs and have a drink or two. Or three. And there had been altogether too much drinking over the last six weeks or so. He was no longer a young man who could toss them off one after the other, the way he had when he had been an officer on leave in Berlin in '39, when the scent of victory had been in the air and everywhere you heard the Führer's voice, saw his blazing, commanding eyes –

The boy . . . the cursed boy!

'Be honest,' he said aloud, and the sound of his own voice in the quiet room made him jump a little. He was not in the habit of talking to himself, but neither was it the first time he had ever done so. He remembered doing it off and on during the last few weeks at Patin, when everything had come down around their ears and in the east the sound of Russian thunder grew louder first every day and then every hour. It had been natural enough to talk to himself then. He had been under stress, and people under stress often do strange things – cup their testicles through the pockets of their pants, click their teeth together . . . Wolff had been a great teeth-clicker. He grinned as he did it. Huffman had been a finger-snapper and a thigh-patter, creating fast, intricate rhythms that he seemed utterly unaware of. He, Kurt Dussander, had sometimes talked to himself. But now –

'You are under stress again,' he said aloud. He was aware that he had spoken in German this time. He hadn't spoken German in many years, but the language now seemed warm and comfortable. It lulled him, eased him. It was sweet and dark.

'Yes. You are under stress. Because of the boy. But be honest with yourself. It is too early in the morning to tell lies. You have not entirely regretted talking. At first you were terrified that the boy could not or would not keep his secret. He would have to tell a friend, who would tell another friend, and that friend would tell two. But if he has kept it this long, he will keep it longer. If I am taken away, he loses his . . . his talking book. Is that what I am to him? I think so.'

He fell silent, but his thoughts went on. He had been lonely – no one would ever know just how lonely. There had been times when he thought almost seriously of suicide. He made a bad hermit. The voices he heard came from the radio. The only people who visited were on the other side of a dirty glass square. He was an old man, and although he was afraid of death, he was more afraid of being an old man who is alone.

His bladder sometimes tricked him. He would be halfway to the bathroom when a dark stain spread on his pants. In wet weather his joints would first throb and then begin to cry out, and there had been days when he had chewed an entire tin of Arthritis Pain Formula between sunrise and sunset . . . and still the aspirin only subdued the aches, and even such acts as taking a book from the shelf or switching the TV channel became an essay in pain. His eyes were bad; sometimes he knocked things over, barked his shins, bumped his head. He lived in fear of breaking a bone and not being able to get to the telephone, and he lived in fear of getting there and having some doctor uncover his real past as he became suspicious of Mr Denker's nonexistent medical history.

The boy had alleviated some of those things. When the boy was here, he could call back the old days. His memory of those days was perversely clear; he spilled out a seemingly endless catalogue of names and events, even the weather of such and such a day. He remembered Private Henreid, who manned a machine-gun in the north-east tower and the wen Private Henreid had had between his eyes. Some of the men called him Three-Eyes, or Old Cyclops. He remembered Kessel, who had a picture of his girlfriend naked, lying on a sofa with her hands behind her head. Kessel charged the men to look at it. He remembered the names of the doctors and their experiments – thresholds of pain, the brainwaves of dying men and women, physiological retardation, effects of different sorts of radiation, dozens more. *Hundreds* more.

He supposed he talked to the boy as all old men talk, but he guessed he was luckier than most old men, who had impatience, uninterest, or outright rudeness for an audience. *His* audience was endlessly fascinated.

Were a few bad dreams too high a price to pay?

He crushed out his cigarette, lay looking at the ceiling for a moment, and then swung his feet out onto the floor. He and the boy were loathesome, he supposed, feeding off each other . . . eating each other. If his own belly was sometimes sour with the dark but rich food they partook of in his afternoon kitchen, what was the boy's like? Did he sleep well? Perhaps not. Lately Dussander thought the boy looked rather pale, and thinner than when he had first come into Dussander's life.

He walked across the bedroom and opened the closet door. He brushed hangers to the right, reached into the shadows, and brought out the sham uniform. It hung from his hand like a vulture-skin. He touched it with his other hand. Touched it . . . and then stroked it.

After a very long time he took it down and put it on, dressing slowly, not looking into the mirror until the uniform was completely buttoned and belted (and the sham fly zipped).

He looked at himself in the mirror, then, and nodded.

He went back to bed, lay down, and smoked another cigarette. When it was finished, he felt sleepy again. He turned off the bedlamp, not believing it, that it could be this easy.

But he was asleep five minutes later, and this time his sleep was dreamless.

8

February, 1975.

After dinner, Dick Bowden produced a cognac that Dussander privately thought dreadful. But of course he smiled broadly and complimented it extravagantly. Bowden's wife served the boy a chocolate malted. The boy had been unusually quiet all through the meal. Uneasy? Yes. For some reason the boy seemed very uneasy.

Dussander had charmed Dick and Monica Bowden from the moment he and the boy had arrived. The boy had told his parents that Mr Denker's vision was much worse than it actually was (which made poor old Mr Denker in need of a seeing-eye dog, Dussander thought dryly), because that explained all the reading the boy had supposedly been doing. Dussander had been very careful about that, and he thought there had been no slips.

He was dressed in his best suit, and although the evening was damp, his arthritis had been remarkably mellow – nothing but an occasional twinge. For some absurd reason the boy had wanted him to leave his umbrella home, but Dussander had insisted. All in all, he had had a pleasant and rather exciting evening. Dreadful cognac or no, he had not been out to dinner in nine years.

During the meal he had discussed the Essen Motor Works, the rebuilding of postwar Germany – Bowden had asked several intelligent questions about that, and had seemed impressed by Dussander's answers – and German writers. Monica Bowden had asked him how he had happened to come to America so late in life and Dussander, adopting the proper expression of myopic sorrow, had explained about the death of his fictitious wife. Monica Bowden was meltingly sympathetic.

And now, over the absurd cognac, Dick Bowden said: 'If this is too personal, Mr Denker, please don't answer . . . but I couldn't help wondering what you did in the war.'

The boy stiffened ever so slightly.

Dussander smiled and felt for his cigarettes. He could see them perfectly well, but it was important to make not the tiniest slip. Monica put them in his hand.

'Thank you, dear lady. The meal was superb. You are a fine cook. My own wife never did better.'

Monica thanked him and looked flustered. Todd gave her an irritated look.

'Not personal at all,' Dussander said, lighting his cigarette and turning to Bowden. 'I was in the reserves from 1943 on, as were all able-bodied men too old to be in the active services. By then the handwriting was on the wall for the Third Reich, and for the madmen who created it. One madman in particular, of course.'

He blew out his match and looked solemn.

'There was great relief when the tide turned against Hitler. Great relief. Of course,' and here he looked at Bowden disarmingly, as man to man, 'one was careful not to express such a sentiment. Not aloud.'

'I suppose not,' Dick Bowden said respectfully.

'No,' Dussander said gravely. 'Not aloud. I remember one evening when four or five of us, all friends, stopped at a local *ratskeller* after work for a drink – by then there was not always *schnapps*, or even beer, but it so happened that night there were both. We had all known each other for upwards of twenty years. One of our number, Hans Hassler, mentioned in passing that perhaps the Führer had been ill-advised to open a second front against the Russians. I said, "Hans, God in Heaven, watch what you say!" Poor Hans went pale and changed the subject entirely. Yet three days later he was gone. I never saw him again, nor, as far as I know, did anyone else who was sitting at our table that night.'

'How awful!' Monica said breathlessly. 'More cognac, Mr Denker?'

'No thank you,' he smiled at her. 'My wife had a saying from her mother: "One must never overdo the sublime."'

Todd's small, troubled frown deepened slightly.

'Do you think he was sent to one of the camps?' Dick asked. 'Your friend Hessler?'

'*Hassler*,' Dussander corrected gently. He grew grave. 'Many were. The camps . . . they will be the shame of the German people for a thousand years to come. They are Hitler's real legacy.'

'Oh, I think that's too harsh,' Bowden said, lighting his pipe and puffing out a choking cloud of Cherry Blend. 'According to what I've read, the majority of the German people had no idea of what was going on. The locals around Auschwitz thought it was a sausage plant.'

'Ugh, how *terrible*,' Monica said, and pulled a grimacing that's-enough-of-that expression at her husband. Then she turned to Dussander and smiled. 'I just love the smell of a pipe, Mr Denker, don't you?'

'Indeed I do, madam,' Dussander said. He had just gotten an almost insurmountable urge to sneeze under control.

Bowden suddenly reached across the table and clapped

his son on the shoulder. Todd jumped. 'You're awfully quiet tonight, son. Feeling all right?'

Todd offered a peculiar smile that seemed divided between his father and Dussander. 'I feel okay. I've heard most of these stories before, remember.'

'Todd!' Monica said. 'That's hardly –'

'The boy is only being honest,' Dussander said. 'A privilege of boys which men often have to give up. Yes, Mr Bowden?'

Dick laughed and nodded.

'Perhaps I could get Todd to walk back to my house with me now,' Dussander said. 'I'm sure he has his studies.'

'Todd is a very apt pupil,' Monica said, but she spoke almost automatically, looking at Todd in a puzzled sort of way. 'All As and Bs, usually. He got a C in this last quarter, but he's promised to bring his French up to snuff on his March report. Right, Todd-baby?'

Todd offered the peculiar smile again and nodded.

'No need for you to walk,' Dick said. 'I'll be glad to run you back to your place.'

'I walk for the air and the exercise,' Dussander said. 'Really, I must insist . . . unless Todd prefers not to.'

'Oh, no, I'd like a walk,' Todd said, and his mother and father beamed at him.

They were almost to Dussander's corner when Dussander broke the silence. It was drizzling, and he hoisted his umbrella over both of them. And yet still his arthritis lay quiet, dozing. It was amazing.

'You are like my arthritis,' he said.

Todd's head came up. 'Huh?'

'Neither of you have had much to say tonight. What's got your tongue, boy? Cat or cormorant?'

'Nothing,' Todd muttered. They turned down Dussander's street.

'Perhaps I could guess,' Dussander said, not without a touch of malice. 'When you came to get me, you were afraid I might make a slip . . . "let the cat out of the bag," you say here. Yet you were determined to go through with the dinner because you had run out of excuses to put your parents off. Now you are disconcerted that all went well. Is that not the truth?'

'Who cares?' Todd said, and shrugged sullenly.

'Why shouldn't it go well?' Dussander demanded. 'I was dissembling before you were born. You keep a secret well enough, I give you that. I give it to you most graciously. But did you see me tonight? I charmed them. *Charmed* them!'

Todd suddenly burst out: 'You didn't have to do that!'

Dussander came to a complete stop, staring at Todd.

'Not do it? *Not?* I thought that was what you wanted, boy! Certainly they will offer no objections if you continue to come over and "read" to me.'

'You're sure taking a lot for granted!' Todd said hotly. 'Maybe I've got all I want from you. Do you think there's anybody *forcing* me to come over to your scuzzy house and watch you slop up booze like those old wino pushbags that hang around the old trainyards? Is that what you think?' His voice had risen and taken on a thin, wavering, hysterical note. 'Because there's nobody *forcing* me. If I want to come, I'll come, and if I don't, I won't.'

'Lower your voice. People will hear.'

'Who cares?' Todd said, but he began to walk again. This time he deliberately walked outside the umbrella's span.

'No, nobody forces you to come,' Dussander said. And then he took a calculated shot in the dark: 'In fact, you are welcome to stay away. Believe me, boy, I have no scruples about drinking alone. None at all.'

Todd looked at him scornfully. 'You'd like that, wouldn't you?'

Dussander only smiled noncommittally.

'Well, don't count on it.' They had reached the concrete walk leading up to Dussander's stoop. Dussander fumbled in his pocket for his latchkey. The arthritis flared a dim red in the joints of his fingers and then subsided, waiting. Now Dussander thought he understood what it was waiting for: for him to be alone again. Then it could come out.

'I'll tell you something,' Todd said. He sounded oddly breathless. 'If they knew what you were, if I ever told them, they'd spit on you and then kick you out on your skinny old ass. My mom might even take a butcher's knife to you. Her mother was part Jewish, she told me once.'

Dussander looked at Todd closely in the drizzling dark. The boy's face was turned defiantly up to his, but the skin was pallid, the sockets under the eyes dark and slightly hollowed — the skin-tones of someone who has brooded long while others are asleep.

'I am sure they would have nothing but revulsion for me,' Dussander said, although he privately thought that the elder Bowden might stay his revulsion to ask many of the questions his son had asked already. 'Nothing but revulsion. But what would they feel for you, boy, when I told them you had known about me for eight months . . . and said nothing?'

Todd stared at him wordlessly in the dark.

'Come and see me if you please,' Dussander said indifferently, 'and stay home if you don't. Goodnight, boy.'

He went up the walk to his front door, leaving Todd standing in the drizzle and looking after him with his mouth slightly ajar.

The next morning at breakfast, Monica said: 'Your dad liked Mr Denker a lot, Todd. He said he reminded him of your grandfather.'

Todd muttered something unintelligible around his toast. Monica looked at her son and wondered if he had been sleeping well. He looked pale. And his grades had taken that inexplicable dip. Todd *never* got Cs.

'You feeling okay these days, Todd?'

He looked at her blankly for a moment, and then that radiant smile spread over his face, charming her . . . comforting her. There was a dab of strawberry preserve on his chin. 'Sure,' he said. 'Four-oh.'

'Todd-baby,' she said.

'Monica-baby,' he responded, and they both started to laugh.

9

March, 1975.

'Kitty-kitty,' Dussander said. '*Heeere*, kitty-kitty. Puss-puss? Puss-puss?'

He was sitting on his back stoop, a pink plastic bowl by his right foot. The bowl was full of milk. It was 1.30 in the afternoon; the day was hazy and hot. Brush-fires far to the west tinged the air with an autumnal smell that jagged oddly

195

against the calendar. If the boy was coming, he would be here in another hour. But the boy didn't always come now. Instead of seven days a week he came sometimes only four times, or five. An intuition had grown in him, little by little, and his intuition told him that the boy was having troubles of his own.

'Kitty-kitty,' Dussander coaxed. The stray cat was at the far end of the yard, sitting in the ragged verge of weeds by Dussander's fence. It was a tom, and every bit as ragged as the weeds it sat in. Every time he spoke, the cat's ears cocked forward. Its eyes never left the pink bowl filled with milk.

Perhaps, Dussander thought, the boy was having troubles with his studies. Or bad dreams. Or both.

The last made him smile.

'Kitty-kitty,' he called softly. The cat's ears cocked forward again. It didn't move, not yet, but it continued to study the milk.

Dussander had certainly been afflicted with problems of his own. For three weeks or so he had worn the SS uniform to bed like grotesque pyjamas, and the uniform had warded off the insomnia and the bad dreams. His sleep had been – at first – as sound as a lumberjack's. Then the dreams had returned, not little by little, but all at once, and worse than ever before. Dreams of running as well as the dreams of the eyes. Running through a wet, unseen jungle where heavy leaves and damp fronds struck his face, leaving trickles that felt like sap . . . or blood. Running and running, the luminous eyes always around him, peering soullessly at him, until he broke into a clearing. In the darkness he sensed rather than saw the steep rise that began on the clearing's far side. At the top of that rise was Patin, its low cement buildings

196

and yards surrounded by barbed wire and electrified wire, its sentry towers standing like Martian dreadnoughts straight out of *War of the Worlds*. And in the middle, huge stacks billowed smoke against the sky, and below these brick columns were the furnaces, stoked and ready to go, glowing in the night like the eyes of fierce demons. They had told the inhabitants of the area that the Patin inmates made clothes and candles, and of course the locals had believed that no more than the locals around Auschwitz had believed that the camp was a sausage factory. It didn't matter.

Looking back over his shoulder in the dream, he would at last see *them* coming out of hiding, the restless dead, the *Juden*, shambling towards him with blue numbers glaring from the livid flesh of their outstretched arms, their hands hooked into talons, their faces no longer expressionless but animated with hate, lively with vengeance, vivacious with murder. Toddlers ran beside their mothers and grandfathers were borne up by their middle-aged children. And the dominant expression on all their faces was desperation.

Desperation? Yes. Because in the dreams he knew (and so did they) that if he could climb the hill, he would be safe. Down here in these wet and swampy lowlands, in this jungle where the night-flowering plants extruded blood instead of sap, he was a hunted animal . . . prey. But up there, he was in command. If this was a jungle, then the camp at the top of the hill was a zoo, all the wild animals safely in cages, he the head keeper whose job it was to decide which would be fed, which would live, which would be handed over to the vivisectionists, which would be taken to the knacker's in the remover's van.

He would begin to run up the hill, running in all the

slowness of nightmare. He would feel the first skeletal hands close about his neck, feel their cold and stinking breath, smell their decay, hear their birdlike cries of triumph as they pulled him down with salvation not only in sight but almost at hand –

'Kitty-kitty,' Dussander called. 'Milk. Nice milk.'

The cat came at last. It crossed half of the back yard and then sat again, but lightly, its tail twitching with worry. It didn't trust him; no. But Dussander knew the cat could smell the milk and so he was sanguine. Sooner or later it would come.

At Patin there had never been a contraband problem. Some of the prisoners came in with their valuables poked far up their asses in small chamois bags (and how often their valuables turned out not to be valuable at all – photographs, locks of hair, fake jewellery), often pushed up with sticks until they were past the point where even the long fingers of the trusty they had called Stinky-Thumbs could reach. One woman, he remembered, had had a small diamond, flawed, it turned out, really not valuable at all – but it had been in her family for six generations, passed from mother to eldest daughter (or so she said, but of course she was a Jew and all of them lied). She swallowed it before entering Patin. When it came out in her waste, she swallowed it again. She kept doing this, although eventually the diamond began to cut her insides and she bled.

There had been other ruses, although most only involved petty items such as a hoard of tobacco or a hair-ribbon or two. It didn't matter. In the room Dussander used for prisoner interrogations there was a hotplate and a homely kitchen table covered with a red checked cloth much like the one in his own kitchen. There was always a pot of lamb stew bubbling mellowly away on that hotplate. When contraband was suspected (and when was it not . . .) a member of the suspected clique would be brought to that room. Dussander would stand them by the hotplate, where the rich fumes from the stew wafted. Gently, he would ask them *Who*. Who is hiding gold? Who is hiding jewellery? Who has tobacco? Who gave the Givenet woman the pill for her baby? Who? The stew was never specifically promised; but always the aroma eventually loosened their tongues. Of course, a truncheon would have done the same, or a gun-barrel jammed into their filthy crotches, but the stew was . . . was *elegant*. Yes.

'Kitty-kitty,' Dussander called. The cat's ears cocked forward. It half-rose, than half-remembered some long-ago kick, or perhaps a match that had burned its whiskers, and it settled back on its haunches. But soon it would move.

He had found a way of propitiating his nightmare. It was, in a way, no more than wearing the SS uniform . . . but raised to a greater power. Dussander was pleased with himself, only sorry that he had never thought of it before. He supposed he had the boy to thank for this new method of quieting himself, for showing him that the key to the past's terrors was not in rejection but in contemplation and even something like a friend's embrace. It was true that before the boy's unexpected arrival last summer he hadn't had any bad dreams for a long time, but he believed now that he had come to a coward's terms with his past. He had been forced to give up a part of himself. Now he had reclaimed it.

'Kitty-kitty,' called Dussander, and a smile broke on his face, a kindly smile, a reassuring smile, the smile of all old men who have somehow come through the cruel courses of life to a safe place, still relatively intact, and with at least some wisdom.

The tom rose from its haunches, hesitated only a moment

longer, and then trotted across the remainder of the back yard with lithe grace. It mounted the steps, gave Dussander a final mistrustful look, laying back its chewed and scabby ears; then it began to drink the milk.

'*Nice* milk,' Dussander said, pulling on the Playtex rubber gloves that had lain in his lap all the while. '*Nice* milk for a *nice* kitty.' He had bought these gloves in the supermarket. He had stood in the express lane, and older women had looked at him approvingly, even speculatively. The gloves were advertised on TV. They had cuffs. They were so flexible you could pick up a dime while you were wearing them.

He stroked the cat's back with one green finger and talked to it soothingly. Its back began to arch with the rhythm of his strokes.

Just before the bowl was empty, he seized the cat.

It came electrically alive in his clenching hands, twisting and jerking, clawing at the rubber. Its body lashed limberly back and forth, and Dussander had no doubt that if its teeth or claws got into him, it would come off the winner. It was an old campaigner. It takes one to know one, Dussander thought, grinning.

Holding the cat prudently away from his body, the painful grin stamped on his face, Dussander pushed the back door open with his foot and went into the kitchen. The cat yowled and twisted and ripped at the rubber gloves. Its feral, triangular head flashed down and fastened on one green thumb.

'Nasty kitty,' Dussander said reproachfully.

The oven door stood open. Dussander threw the cat inside. Its claws made a ripping, prickly sound as they disengaged from the gloves. Dussander slammed the oven door shut with one knee, provoking a painful twinge from his arthritis. Yet he continued to grin. Breathing hard, nearly panting, he propped himself against the stove for a moment, his head hanging down. It was a gas stove. He rarely used it for anything fancier than TV dinners, and now, killing stray cats.

Faintly, rising up through the gas burners, he could hear the cat scratching and yowling to be let out.

Dussander twisted the oven dial over to 500°. There was an audible *pop!* as the oven pilot light lit two double rows of hissing gas. The cat stopped yowling and began to scream. It sounded . . . yes . . . almost like a young boy. A young boy in terrible pain. The thought made Dussander smile even more broadly. His heart thundered in his chest. The cat scratched and whirled madly in the oven, still screaming. Soon, a hot, furry, burning smell began to seep out of the oven and into the room.

He scraped the remains of the cat out of the oven half an hour later, using a barbecue fork he had acquired for two dollars and ninety-eight cents at the Grant's in the shopping centre a mile away.

The cat's roasted carcass went into an empty flour sack. He took the sack down to the cellar. The cellar floor had never been cemented. Shortly, Dussander came back up. He sprayed the kitchen with Glade until it reeked of artificial pine scent. He opened all the windows. He washed the barbecue fork and hung it up on the pegboard. Then he sat down to wait and see if the boy would come. He smiled and smiled.

Todd did come, about five minutes after Dussander had given up on him for the afternoon. He was wearing a warmup jacket with his school colours on it; he was also wearing a San Diego Padres baseball cap. He carried his schoolbooks under his arm.

'Yucka-ducka,' he said, coming into the kitchen and wrinkling his nose. 'What's that smell? It's awful.'

'I tried the oven,' Dussander said, lighting a cigarette. 'I'm afraid I burned my supper. I had to throw it out.'

One day late in the month the boy came much earlier than usual, long before school usually let out. Dussander was sitting in the kitchen, drinking Ancient Age bourbon from a chipped and discoloured cup that had the words HERE'S YER CAWFEE MAW, HAW! HAW! HAW! written around the rim. He had his rocker out in the kitchen now and he was just drinking and rocking, rocking and drinking, bumping his slippers on the faded linoleum. He was pleasantly high. There had been no more bad dreams at all until just last night. Not since the tomcat with the chewed ears. Last night's had been particularly horrible, though. That could not be denied. *They* had dragged him down after he had gotten halfway up the hill, and *they* had begun to do unspeakable things to him before he was able to wake himself up. Yet, after his initial thrashing return to the world of real things, he had been confident. He could end the dreams whenever he wished. Perhaps a cat would not be enough this time. But there was always the dog pound. Yes. Always the pound.

Todd came abruptly into the kitchen, his face pale and shiny and strained. He had lost weight, all right, Dussander thought. And there was a queer white look in his eyes that Dussander did not like at all.

'You're going to help me,' Todd said suddenly and defiantly.

202

'Really?' Dussander said mildly, but sudden apprehension leaped inside of him. He didn't let his face change as Todd slammed his books down on the table with a sudden, vicious overhand stroke. One of them spun-skated across the oilcloth and landed in a tent on the floor by Dussander's foot.

'Yes, you're fucking-A right!' Todd said shrilly. 'You better believe it! Because this is your fault! All your fault!' Hectic spots of red mounted into his cheeks. 'But you're going to have to help me get out of it, because I've got the goods on you! *I've got you right where I want you!*'

'I'll help you in any way I can,' Dussander said quietly. He saw that he had folded his hands neatly in front of himself without even thinking about it – just as he had once done. He leaned forward in the rocker until his chin was directly over his folded hands – as he had once done. His face was calm and friendly and inquiring; none of his growing apprehension showed. Sitting just so, he could almost imagine a pot of lamb stew simmering on the stove behind him. 'Tell me what the trouble is.'

'This is the fucking *trouble*,' Todd said viciously, and threw a folder at Dussander. It bounced off his chest and landed in his lap, and he was momentarily surprised by the heat of the anger which leaped up in him; the urge to rise and backhand the boy smartly. Instead, he kept the mild expression on his face. It was the boy's school-card, he saw, although the school seemed to be at ridiculous pains to hide the fact. Instead of a school-card, or a Grade Report, it was called a 'Quarterly Progess Report'. He grunted at that, and opened the card.

A typed half-sheet of paper fell out. Dussander put it aside for later examination and turned his attention to the boy's grades first.

'You seem to have fallen on the rocks, my boy,' Dussander said, not without some pleasure. The boy had passed only English and American History. Every other grade was an F.

'It's not my fault,' Todd hissed venomously. 'It's *your* fault. All those *stories*. I have nightmares about them, do you know that? I sit down and open my books and I start thinking about whatever you told me that day and the next thing I know, my mother's telling me it's time to go to bed. Well, that's not my fault! *It isn't! You hear me? It isn't!*'

'I hear you very well,' Dussander said, and read the typed note that had been tucked into Todd's card.

Dear Mr and Mrs Bowden,

This note is to suggest that we have a group conference concerning Todd's second- and third-quarter grades. In light of Todd's previous good work in this school, his current grades suggest a specific problem which may be affecting his academic performance in a deleterious way. Such a problem can often be solved by a frank and open discussion.

I should point out that although Todd has passed the half-year, his final grades may be failing in some cases unless his work improves radically in the fourth quarter. Failing grades would entail summer school to avoid being kept back and causing a major scheduling problem.

I must also note that Todd is in the college division, and that his work so far this year is far below college acceptance levels. It is also below the level of academic ability assumed by the SAT tests.

Please be assured that I am ready to work out a

mutually convenient time for us to meet. In a case
such as this, earlier is usually better.
    Sincerely yours,
    Edward French

'Who is this Edward French?' Dussander asked, slipping the
note back inside the card (part of him still marvelled at the
American love of jargon; such a rolling missive to inform
the parents that their son was flunking out!) and then
refolding his hands. His premonition of disaster was stronger
than ever, but he refused to give in to it. A year before, he
would have done; a year ago he had been ready for disaster.
Now he was not, but it seemed that the cursed boy had
brought it to him anyway. 'Is he your headmaster?'

'Rubber Ed? Hell, no. He's the guidance counsellor.'

'*Guidance* consellor? What is that?'

'You can figure it out,' Todd said. He was nearly hysterical. 'You read the goddam note!' He walked rapidly around
the room, shooting sharp, quick glances at Dussander. 'Well,
I'm not going to let any of this shit go down. I'm just
not. I'm not going to any summer school. My dad and
mom are going to Hawaii this summer and I'm going with
them.' He pointed at the card on the table. 'Do you know
what my dad will do if he sees that?'

Dussander shook his head.

'He'll get everything out of me. *Everything.* He'll know
it was you. It couldn't be anything else, because nothing else
has changed. He'll poke and pry and he'll get it all out of
me. And then . . . then I'll . . . I'll be in Dutch.'

He stared at Dussander resentfully.

'They'll watch me. Hell, they might make me see a doctor,

I don't know. How should *I* know? But I'm not getting in Dutch. And I'm not going to any fucking summer school.'

'Or to the reformatory,' Dussander said. He said it very quietly.

Todd stopped circling the room. His face became very still. His cheeks and forehead, already pale, became even whiter. He stared at Dussander, and had to try twice before he could speak. '*What? What* did you just say?'

'My dear boy,' Dussander said, assuming an air of great patience, 'for the last five minutes I have listened to you pule and whine, and what all your puling and whining comes down to is this. *You* are in trouble. *You* might be found out. *You* might find yourself in adverse circumstances.' Seeing that he had the boy's complete attention − at last − Dussander sipped reflectively from his cup.

'My boy,' he went on, 'that is a very dangerous attitude for you to have. And dangerous for me. The potential harm is much greater for me. You worry about your school-card. Pah! *This* for your school-card.'

He flicked it off the table and onto the floor with one yellow finger.

'I am worried about my *life*!'

Todd did not reply; he simply went on looking at Dussander with that white-eyed, slightly crazed stare.

'The Israelis will not scruple at the fact that I am seventy-six. The death penalty is still very much in favour over there, you know, especially when the man in the dock is a Nazi war criminal associated with the camps.'

'You're a US citizen,' Todd said. 'America wouldn't let them take you. I read up on that. I −'

'You read, but you don't *listen*! I am *not* a US citizen! My papers came from *la cosa nostra*. I would be deported, and Mossad agents would be waiting for me wherever I deplaned.'

'I wish they *would* hang you,' Todd muttered, curling his hands into his fists and staring down at them. 'I was crazy to get mixed up with you in the first place.'

'No doubt,' Dussander said, and smiled thinly. 'But you *are* mixed up with me. We must live in the present, boy, not in the past of "I-should-have-nevers". You must realize that your fate and my own are now inextricably entwined. If you "blow the horn on me", as your saying goes, do you think I will hesitate to blow the horn on you? Seven hundred thousand died at Patin. To the world at large I am a criminal, a monster, even the butcher your scandal-rags would have me. You are an accessory to all of that, my boy. You have criminal knowledge of an illegal alien, but you have not reported it. And if I am caught, I will tell the world all about you. When the reporters put their microphones in my face, it will be your name I'll repeat over and over again. "Todd Bowden, yes, that is his name . . . how long? Almost a year. He wanted to know everything . . . all the gooshy parts. That's how he put it, yes: 'All the gooshy parts'."'

Todd's breath had stopped. His skin appeared transparent. Dussander smiled at him. He sipped bourbon.

'I think they will put you in jail. They may call it a reformatory, or a correctional facility – there may be a fancy name for it, like this "Quarterly Progress Report" –' his lip curled '– but no matter what they call it, there will be bars on the windows.'

Todd wet his lips. 'I'd call you a liar. I'd tell them I just found out. They'd believe me, not you. You just better remember that.'

STEPHEN KING

Dussander's thin smile remained. 'I thought you told me your father would get it all out of you.'

Todd spoke slowly, as a person speaks when realization and verbalization occur simultaneously. 'Maybe not. Maybe not this time. This isn't just breaking a window with a rock.'

Dussander winced inwardly. He suspected that the boy's judgement was right – with so much at stake, he might indeed be able to convince his father. After all, when faced with such an unpleasant truth, what parent would not want to be convinced?

'Perhaps. Perhaps not. But how are you going to explain all those books you had to read to me because poor Mr Denker is half blind? My eyes are not what they were, but I can still read fine print with my spectacles. I can prove it.'

'I'd say you fooled me!'

'Will you? And what reason will you be able to give for my fooling?'

'For . . . for friendship. Because you were lonely.'

That, Dussander reflected, was just close enough to the truth to be believable. And once, in the beginning, the boy might have been able to bring it off. But now he was ragged; now he was coming apart in strings like a coat that has reached the end of its useful service. If a child shot off his cap pistol across the street, this boy would jump into the air and scream like a girl.

'Your school-card will also support my side of it,' Dussander said. 'It was not *Robinson Crusoe* that caused your grades to fall down so badly, my boy, was it?'

'Shut up, why don't you? Just shut up about it!'

'No,' Dussander said. 'I won't shut up about it.' He lit a cigarette, scratching the wooden match alight on the gas oven door. 'Not until I make you see the simple truth. We are in this together, sink or swim.' He looked at Todd through the raftering smoke, not smiling, his old, lined face reptilian. 'I will drag you down, boy. I promise you that. If anything comes out, *everything* will come out. That is my promise to you.'

Todd stared at him sullenly and didn't reply.

'Now,' Dussander said briskly, with the air of a man who has put a necessary unpleasantness behind him, 'the question is, what are we going to do about this situation? Have you any ideas?'

'This will fix the report card,' Todd said, and took a new bottle of ink eradicator from his jacket pocket. 'About that fucking letter, I don't know.'

Dussander looked at the ink eradicator approvingly. He had falsified a few reports of his own in his time. When the quotas had gone up to the point of fantasy . . . and far, far beyond. And – more like the situation they were now in – there had been the matter of the invoices . . . those which enumerated the spoils of war. Each week he would check the boxes of valuables, all of them to be sent back to Berlin in special train-cars that were like big Padd safes on wheels. On the side of each box was a manilla envelope, and inside the envelope there had been a verified invoice of that box's contents. So many rings, necklaces, chokers, so many grams of gold. Dussander, however, had had his own box of valuables – not very valuable valuables, but not insignificant, either. Jades. Tourmalines. Opals. A few flawed pearls. Industrial diamonds. And when he saw an item invoiced for Berlin that caught his eye or seemed a good investment, he would remove it, replace it with an item from his own box, and use ink eradicator on the invoice, changing their item for his. He had developed into a fairly expert forger . . . a talent that had come in handy more than once after the war was over.

'Good,' he told Todd. 'As for this other matter . . .'

Dussander began to rock again, sipping from his cup. Todd pulled a chair up to the table and began to go to work on his report-card, which he had picked up from the floor without a word. Dussander's outward calm had had its effect on him and now he worked silently, his head bent studiously over the card, like any American boy who has set out to do the best by God job he can, whether that job be planting corn, pitching a no-hitter in the Little League World Series, or forging grades on his report-card.

Dussander looked at the nape of his neck, lightly tanned and cleanly exposed between the fall of his hair and the round neck of his tee-shirt. His eyes drifted from there to the top counter drawer where he kept the butcher knives. One quick thrust – he knew where to put it – and the boy's spinal cord would be severed. His lips would be sealed forever. Dussander smiled regretfully. There would be questions asked if the boy disappeared. Too many of them. Some directed at him. Even if there was no letter with a friend, close scrutiny was something he could not afford. Too bad.

'This man French,' he said, tapping the letter. 'Does he know your parents in a social way?'

'Him?' Todd edged the word with contempt. 'My mom and dad don't go anywhere that he could even get in.'

'Has he ever met them in his professional capacity? Has he ever had conferences with them before?'

'No. I've always been near the top of my classes. Until now.'

'So what does he know about them?' Dussander said, looking dreamily into his cup, which was now nearly empty.

'Oh, he knows about *you*. He no doubt has all the records on you that he can use. Back to the fights you had in the kindergarten play yard. But what does he know about *them*?'

Todd put his pen and the small bottle of ink eradicator away. 'Well, he knows their names. Of course. And their ages. He knows we're all Methodists. We don't go much, but he'd know that's what we are, because it's on the forms. He must know what my dad does for a living; that's on the forms, too. All that stuff they have to fill out every year. And I'm pretty sure that's all.'

'Would he know if your parents were having troubles at home?'

'What's that supposed to mean?'

Dussander tossed off the last of the bourbon in his cup. 'Squabbles. Fights. Your father sleeping on the couch. Your mother drinking too much.' His eyes gleamed. 'A divorce brewing.'

Indignantly, Todd said: 'There's nothing like that going on! No way!'

'I never said there was. But just think, boy. Suppose that things at your house were "going to hell in a streetcar", as the saying is.'

Todd only looked at him, frowning.

'You would be worried about them,' Dussander said. 'Very worried. You would lose your appetite. You would sleep poorly. Saddest of all, your schoolwork would suffer. True? Very sad for the children, when there are troubles in the home.'

Understanding dawned in the boy's eyes – understanding and something like dumb gratitude. Dussander was gratified.

'Yes, it is an unhappy situation when a family totters on the edge of destruction,' Dussander said grandly, pouring more bourbon. He was getting quite drunk. 'The daytime television dramas, they make this absolutely clear. There is acrimony. Backbiting and lies. Most of all, there is pain. Pain, my boy. You have no idea of the hell your parents are going through. They are so swallowed up by their own troubles that they have little time for the problems of their own son. His problems seem minor compared to theirs, *hein*? Someday, when the scars have begun to heal, they will no doubt take a fuller interest in him once again. But now the only concession they can make is to send the boy's kindly grandfather to Mr French.'

Todd's eyes had been gradually brightening to a glow that was nearly fervid. 'Might work,' he was muttering. 'Might, yeah, might work, might –' He broke off suddenly. His eyes darkened again. 'No, it won't. You don't look like me, not even a little bit. Rubber Ed will never believe it.'

'Himmel! *Gott im Himmel!*' Dussander cried, getting to his feet, crossing the kitchen (a bit unsteadily), opening one of the cupboards, and pulling down his bottle of Ancient Age. He spun off the cap and poured liberally. 'For a smart boy, you are such a *Dummkopf*. When do grandfathers ever look like their grandsons? Huh? I am bald.' He pronounced it *balt*. 'Are you bald?'

Approaching the table again, he reached out with surprising quickness, snatched an abundant handful of Todd's blond hair, and pulled briskly.

'Cut it out!' Todd snapped, but he smiled a little.

'Besides,' Dussander said, settling back into his rocker, 'you have blond hair and blue eyes. My eyes are blue, and before my hair turned white and fell out, it was blond. You can tell me your whole family history. Your aunts and uncles. The people your father works with. Your mother's little hobbies. I will remember. I will study and remember. Two days later it will all be forgotten again – these days my memory is like a cloth bag filled with water – but I will remember for long enough.' He smiled grimly. 'In my time I have stayed ahead of Wiesenthal and pulled the wool over the eyes of Himmler himself. If I cannot fool one American public school teacher, I will pull my winding shroud around me and crawl down into my grave.'

'Maybe,' Todd said slowly, and Dussander could see he had already accepted it. His eyes were luminous with relief.

'There is another resemblance,' Dussander said.

'There is?'

'You said your mother was one-eighth a Jew. My mother was *all* Jewish. We are both kikes, my boy. We are two mockies sitting in the kitchen, just like in the old joke.'

He suddenly grabbed his nose between the thumb and index finger of his right hand. At the same time he reached over the table and grabbed the boy's nose with his left hand.

'And it shows!' he roared. 'It shows!'

He began to cackle with laughter, the rocking chair squeaking back and forth. Todd looked at him, puzzled and a little frightened, but after a bit he began to laugh, too. In Dussander's kitchen they laughed and laughed, Dussander by the open window where the warm California breeze wafted in, and Todd rocked back on the rear legs of his kitchen chair, so that its back rested against the oven door, the white enamel of which was crisscrossed by the dark, charred-looking streaks made by Dussander's wooden matches as he struck them alight.

★   ★   ★

Rubber Ed French (his nickname, Todd had explained to Dussander, referred to the rubbers he always wore over his sneakers during wet weather) was a slight man who made an affectation of always wearing Keds to school. It was a touch of informality which he thought would endear him to the one hundred and six children between the ages of twelve and fourteen who made up his counselling load. He had five pairs of Keds, ranging in colour from Fast Track Blue to Screaming Yellow Zonkers, totally unaware that behind his back he was known not only as Rubber Ed but as Sneaker Pete and The Ked Man, as in The Ked Man Cometh. He had been known as Pucker in college, and he would have been most humiliated of all to learn that even that shameful fact had somehow gotten out.

He rarely wore ties, preferring turtle-neck sweaters. He had been wearing these ever since the early sixties, when David McCallum had popularized them in *The Man from U.N.C.L.E.* In his college days his classmates had been known to spy him crossing the quad and remark, 'Here comes Pucker in his U.N.C.L.E. sweater.' He had majored in Education Psychology, and he privately considered himself to be the only good guidance counsellor he had ever met. He had real *rapport* with his kids. He could *get right down to it* with them; he could *rap* with them and be silently sympathetic if they had to do some shouting and *kick out the jams*. He could *get into their hangups* because he understood what a *bummer* it was to be thirteen when someone was *doing a number on your head* and you couldn't *get your shit together*.

The thing was, he had a damned hard time remembering what it had been like to be thirteen himself. He supposed that was the ultimate price you had to pay for growing up in the fifties. That, and entering the brave new world of the sixties nicknamed Pucker.

Now, as Todd Bowden's grandfather came into his office, closing the pebbled-glass door firmly behind him, Rubber Ed stood up respectfully but was careful not to come around his desk to greet the old man. He was aware of his sneakers. Sometimes the old-timers didn't understand that the sneakers were a psychological aid with kids who had teacher hangups – which was to say that some of the older folks couldn't get behind a guidance counsellor in Keds.

This is one fine-looking dude, Rubber Ed thought. His white hair was carefully brushed back. His three-piece suit was spotlessly clean. His dove-grey tie was impeccably knotted. In his left hand he held a furled black umbrella (outside, a light drizzle had been falling since the weekend) in a manner that was almost military. A few years ago Rubber Ed and his wife had gone on a Dorothy Sayers jag, reading everything by that estimable lady that they could lay their hands upon. It occurred to him now that this was her brain-child, Lord Peter Wimsey, to the life. It was Wimsey at seventy-five, years after both Bunter and Harriet Vane had passed on to their rewards. He made a mental note to tell Sondra about this when he got home.

'Mr Bowden,' he said respectfully, and offered his hand.

'A pleasure,' Bowden said, and shook it. Rubber Ed was careful not to put on the firm and uncompromising pressure he applied to the hands of the fathers he saw; it was obvious from the gingerly way the old boy offered it that he had arthritis.

'A pleasure, Mr French,' Bowden repeated, and took a seat, carefully pulling up the knees of his trousers. He propped the umbrella between his feet and leaned on it, looking like an elderly, extremely urbane vulture that had come in to roost in Rubber Ed French's office. He had the slightest touch of an accent, Rubber Ed thought, but it wasn't the clipped intonation of the British upper class, as Wimsey's would have been; it was broader, more European. Anyway, the resemblance to Todd was quite striking. Especially through the nose and eyes.

'I'm glad you could come,' Rubber Ed told him, resuming his own seat, 'although in these cases the student's mother or father –'

This was the opening gambit, of course. Almost ten years of experience in the counselling business had convinced him that when an aunt or an uncle or a grandparent showed up for a conference, it usually meant trouble at home – the sort of trouble that invariably turned out to be the root of the problem. To Rubber Ed, this came as a relief. Domestic problems were bad, but for a boy of Todd's intelligence, *a heavy drug trip* would have been much, much worse.

'Yes, of course,' Bowden said, managing to look both sorrowful and angry at the same time. 'My son and his wife asked me if I could come and talk this sorry business over with you, Mr French. Todd is a good boy, believe me. This trouble with his school marks is only temporary.'

'Well, we all hope so, don't we, Mr Bowden? Smoke if you like. It's supposed to be off-limits on school property, but I'll never tell.'

'Thank you.'

Mr Bowden took a half-crushed package of Camel cigarettes from his inner pocket, put one of the last two zigzagging smokes in his mouth, found a Diamond Blue-Tip match, scratched it on the heel of one black shoe, and lit up. He coughed an old man's dank cough over the first drag, shook the match out, and put the blackened stump into the ashtray Rubber Ed had produced. Rubber Ed watched this ritual, which seemed almost as formal as the old man's shoes, with frank fascination.

'Where to begin,' Bowden said, his distressed face looking at Rubber Ed through a swirling raft of cigarette smoke.

'Well,' Rubber Ed said kindly, 'the very fact that you're here instead of Todd's parents tells me something, you know.'

'Yes, I suppose it does. Very well.' He folded his hands. The Camel protruded from between the second and third fingers of his right. He straightened his back and lifted his chin. There was something almost Prussian in his mental coming to terms, Rubber Ed thought, something that made him think of all those war movies he'd seen as a kid.

'My son and my daughter-in-law are having troubles in their home,' Bowden said, biting off each word precisely. 'Rather bad troubles, I should think.' His eyes, old but amazingly bright, watched as Rubber Ed opened the folder centred in front of him on the desk blotter. There were sheets of paper inside, but not many.

'And you feel that these troubles are affecting Todd's academic performance?'

Bowden leaned forward perhaps six inches. His blue eyes never left Rubber Ed's brown ones. There was a heavily charged pause, and then Bowden said: 'The mother drinks.'

He resumed his former ramrod-straight position.

'Oh,' Rubber Ed said.

'Yes,' Bowden replied, nodding grimly. 'The boy has told me that he has come home on two occasions and has found her sprawled out on the kitchen table. He knows how my son feels about her drinking problem, and so the boy has put dinner in the oven himself on these occasions, and has gotten her to drink enough black coffee so she will at least be awake when Richard comes home.'

'That's bad,' Rubber Ed said, although he had heard worse – mothers with heroin habits, fathers who had abruptly taken it into their heads to start banging their daughters . . . or their sons. 'Has Mrs Bowden thought about getting professional help for her problem?'

'The boy has tried to persuade her that would be the best course. She is much ashamed, I think. If she was given a little time . . .' He made a gesture with his cigarette that left a dissolving smoke-ring in the air. 'You understand?'

'Yes, of course,' Rubber Ed nodded, privately admiring the gesture that had produced the smoke-ring. 'Your son . . . Todd's father . . .'

'He is not without blame,' Bowden said harshly. 'The hours he works, the meals he has missed, the nights when he must leave suddenly . . . I tell you, Mr French, he is more married to his job than he is to Monica. I was raised to believe that a man's family came before everything. Was it not the same for you?'

'It sure was,' Rubber Ed responded heartily. His father had been a night watchman for a large Los Angeles department store and he had really only seen his pop on weekends and vacations.

'That is another side of the problem,' Bowden said.

Rubber Ed nodded and thought for a moment. 'What about your other son, Mr Bowden? Uh . . .' He looked down at the folder. 'Harold. Todd's uncle.'

'Harry and Deborah are in Minnesota now,' Bowden said,

quite truthfully. 'He has a position there at the University medical school. It would be quite difficult for him to leave, and very unfair to ask him.' His face took on a righteous cast. 'Harry and his wife are quite happily married.'

'I see.' Rubber Ed looked at the file again for a moment and then closed it. 'Mr Bowden, I appreciate your frankness. I'll be just as frank with you.'

'Thank you,' Bowden said stiffly.

'We can't do as much for our students in the counselling area as we would like. There are six counsellors here, and we're each carrying a load of over a hundred students. My newest colleague, Hepburn, has a hundred and fifteen. At this age, in our society, all children need help.'

'Of course.' Bowden mashed his cigarette brutally into the ashtray and folded his hands once more.

'Sometimes bad problems get by us. Home environment and drugs are the two most common. At least Todd isn't mixed up with speed or mescaline or PCP.'

'God forbid.'

'Sometimes,' Rubber Ed went on, 'there's simply nothing we can do. It's depressing, but it's a fact of life. Usually the ones that are first to get spit out of the machine we're running here are the class troublemakers, the sullen, uncommunicative kids, the ones who refuse to even try. They are simply warm bodies waiting for the system to buck them up through the grades or waiting to get old enough so they can quit without their parents' permission and join the army or get a job at the Speedy-Boy Carwash or marry their boyfriends. You understand? I'm being blunt. Our system is, as they say, not all it's cracked up to be.'

'I appreciate your frankness.'

'But it hurts when you see the machine starting to mash up someone like Todd. He ran out a 92 average for last year's work, and that puts him in the ninety-fifth percentile. His English averages are even better. He shows a flair for writing, and that's something special in a generation of kids that thinks culture begins in front of the TV and ends in the neighbourhood movie theatre. I was talking to the woman who had Todd in Comp last year. She said Todd passed in the finest term-paper she'd seen in twenty years of teaching. It was on the German death-camps during World War II. She gave him the only A-plus she's ever given a composition student.'

'I have read it,' Bowden said. 'It is very fine.'

'He has also demonstrated above-average ability in the life sciences and social sciences, and while he's not going to be one of the great math whizzes of the century, all the notes I have indicate that he's given it the good old college try . . . until this year. Until this year. That's the whole story, in a nutshell.'

'Yes.'

'I hate like *hell* to see Todd go down the tubes this way, Mr Bowden. And summer school . . . well, I said I'd be frank. Summer school often does a boy like Todd more harm than good. Your usual junior high school summer session is a zoo. All the monkeys and the laughing hyenas are in attendance, plus a full complement of dodo birds. Bad company for a boy like Todd.'

'Certainly.'

'So let's get to the bottom line, shall we? I suggest a series of appointments for Mr and Mrs Bowden at the Counselling Centre downtown. Everything in confidence, of course. The man in charge down there, Harry Ackerman, is a good friend of mine. And I don't think Todd should go to them with the idea; I think you should.' Rubber Ed smiled widely. 'Maybe we can get everybody back on track by June. It's not impossible.'

But Bowden looked positively alarmed by this idea.

'I believe they might resent the boy if I took that proposal to them now,' he said. 'Things are very delicate. They could go either way. The boy has promised me he will work harder in his studies. He is very alarmed at this drop in his marks.' He smiled thinly, a smile Ed French could not quite interpret. 'More alarmed than you know.'

'But –'

'And they would resent *me*,' Bowden pressed on quickly. 'God knows they would. Monica already regards me as something of a meddler. I try not to be, but you see the situation. I feel that things are best left alone . . . for now.'

'I've had a great deal of experience in these matters,' Rubber Ed told Bowden. He folded his hands on Todd's file and looked at the old man earnestly. 'I really think counselling is in order here. You'll understand that my interest in the marital problems your son and daughter-in-law are having begins and ends with the effect they're having on Todd . . . and right now, they're having quite an effect.'

'Let me make a counter-proposal,' Bowden said. 'You have, I believe, a system of marking halfway through each quarter?'

'Yes,' Rubber Ed agreed cautiously. 'Interpretation of Progress cards – IOP Cards. The kids, of course, call them Flunk Cards. They only get them if their grade in a given course is below 78 halfway through the quarter. In other words, we give out IOP cards to kids who are pulling a D or an F in a given course.'

'Very good,' Bowden said. 'Then what I suggest is this: If the boy gets one of those cards . . . even *one* –' He held up one gnarled finger '– I will approach my son and his wife about your counselling. I will go further.' He pronounced it *furdah*. 'If the boy receives one of your Flunk Cards in April –'

'We give them out the first week in May, actually.'

'Yes? If he receives one then, I guarantee that they will accept the counselling proposal. They are worried about their son, Mr French. But now they are so wrapped up in their own problem that . . .' He shrugged.

'I understand.'

'So let us give them that long to solve their own problems. Pulling one's self up by one's own shoelaces . . . that is the American way, is it not?'

'Yes, I guess it is,' Rubber Ed told him after a moment's thought . . . and after a quick glance at the clock, which told him he had another appointment in five minutes. 'I'll accept that.'

He stood, and Bowden stood with him. They shook hands again, Rubber Ed being carefully mindful of the old party's arthritis.

'But in all fairness, I ought to tell you that very few students can pull out of an eighteen-week tailspin in just five weeks of classes. There's a huge amount of ground to be made up – a *huge* amount. I suspect you'll have to come through on your guarantee, Mr Bowden.'

Bowden offered his thin, disconcerting smile again. 'Do you?' was all he said.

Something had troubled Rubber Ed through the entire interview, and he put his finger on it during lunch in the cafeteria, more than an hour after 'Lord Peter' had left, umbrella once again neatly tucked under his arm.

He and Todd's grandfather had talked for fifteen minutes at least, probably closer to twenty, and Ed didn't think the old man had once referred to his grandson by name.

Todd pedalled breathlessly up Dussander's walk and parked his bike on its kickstand. School had let out only fifteen minutes before. He took the front steps at one jump, used his doorkey, and hurried down the hall to the sunlit kitchen. His face was a hopeful landscape of hopeful sunshine and gloomy clouds. He stood in the kitchen doorway for a moment, his stomach and his vocal cords knotted, watching Dussander as he rocked with his cupful of bourbon in his lap. He was still dressed in his best, although he had pulled his tie down two inches and loosened the top button of his shirt. He looked at Todd expressionlessly, his lizard-like eyes at halfmast.

'Well,' Todd finally managed.

Dussander left him hanging a moment longer, a moment that seemed at least ten years long to Todd. Then, deliberately, Dussander set his cup on the table next to his bottle of Ancient Age and said:

'The fool believed everything.'

Todd let out his pentup breath in a whooping gust of relief.

Before he could draw another breath in, Dussander added: 'He wanted your poor, troubled parents to attend counselling sessions downtown with a friend of his. He was really quite insistent.'

'Jesus! Did you . . . what did you . . . how did you handle it?'

'I thought quickly,' Dussander replied. 'Like the little girl in the Saki story, invention on short notice is one of my strong points. I promised him your parents would go in for such counselling if you received one Flunk Card when they are given out the first week of May.'

The blood fell out of Todd's face.

'You did *what*?' he nearly screamed. 'I've already flunked two algebra quizzes and a history test since the marking period started!' He advanced into the room, his pale face now growing shiny with breaking sweat. 'There was a French quiz this afternoon and I flunked that too . . . I know I did. All I could think about was that godamned Rubber Ed and whether or not you were taking care of him. You took care of him, all right,' he finished bitterly. 'Not get one Flunk Card? I'll probably get five or six.'

'It was the best I could do without arousing suspicions,' Dussander said. 'This French, fool that he is, is only doing his job. Now you will do yours.'

'What's that supposed to mean?' Todd's face was ugly and thunderous, his voice truculent.

'You will work. In the next four weeks you will work harder than you have ever worked in your life. Furthermore, on Monday you will go to each of your instructors and apologize to them for your poor showing thus far. You will —'

'It's impossible,' Todd said. 'You don't get it, man. It's *impossible*. I'm at least five weeks behind in science and history. In algebra it's more like ten.'

'Nevertheless,' Dussander said. He poured more bourbon.

'You think you're pretty smart, don't you?' Todd shouted at him. 'Well, I don't take orders from you. The days when you gave orders are long over. *Do you get it?*' He lowered his voice abruptly. 'The most lethal thing you've got around the house these days is a Shell No-Pest Strip. You're nothing but a broken-down old man who farts rotten eggs if he eats a taco. I bet you even pee in your bed.'

'Listen to me, snotnose,' Dussander said quietly.

Todd's head jerked angrily around at that.

'Before today,' Dussander said carefully, 'it was possible, *just barely* possible, that you could have denounced me and come out clean yourself. I don't believe you would have been up to the job with your nerves in their present state, but never mind that. It would have been technically possible. But now things have changed. Today I impersonated your grandfather, one Victor Bowden. No one can have the slightest doubt that I did it with . . . how is the word? . . . your connivance. If it comes out now, boy, you will look blacker than ever. And you will have no defence. I took care of that today.'

'I wish –'

'You *wish*! You *wish*!' Dussander roared. 'Never mind your wishes, your wishes make me *sick*, your wishes are no more than little piles of dogshit in the gutter! *All I want from you is to know if you understand the situation we are in!*'

'I understand it,' Todd muttered. His fists had been tightly clenched while Dussander shouted at him – he was not used to being shouted at. Now he opened his hands and dully observed that he had dug bleeding half-moons into his palms. The cuts would have been worse, he supposed, but in the last four months or so he had taken up biting his nails.

'Good. Then you will make your sweet apologies, and you will study. In your free time at school you will study.

During your lunch hours you will study. After school you will come here and study, and on your weekends you will come here and do more of the same.'

'Not here,' Todd said quickly. 'At home.'

'No. At home you will dawdle and daydream as you have all along. If you are here I can stand over you if I have to and watch you. I can protect my own interests in this matter. I can quiz you. I can listen to your lessons.'

'If I don't want to come here, you can't make me.'

Dussander drank. 'That is true. Things will then go on as they have. You will fail. This guidance person, French, will expect me to make good on my promise. When I don't, he will call your parents. They will find out that kindly Mr Denker impersonated your grandfather at your request. They will find out about the altered grades. They —'

'Oh, shut up. I'll come.'

'You're already here. Begin with algebra.'

'No *way*! It's Friday afternoon!'

'You study *every* afternoon now,' Dussander said softly. 'Begin with algebra.'

Todd stared at him — only for a moment before dropping his eyes and fumbling his algebra text out of his bookbag — and Dussander saw murder in the boy's eyes. Not figurative murder; literal murder. It had been years since he had seen that dark, burning, speculative glance, but one never forgot it. He supposed he would have seen it in his own eyes if there had been a mirror at hand on the day he had looked at the white and defenceless nape of the boy's neck.

I must protect myself, he thought with some amazement. *One underestimates at one's own risk.*

226

He drank his bourbon and rocked and watched the boy study.

It was nearly five o'clock when Todd biked home. He felt washed out, hot-eyed, drained, impotently angry. Every time his eyes had wandered from the printed page — from the maddening, incomprehensible, fucking *stupid* world of sets, subsets, ordered pairs, and Cartesian co-ordinates — Dussander's sharp old man's voice had spoken. Otherwise he had remained completely silent . . . except for the maddening bump of his slippers on the floor and the squeak of the rocker. He sat there like a vulture waiting for its prey to expire. Why had he ever gotten into this? *How* had he gotten into it? This was a mess, a terrible mess. He had picked up some ground this afternoon — some of the set theory that had stumped him so badly just before the Christmas break had fallen into place with an almost audible click — but it was impossible to think he could pick up enough to scrape through next week's algebra test with even a D.

It was five weeks until the end of the world.

On the corner he saw a bluejay lying on the sidewalk, its beak slowly opening and closing. It was trying vainly to get onto its birdy-feet and hop away. One of its wings had been crushed, and Todd supposed a passing car had hit it and flipped it up onto the sidewalk like a tiddlywink. One of its beady eyes stared up at him.

Todd looked at it for a long time, holding the grips of his bike's apehanger handlebars lightly. Some of the warmth had gone out of the day and the air felt almost chilly. He supposed his friends had spent the afternoon goofing off down at the Babe Ruth diamond on Walnut Street, maybe playing a little one-on-one, more likely playing pepper or three-flies-six-grounders or rolly-bat. It was the time of year when you started working your way up to baseball. There was some talk about getting up their own sandlot team this year to compete in the informal city league; there were dads enough willing to shlepp them around to games. Todd, of course, would pitch. He had been a Little League pitching star until he had grown out of the Senior Little League division last year. *Would have pitched.*

So what? He'd just have to tell them no. He'd just have to tell them: *Guys, I got mixed up with this war criminal. I got him right by the balls, and then – ha-ha, this'll killya, guys – then I found out he was holding my balls as tight as I was holding his. I started having funny dreams and the cold sweats. My grades went to hell and I changed them on my report card so my folks wouldn't find out and now I've got to hit the books really hard for the first time in my life. I'm not afraid of getting grounded, though. I'm afraid of going to the reformatory. And that's why I can't play any sandlot with you guys this year. You see how it is, guys.*

A thin smile, much like Dussander's and not at all like his former broad grin, touched his lips. There was no sunshine in it; it was a shady smile. There was no fun in it; no confidence. It merely said, *You see how it is, guys.*

He rolled his bike forward over the jay with exquisite slowness, hearing the newspaper crackle of its feathers and the crunch of its small hollow bones as they fractured inside it. He reversed, rolling over it again. It was still twitching. He rolled over it again, a single bloody feather stuck in his front tyre, revolving up and down, up and down. By then the bird had stopped moving, the bird had kicked the bucket, the bird had punched out, the bird had gone to the great aviary in the sky, but Todd kept going forward and backward across its mashed body just the same. He did it for almost five minutes, and that thin smile never left his face. *You see how it is, guys.*

10

April, 1975.

The old man stood halfway down the compound's aisle, smiling broadly, as Dave Klingerman walked up to meet him. The frenzied barking that filled the air didn't seem to bother him in the slightest, nor the smells of fur and urine, nor the hundred different strays yapping and howling in their cages, dashing back and forth, leaping against the mesh. Klingerman pegged the old guy as a dog-lover right off the bat. His smile was sweet and pleasant. He offered Dave a swollen, arthritis-bunched hand carefully, and Klingerman shook it in the same spirit.

'Hello, sir!' he said, speaking up. 'Noisy as hell, isn't it?'

'I don't mind,' the old man said. 'Not at all. My name is Arthur Denker.'

'Klingerman. Dave Klingerman.'

'I am pleased to meet you, sir. I read in the paper — I could not believe it — that you *give* dogs away here. Perhaps I misunderstood. In fact I think I must have misunderstood.'

'No, we give 'em away, all right,' Dave said. 'If we can't we have to destroy 'em. Sixty days, that's what the state gives us. Shame. Come on in the office here. Quieter. Smells better, too.'

In the office, Dave heard a story that was familiar (but nonetheless affecting): Arthur Denker was in his seventies. He had come to California when his wife died. He was not rich, but he tended what he did have with great care. He

229

was lonely. His only friend was the boy who sometimes came to his house and read to him. In Germany he had owned a beautiful St Bernard. Now, in Santa Donato, he had a house with a good-sized back yard. The yard was fenced. And he had read in the paper . . . would it be possible that he could . . .

'Well, we don't have any Bernards,' Dave said. 'They go fast because they're so good with kids –'

'Oh, I understand. I didn't mean that –'

'—but I do have a half-grown Shepherd pup. How would that be?'

Mr Denker's eyes grew bright, as if he might be on the verge of tears. 'Perfect,' he said. 'That would be perfect.'

'The dog itself is free, but there are a few other charges. Distemper and rabies shots. A city dog licence. All of it goes about twenty-five bucks for most people, but the state pays half if you're over sixty-five – part of the California Golden Ager programme.'

'Golden Ager . . . is that what I am?' Mr Denker said, and laughed. For just a moment – it was silly – Dave felt a kind of chill.

'Uh . . . I guess so, sir.'

'It is very reasonable.'

'Sure, we think so. The same dog would cost you a hundred and twenty-five dollars in a pet shop. But people go to those places instead of here. They are paying for a set of papers, of course, not the dog.' Dave shook his head. 'If they only understood how many fine animals are abandoned every year.'

'And if you can't find a suitable home for them within sixty days, they are destroyed?'

'We put them to sleep, yes.'

'Put them to . . . ? I'm sorry, my English –'

230

'It's a city ordinance,' Dave said. 'Can't have dog-packs running the streets.'

'You shoot them.'

'No, we give them gas. It's very humane. They don't feel a thing.'

'No,' Mr Denker said. 'I am sure they don't.'

Todd's seat in Introduction to Algebra was four desks down in the second row. He sat there, trying to keep his face expressionless, as Mr Storrman passed back the exams. But his ragged fingernails were digging into his palms again, and his entire body seemed to be running with a slow and caustic sweat.

Don't get your hopes up. Don't be such a goddam chump. There's no way you could have passed. You know *you didn't pass.*

Nevertheless, he could not completely squash the foolish hope. It had been the first algebra exam in weeks that looked as if it had been written in something other than Greek. He was sure that in his nervousness (nervousness? no, call it what it had really been: outright terror) he had not done that well, but maybe . . . well, if it had been anyone else but Storrman, who had a Yale padlock for a heart . . .

STOP IT! he commanded himself, and for a moment, a coldly horrible moment, he was positive he had screamed those two words aloud in the classroom. *You flunked, you know you did, not a thing in the world is going to change it.*

Storrman handed him his paper expressionlessly and moved on. Todd laid it face-down on his initial-scarred desk. For a moment he didn't think he possessed sufficient will to even turn it over and know. At last he flipped it with such convulsive suddenness that the exam sheet tore. His tongue stuck to the roof of his mouth as he stared at it. His heart seemed to stop for a moment.

The number 83 was written in a circle at the top of the sheet. Below it was a letter-grade: C Plus. Below the letter grade was a brief notation: *Good improvement! I think I'm twice as relieved as you should be. Check errors carefully. At least three of them are arithmetical rather than conceptual.*

His heartbeat began again, at triple-time. Relief washed over him, but it was not cool – it was hot and complicated and strange. He closed his eyes, not hearing the class as it buzzed over the exam and began the pre-ordained fight for an extra point here or there. Todd saw redness behind his eyes. It pulsed like flowing blood with the rhythm of his heartbeat. In that instant he hated Dussander more than he ever had before. His hands snapped shut into fists and he only wished, wished, wished, that Dussander's scrawny chicken neck could have been between them.

Dick and Monica Bowden had twin beds, separated by a nightstand with a pretty imitation Tiffany lamp standing on it. Their room was done in genuine redwood, and the walls were comfortably lined with books. Across the room, nestled between two ivory bookends (bull elephants on their hind legs) was a round Sony TV. Dick was watching Johnny Carson with the earplugs in while Monica read the new Michael Crichton that had come from the book club that day.

'Dick?' She put a bookmark (THIS IS WHERE I FELL ASLEEP, it said) into the Crichton and closed it.

On the TV, Buddy Hackett had just broken everyone up. Dick smiled.

'Dick?' she said more loudly.

He pulled the earplugs out. 'What?'

'Do you think Todd's all right?'

He looked at her for a moment, frowning, then shook his head a little. '*Je ne comprends pas, chérie.*' His limping French was a joke between them; he had met her in college when he was flunking his language requirement. His father had sent him an extra two hundred dollars to hire a tutor. He had gotten Monica Darrow, picking her name at random from the cards tacked up on the Union bulletin board. By Christmas she had been wearing his pin . . . and he had managed a C in French.

'Well . . . he's lost weight.'

'He looks a little scrawny, sure,' Dick said. He put the TV earplugs in his lap, where they emitted tiny squawking sounds. 'He's growing up, Monica.'

'So soon?' she asked uneasily.

He laughed. 'So soon. I shot up seven inches as a teenager – from a five-foot-six shrimp at twelve to the beautiful six-foot-one mass of muscle you see before you today. My mother said that when I was fourteen you could hear me growing in the night.'

'Good thing not all of you grew that much.'

'It's all in how you use it.'

'Want to use it tonight?'

'The wench grows bold,' Dick Bowden said, and threw the earplugs across the room.

After, as he was drifting off to sleep:

'Dick, he's having bad dreams, too.'

'Nightmares?' he muttered.

'Nightmares. I've heard him moaning in his sleep two or

three times when I've gone down to use the bathroom in the night. I didn't want to wake him up. It's silly, but my grandmother used to say you could drive a person insane if you woke them up in the middle of a bad dream.'

'She was the Polack, wasn't she?'

'The Polack, yeah, the Polack. The mockie, why don't you say? Nice talk!'

'You know what I mean. Why don't you just use the upstairs john?' He had put it in himself two years ago.

'You know the flush always wakes you up,' she said.

'So don't flush it.'

'Dick, that's nasty.'

He sighed.

'Sometimes when I go in, he's sweating. And the sheets are damp.'

He grinned in the dark. 'I bet.'

'What's *that* . . . oh.' She slapped him lightly. 'That's nasty, too. Besides, he's only thirteen.'

'Fourteen next month. He's not too young. A little precocious, maybe, but not too young.'

'How old were you?'

'Fourteen or fifteen. I don't remember exactly. But I remember I woke up thinking I'd died and gone to heaven.'

'But you were older than Todd is now.'

'All that stuff's happening younger. It must be the milk . . . or the fluoride. Do you know they have sanitary napkin dispensers in all the girls' rooms of the school we built in Jackson Park last year? And that's a *grammar school*. Now your average sixth-grader is only ten. How old were you when you started?'

'I don't remember,' she said. 'All I know is Todd's dreams don't sound like . . . like he died and went to heaven.'

'Have you asked him about them?'

'Once. About six weeks ago. You were off playing golf with that horrible Ernie Jacobs.'

'That horrible Ernie Jacobs is going to make me a full partner by 1977, if he doesn't screw himself to death with that high yellow secretary of his before then. Besides, he always pays the greens' fees. What did Todd say?'

'That he didn't remember. But a sort of . . . shadow crossed his face. I think he *did* remember.'

'Monica, I don't remember everything from my dear dead youth, but one thing I do remember is that wet dreams are not always pleasant. In fact, they can be downright unpleasant.'

'How can that be?'

'Guilt. All kinds of guilt. Some of it maybe all the way from babyhood, when it was made very clear to him that wetting the bed was wrong. Then there's the sex thing. Who knows what brings a wet dream on? Copping a feel on the bus? Looking up a girl's skirt in study hall? I don't know. The only one I can really remember was going off the high board at the YMCA pool on co-ed day and losing my trunks when I hit the water.'

'You got off on that?' she asked, giggling a little.

'Yeah. So if the kid doesn't want to talk to you about his John Thomas problems, don't force him.'

'We did our damn best to raise him without all those needless guilts.'

'You can't escape them. He brings them home from school like the colds he used to pick up in the first grade. From his friends, or the way his teachers mince around certain subjects. He probably got it from my dad, too. "Don't touch it in the night, Todd, or your hands'll grow hair and you'll go blind and you'll start to lose your memory, and after a while your thing will turn black and rot off. So be careful, Todd." '

'Dick Bowden! Your dad would never −'

'He wouldn't? Hell, he *did*. Just like your Jewish-Polack grandmother told you that waking somebody up in the middle of a nightmare might drive them nuts. He also told me to always wipe off the ring of a public toilet before I sat on it so I wouldn't get "other people's germs". I guess that was his way of saying syphilis. I bet your grandmother laid that one on you, too.'

'No, my mother,' she said absently. 'And she told me to always flush. Which is why I go downstairs.'

'It still wakes me up,' Dick mumbled.

'What?'

'Nothing.'

This time he had actually drifted halfway over the threshold of sleep when she spoke his name again.

'*What?*' he asked, a little impatiently.

'You don't suppose . . . oh, never mind. Go back to sleep.'

'No, go on, finish. I'm awake again. I don't suppose what?'

'That old man. Mr Denker. You don't think Todd's seeing too much of him, do you? Maybe he's . . . oh, I don't know . . . filling Todd up with a lot of stories.'

'The real heavy horrors,' Dick said. 'The day the Essen Motor Works dropped below quota.' He snickered.

'It was just an idea,' she said, a little stiffly. The covers rustled as she turned over on her side. 'Sorry I bothered you.'

He put a hand on her bare shoulder. 'I'll tell you something, babe,' he said, and stopped for a moment, thinking carefully, choosing his words. 'I've been worried about Todd too, sometimes. Not the same things you've been worried about, but worried is worried, right?'

She turned back to him. 'About what?'

'Well, I grew up a lot different than he's growing up. My dad had the store. Vic the Grocer, everyone called him. He had a book where he kept the names of the people who owed him, and how much they owed. You know what he called it?'

'No.' Dick rarely talked about his boyhood; she had always thought it was because he hadn't enjoyed it. She listened carefully now.

'He called it the Left Hand Book. He said the right hand was business, but the right hand should never know what the left hand was doing. He said if the right hand *did* know, it would probably grab a meat-cleaver and chop the left hand right off.'

'You never told me that.'

'Well, I didn't like the old man very much when we first got married, and the truth is I still spend a lot of time not liking him. I couldn't understand why I had to wear pants from the Goodwill box while Mrs Mazursky could get a ham on credit with that same old story about how her husband was going back to work next week. The only work that fucking wino Bill Mazursky ever had was holding onto a twelve-cent bottle of musky so it wouldn't fly away.

'All I ever wanted in those days was to get out of the neighbourhood and away from my old man's life. So I made grades and played sports I didn't really like and got a scholarship at UCLA. And I made damn sure I stayed in the top ten per cent of my classes because the only Left Hand Book the colleges kept in those days was for the GIs that fought in the war. My dad sent me money for my textbooks, but the only other money I ever took from him was the time I wrote home in a panic because I was flunking funnybook French. I met you. And I found out later from Mr Henreid down the block that my dad put a lien on his car to scare up that two hundred bucks.

'And now I've got you, and we've got Todd. I've always thought he was a damned fine boy, and I've tried to make sure he's always had everything he ever needed . . . anything that would help him grow into a fine man. I used to laugh at that old wheeze about a man wanting his son to be better than he was, but as I get older it seems less funny and more true. I never want Todd to have to wear pants from a Goodwill box because some wino's wife got a ham on credit. You understand?'

'Yes, of course I do,' she said quietly.

'Then, about ten years ago, just before my old man finally got tired of fighting off the urban renewal guys and retired, he had a minor stroke. He was in the hospital for ten days. And the people from the neighbourhood, the guineas and the krauts, even some of the jigs that started to move in around 1955 or so – they paid his bill. Every fucking cent. I couldn't believe it. They kept the store open, too. Fiona Castellano got four or five of her friends who were out of work to come in on shifts. When my old man got back, the books balanced out to the cent.'

'Wow,' she said, very softly.

'You know what he said to me? My old man? That he'd always been afraid of getting old – of being scared and hurting and all by himself. Of having to go into the hospital and not being able to make ends meet anymore. Of dying. He said that after the stroke he wasn't scared anymore. He said he thought he could die well. "You mean die happy, pop?" I asked him. "No," he said. "I don't think anyone dies happy, Dickie." He always called me Dickie, still does, and that's another thing I guess I'll never be able to like. He said he didn't think anyone died happy, but you could die well. That impressed me.'

He was silent for a long, thoughtful time.

'The last five or six years I've been able to get some perspective on my old man. Maybe because he's down there in Sandoro and out of my hair. I started thinking that maybe the Left Hand Book wasn't such a bad idea. That was when I started to worry about Todd. I kept wanting to tell him about how there was maybe something more to life than me being able to take all of you to Hawaii for a month or being able to buy Todd pants that don't smell like the mothballs they used to put in the Goodwill box. I could never figure out how to tell him those things. But I think maybe he knows. And it takes a load off my mind.'

'Reading to Mr Denker, you mean?'

'Yes. He's not getting anything for that. Denker can't pay him. Here's this old guy, thousands of miles from any friends or relatives that might still be living, here's this guy that's everything my father was afraid of. And there's Todd.'

'I never thought of it just like that.'

'Have you noticed the way Todd gets when you talk to him about that old man?'

'He gets very quiet.'

'Sure. He gets tongue-tied and embarrassed, like he was doing something nasty. Just like my pop used to when someone tried to thank him for laying some credit on them. We're Todd's right hand, that's all. You and me and all the rest – the house, the ski-trips to Tahoe, the Thunderbird in the garage, his colour TV. All his right hand. And he doesn't want us to see what his left hand is up to.'

'You don't think he's seeing too much of Denker, then?'

'Honey, look at his grades! If *they* were falling off, I'd be the first one to say hey, enough is enough, already, don't go overboard. His grades are the first place trouble would show up. And how have they been?'

'As good as ever, after that first slip.'

'So what are we talking about? Listen, I've got a conference at nine, babe. If I don't get some sleep, I'm going to be sloppy.'

'Sure, go to sleep,' she said indulgently, and as he turned over, she kissed him lightly on one shoulderblade. 'I love you.'

'Love you too,' he said comfortably, and closed his eyes. 'Everything's fine, Monica. You worry too much.'

'I know I do. Goodnight.'

They slept.

'Stop looking out the window,' Dussander said. 'There is nothing out there to interest you.'

Todd looked at him sullenly. His history text was open on the table, showing a colour plate of Teddy Roosevelt cresting San Juan Hill. Helpless Cubans were falling away from the hooves of Teddy's horses. Teddy was grinning a wide American grin, the grin of a man who knew that God was in His heaven and everything was bully. Todd Bowden was not grinning.

'You like being a slave-driver, don't you?' he asked.

'I like being a free man,' Dussander said. 'Study.'

'Suck my cock.'

'As a boy,' Dussander said, 'I would have had my mouth washed out with lye soap for saying such a thing.'

'Times change.'

'Do they?' Dussander sipped his bourbon. 'Study.'

Todd stared at Dussander. 'You're nothing but a goddamned rummy. You know that?'

'Study.'

'*Shut up!*' Todd slammed his book shut. It made a rifle-crack sound in Dussander's kitchen. 'I can never catch up, anyway. Not in time for the test. There's fifty pages of this shit left, all the way up to World War I. I'll make a crib in Study Hall 2 tomorrow.'

Harshly, Dussander said: 'You will do no such thing!'

'Why not? Who's going to stop me? You?'

'Boy, you are still having a hard time comprehending the stakes we play for. Do you think I enjoy keeping your snivelling brat nose in your books?' His voice rose, whipsawing, demanding, commanding. 'Do you think I enjoy listening to your tantrums, your kindergarten swears? "Suck my cock",' Dussander mimicked savagely in a high, falsetto voice that made Todd flush darkly. '"Suck my cock, so what, who cares, I'll do it tomorrow, suck my cock"!'

'Well, you *like* it!' Todd shouted back. 'Yeah, you *like* it! The only time you don't feel like a zombie is when you're on my back! So give me a fucking break!'

'If you are caught with one of these cribbing papers, what do you think will happen? Who will be told first?'

Todd looked at his hands with their ragged, bitten fingernails and said nothing.

'Who?'

'Jesus, you know. Rubber Ed. Then my folks, I guess.'

Dussander nodded. 'Me, I guess that too. Study. Put your cribbing paper in your head, where it belongs.'

'I hate you,' Todd said dully. 'I really do.' But he opened his book again and Teddy Roosevelt grinned up at him, Teddy galloping into the twentieth century with his sabre in his hand, Cubans falling back in disarray before him – possibly before the force of his fierce American grin.

Dussander began to rock again. He held his teacup of bourbon in his hands. 'That's a good boy,' he said, almost tenderly.

Todd had his first wet-dream on the last night of April, and awoke to the sound of rain whispering secretly through the leaves and branches of the tree outside his window.

In the dream, he had been in one of the Patin laboratories. He was standing at the end of a long, low table. A lush young girl of amazing beauty had been secured to this table with clamps. Dussander was assisting him. Dussander wore a white butcher's apron and nothing else. When he pivoted to turn on the monitoring equipment, Todd could see Dussander's scrawny buttocks grinding at each other like misshapen white stones.

He handed something to Todd, something he recognized immediately, although he had never actually seen one. It was a dildo. The tip of it was polished metal, winking in the light of the overhead fluorescents like heartless chrome. The dildo was hollow. Snaking out of it was a black electrical cord that ended in a red rubber bulb.

'Go ahead,' Dussander said. 'The Führer says it's all right. He says it's your reward for studying.'

Todd looked down at himself and saw that he was naked. His small penis was fully erect, jutting plumply up at an angle from the thin peachdown of his pubic hair. He slipped the dildo on. The fit was tight but there was some sort of

lubricant in there. The friction was pleasant. No; it was more than pleasant. It was delightful.

He looked down at the girl and felt a strange shift in his thoughts . . . as if they had slipped into a perfect groove. Suddenly all things seemed right. Doors had been opened. He would go through them. He took the red bulb in his left hand, put his knees on the table, and paused for just a moment, gauging the angle while his Norseman's prick made his own angle up and out from his slight boy's body.

Dimly, far off, he could hear Dussander reciting: 'Test run eighty-four. Electricity, sexual stimulus, metabolism. Based on the Thyssen theories of negative reinforcement. Subject is a young Jewish girl, approximately sixteen years of age, no scars, no identifying marks, no known disabilities –'

She cried out when the tip of the dildo touched her. Todd found the cry pleasant, as he did her fruitless struggles to free herself, or, lacking that, to at least bring her legs together.

This is what they can't show in those magazines about the war, he thought, *but it's there, just the same.*

He thrust forward suddenly, parting her with no grace. She shrieked like a firebell.

After her initial thrashing and efforts to expel him, she lay perfectly still, enduring. The lubricated interior of the dildo pulled and slid against Todd's engorgement. Delightful. Heavenly. His fingers toyed with the rubber bulb in his left hand.

Far away, Dussander recited pulse, blood pressure, respiration, alpha waves, beta waves, stroke count.

As the climax began to build inside him, Todd became perfectly still and squeezed the bulb. Her eyes, which had been closed, flew open, bulging. Her tongue fluttered in the pink cavity of her mouth. Her arms and legs thrummed.

But the real action was in her torso, rising and falling, vibrating, every muscle
    (oh every muscle every muscle moves tightens closes every)
    every muscle and the sensation at climax was (ecstasy)
    oh it was, it was

(the end of the world thundering outside)

He woke to that sound and the sound of rain. He was huddled on his side in a dark ball, his heart beating at a sprinter's pace. His lower belly was covered with a warm, sticky liquid. There was an instant of panicky horror when he feared he might be bleeding to death . . . and then he realized what it *really* was, and he felt a fainting, nauseated revulsion. Semen. Come. Jizz. Jungle-juice. Words from fences and locker rooms and the walls of gas station bathrooms. There was nothing here he wanted.

His hands balled helplessly into fists. His dream-climax recurred to him, pallid now, senseless, frightening. But nerve-endings still tingled, retreating slowly from their spike-point. That final scene, fading now, was disgusting and yet somehow compulsive, like an unsuspecting bite into a piece of tropical fruit which, you realized (a second too late), had only tasted so amazingly sweet because it was rotten.

It came to him then. What he would have to do.

There was only one way he could get himself back again. He would have to kill Dussander. It was the only way. Games were done; storytime was over. This was survival.

'Kill him and it's all over,' he whispered in the darkness, with the rain in the tree outside and semen drying on his belly. Whispering it made it seem real.

Dussander always kept three or four fifths of Ancient Age

on a shelf over the steep cellar stairs. He would go to the door, open it (half-crocked already, more often than not), and go down two steps. Then he would lean out, put one hand on the shelf, and grip the fresh bottle by the neck with his other hand. The cellar floor was not paved, but the dirt was hard-packed and Dussander, with a machinelike efficiency that Todd now thought of as Prussian rather than German, oiled it once every two months to keep bugs from breeding in the dirt. Cement or no cement, old bones break easily. And old men have accidents. The post-mortem would show that 'Mr Denker' had had a skinful of booze when he 'fell'.

What happened, Todd?

He didn't answer the door so I used the key he made for me. Sometimes he falls asleep. I went into the kitchen and saw the cellar door was open. I went down the stairs and he . . . he . . .

Then, of course, tears.

It would work.

He would have himself back again.

For a long time Todd lay awake in the dark, listening to the thunder retreat westward, out over the Pacific, listening to the secret sound of the rain. He thought he would stay awake the rest of the night, going over it and over it. But he fell asleep only moments later and slept dreamlessly with one fist curled under his chin. He woke on the first of May fully rested for the first time in months.

11

May, 1975.

For Todd, that Friday in the middle of the month was the longest of his life. He sat in class after class, hearing nothing, waiting only for the last five minutes, when the instructor would take out his or her small pile of Flunk Cards and distribute them. Each time an instructor approached Todd's desk with that pile of cards, he grew cold. Each time he or she passed him without stopping, he felt waves of dizziness and a semi-hysteria.

Algebra was the worst. Storrman approached . . . hesitated . . . and just as Todd became convinced he was going to pass on, he laid a Flunk Card face-down on Todd's desk. Todd looked at it coldly, with no feelings at all. Now that it had happened, he was only cold. *Well, that's it,* he thought. *Point, game, set, and match. Unless Dussander can think of something else. And I have my doubts.*

Without much interest, he turned the Flunk Card over to see by how much he had missed his C. It must have been close, but trust old Stony Storrman not to give anyone a break. He saw that the grade-spaces were utterly blank – both the letter-grade space and the numerical-grade space. Written in the COMMENTS section was this message: *I'm sure glad I don't have to give you one of these for real! Chas. Storrman.*

The dizziness came again, more savagely this time, roaring through his head, making it feel like a balloon filled with helium. He gripped the sides of his desk as hard as he could, holding one thought with total obsessive tightness: *You will not faint, not faint, not faint.* Little by little the waves of dizziness passed, and then he had to control an urge to run up the aisle after Storrman, turn him around, and poke his eyes out with the freshly sharpened pencil he held in his hand. And through it all his face remained carefully blank. The only sign that anything at all was going inside was a mild tic in one eyelid.

School let out for the week fifteen minutes later. Todd

walked slowly around the building to the bike-racks, his head down, his hands shoved into his pockets, his books tucked into the crook of his right arm, oblivious of the running, shouting students. He tossed the books into his bike-basket, unlocked the Schwinn, and pedalled away. Towards Dussander's house.

Today, he thought. *Today is your day, old man.*

'And so,' Dussander said, pouring bourbon into his cup as Todd entered the kitchen, 'the accused returns from the dock. How said they, prisoner?' He was wearing his bathrobe and a pair of hairy wool socks that climbed halfway up his shins. Socks like that, Todd thought, would be easy to slip in. He glanced at the bottle of Ancient Age Dussander was currently working. It was down to the last three fingers.

'No Ds, no Fs, no Flunk Cards,' Todd said. 'I'll still have to change some of my grades in June, but maybe just the averages. I'll be getting all As and Bs this quarter if I keep up my work.'

'Oh, you'll keep it up, all right,' Dussander said. 'We will see to it.' He drank and then tipped more bourbon into his cup. 'This calls for a celebration.' His speech was slightly blurred – hardly enough to be noticeable, but Todd knew the old fuck was as drunk as he ever got. Yes, today. It would have to be today.

But he was cool.

'Celebrate pigshit,' he told Dussander.

'I'm afraid the delivery boy hasn't arrived with the beluga and the truffles yet,' Dussander said, ignoring him. 'Help is so unreliable these days. What about a few Ritz crackers and some Velveeta while we wait?'

'Okay,' Todd said. 'What the hell.'

Dussander stood up (one knee banged the table, making him wince) and crossed to the refrigerator. He got out the cheese, took a knife from the drawer and a plate from the cupboard, and a box of Ritz crackers from the breadbox.

'All carefully injected with prussic acid,' he told Todd as he set the cheese and crackers down on the table. He grinned, and Todd saw that he had left out his false teeth again today. Nevertheless, Todd smiled back.

'So quiet today!' Dussander exclaimed. 'I would have expected you to turn handsprings all the way up the hall.' He emptied the last of the bourbon into his cup, sipped, smacked his lips.

'I guess I'm still numb,' Todd said. He bit into a cracker. He had stopped refusing Dussander's food a long time ago. Dussander thought there was a letter with one of Todd's friends – there was not, of course; he had friends, but none he trusted *that* much. He supposed Dussander had guessed that long ago, but he knew Dussander didn't quite dare put his guess to such an extreme test as murder.

'What shall we talk about today?' Dussander enquired, tossing off the last shot. 'I give you the day off from studying, how's that? Uh? Uh?' When he drank, his accent became thicker. It was an accent Todd had come to hate. Now he felt okay about the accent; he felt okay about everything. He felt very cool all over. He looked at his hands, the hands which would give the push, and they looked just as they always did. They were not trembling; they were cool.

'I don't care,' he said. 'Anything you want.'

'Shall I tell you about the special soap we made? Our experiments with enforced homosexuality? Or perhaps you

248